BLOOD IN THE PAINT

Jordanna East

This book is a work of fiction. The characters, incidents, and dialogue are drawn from the author's imagination and are not to be construed as real. Any resemblance to actual events or persons, living or dead, is entirely coincidental.

BLOOD IN THE PAST.

FIRST EDITION
Blood Read Press
Collingswood, NJ 08108

Paperback Edition April 2014
ISBN:
978-0989581035

Dedication

For my darling husband, Justin. All of me loves all of you, too. You're not my muse, but you're so much more.

For my friend, Jill-bug. Your story doesn't end here.

Intro

Files were spread out on the bed around her, the nightstand's dim lamplight casting shadows across papers lined with long, ominous words. Her fingers traced them, searching for answers. Always searching. For weeks, time had passed around her, like a stream around a stone, yet it didn't seem to touch her as she immersed herself in the countless reports. She thumbed through the papers again and again. As the sun began its ascent, she cut her finger. A tiny pinprick of blood fell and dotted one of the papers. She smeared it, thought it a sign that if she just looked harder . . .

1
However Dark It Was.

BLOOD IS RED, but she always wore purple. Each time Lyla Kyle donned her eggplant-colored clothes it was because the memory persisted: the memory of herself, kneeling on the floor of her parents' bedroom, cradling her mother's limp body. The blood had seeped into her blue shirt, staining the fabric a ruddy purple. Her mother's life had bled out and gone, from an act of despair almost exactly a decade ago.

The image kept Lyla strong. It enabled her to channel her rage. *Anything to make you proud, Mom.*

Over the years, Lyla had learned to prepare for death in the same way one would prepare for a date. She would apply her makeup and affix every hair in place, knowing her looks had to be every bit as lethal as her intentions.

The upcoming evening's festivities would play on a loop in Lyla's mind, making sure she remembered everything: lipstick, mini lint-roller, syringes, vials of a deadly chemical, breath mints . . . She loved being in control, savoring every moment.

Lyla had come to enjoy the hours leading up to her ultimate empowerment. The anticipation thrilled her almost as much as the act itself—and it was almost time to act. Almost time to plunge one of the syringes into her date's neck.

Tingling at the thought, she shuddered, then she shooed her excitement away and reined her thoughts back in, returning them instead to the snug, overcrowded Philadelphia nightclub. Her next victim, the man sitting across from her at the high-standing cocktail table, nervously blabbed away, darting his hazel eyes in multiple directions seemingly all it once. He was shouting and yet she could barely hear him.

"I said, nice place you picked. What do you think of the music?"

Lyla just nodded along politely. She always chose popular nightclubs to meet up with her prey, where the patrons were too numerous to count and she and her "date" would never be more than just a couple of faces in a crowd of bodies, writhing in unison to the beat of the bass. It also didn't hurt that the steamy atmosphere, teeming with sexual energy, helped move the night along quickly. The club would always be too crowded, the music would always be too loud, and after a few cocktails, she would always suggest something more intimate. Not because she wanted to converse with them more easily, not because she was interested in her victims' lives, no. Only their demise, and the execution of her grand plan.

Execution. The term was somewhat appropriate, but not entirely accurate. After all, executions were meant to be painless and humane, and Lyla knew her dark little hobby was anything but. *Then again,* she thought, as she continued nodding along with whatever her date was saying, *my weapon of choice is technically one of the chemicals used in lethal injections . . .*

Lyla had justified her craft for years. She did so then, as the man across from her rambled on about the unseasonably cool August weather, and she suppressed a sneer. Men proved to be good-for-nothing charlatans. They were primitive. They were relentless and lived for nothing more than the next conquest, whether it be climbing the social and corporate ladders or bedding the next beautiful woman to strut across their path. Lyla supposed to her date she was the latter—which made her tactic all the easier.

Killing invigorated her. She had found her calling, however dark it was. And dark it was on this cool Friday evening in August as she chatted with a poor, unsuspecting man named Alex.

As he spoke incessantly, the vein in his neck bobbled, and Lyla Kyle was ready to feel invigorated again.

He still seemed nervous. Not only could he not stop yapping or still his flitting eyes, but his hands never seemed to find a comfortable resting place. They jumped from his lap to the table to fussing with his hair and clothes like a teenage girl. *What is his deal? It's not like he knows he's going to die.*

He let the sentence he was stuttering through trail off, possibly noticing Lyla's focus following his hands and not his words. "You know, you look absolutely gorgeous tonight. Did I tell you that? I guess I was trying to think of a more . . . I dunno. Anyway, I almost feel underdressed."

Outward anxiety aside, Alex's Mediterranean features were striking. Lyla definitely wasn't out of his league, so his nervousness must stem from somewhere other than the rarity of being on a date with a beautiful woman.

She was especially drawn to his stubble; its shadow trailed past his jawline, overflowing onto his neck. Under the table, she placed a hand discreetly inside her purse and groped around, lingering, until she'd finally grasped the tortoise-shell eyeglass case within that once belonged to her mother. Her fingertips glided over its smooth surface and danced swiftly around its perimeter until they found the cool, metal clasp. She popped it open, grazed her thumb across the plungers of her syringes, then snapped the case shut. *Yes, I think his stubble will hide the puncture mark quite well.*

Alex gulped his drink, and she smiled sweetly. It would seem he had finally run out of things to say. They sat there, unspeaking, letting the din of the club fill the void around them like a blanket, until, awkwardly, he took her hand in his. His palm was warm and damp though he had just been holding his ice-cold beverage. Alex pulled her to her feet, and twirled her around to a beat he must have heard in his head because it didn't correspond to the song being pumped through the sound system. Lyla tried to steady his step, but he only caused her to stumble as he pulled her close, rocking her off-tempo. She eased him back a few steps, and he admired her figure and stroked her long, dark hair. He didn't care for the rhythm; Lyla could see nothing but a flicker of sexual hunger in his eyes, and she knew right then how easy this would be. *It always was.*

Alex attempted to twirl her again and sent her flailing into a cocktail waitress carrying a tray of drinks. The crash of mixed drinks and beer bottles coupled with the waitress's glare must have quickly reminded Alex they were in a crowded club, and perhaps spinning his date around wasn't the best idea. He dropped Lyla's hand with a pouty reluctance while she stole a glance at the time on his watch.

The waitress collected the shards of broken glass at their feet and the couple reacquainted themselves with their barstools. Annoyed and eager to move on to the next phase of the evening, Lyla wished she could inject Alex right then.

He was the first to interrupt her fantasy. "So, I meant to tell you, seeing as how you're an artist, I happen to be a bit artistic myself."

"Oh, really?" Lyla tried her best to look and sound interested, even going so far as to lean forward, perched on the edge of her seat. "Do tell."

"Well, I'm a freelance web designer. Companies employ me to design the visual layout of their websites. I also do consulting work for various advertising agencies, sometimes even for the companies themselves. Of course, I'm sure it's nothing compared to your work, but I did go to an art school for my degree." His shoulders rolled back, pushing his chest forward; he was confident he was making some sort of impression.

Lyla let him believe he was by continuing to sound intrigued, though she wanted to snort in derision. "No kidding?"

He nodded. "Yep. The Art Institute of Philadelphia."

"Wow, I *am* impressed. *I* didn't even go to art school." Lyla's inflections may have been a bit overplayed, but they were working, nonetheless. Now it was her turn to rope him in. "I mean; I took a few classes here and there, sculpture, photography, art history . . . You know, things like that, electives as an undergrad, but I actually went to medical school."

"Okay, I guess I'm the one who should be impressed. I would never have guessed that." Alex must have noted Lyla's raised eyebrows because he started to eat his words. "I mean, not that I don't think you're smart, or anything like that. I'm sure you're very intelligent. It's just that . . . I didn't know . . . I mean, I didn't . . ."

Although thoroughly amused by his misstep, Lyla had to interrupt his rambling. "It's okay, I know what you meant. Being a doctor is worlds apart from being an artist. But yeah, actually my aunt pushed me down that path, since every pet my parents ever gave me ended up dead and dissected." Lyla let her words linger in the air between them while she sipped from her straw with a smile. Alex laughed, but squirmed in his seat a little, as was her intention. She continued, "I went to UPENN for med school, came within a year of completing my residency at West Philly Gen, and then I dropped out. I just couldn't do it anymore."

"You just dropped out, just like that?"

"Yeah, why?" Lyla felt her face flushing, and not just from the alcohol. Her tone switched from light and airy to sounding gravelly and guarded. "I was going through some family stuff and I needed time to adjust and to express myself. What I didn't need was the rigidity of residency. It was too much to deal with all at once."

"All right, okay." Alex held up two dewy palms, sensing he had hit a nerve. He immediately abandoned the topic. "So, in what other ways do you 'express yourself?' Do you have any other hobbies, besides your artwork?"

Lyla's face softened, and she chuckled at the irony of his question. "Well, I do have one other, but it's somewhat private. Maybe we'll get into that a bit later." She threw him a flirtatious wink. "How 'bout you?"

The question was obligatory; this was the portion of the evening that Lyla hated most. Although he had crammed much of their date with awkward small talk thus far, it was right about now that Alex began telling her about himself: more about his job, his interests, his friends, etc. Lyla didn't care. She didn't care, because as soon as she realized that her soon-to-be victim had family, friends, and coworkers who cared about him, that he was admired by some and liked by others, maybe even loved, she might find it harder to kill him. The slightest hesitation would be detrimental. Therefore, and quite understandably, that's why Lyla tuned Alex out for five minutes or so.

"So, Lyla, enough of me blathering on about myself. Tell me more about you, about your artwork."

Relieved that he'd finally offered an opportunity to return the focus back to her own interests, Lyla responded eagerly. "Well, I do a lot of different things with a lot of different materials, but mostly, I take various objects and dip them in paint to create overlapping textures. I prefer it over just using ordinary paintbrushes. Right now, I'm working on a three-dimensional sculpture of several bodies with exaggerated, elongated, and intertwined limbs, and I'm covering them with a variety of leaf patterns. I actually already have a private collector who's interested in purchasing the piece."

Lyla loved to talk about her artwork. When her husband's death had been ruled an accident almost ten years ago, she was able to collect a sizable life insurance policy which, combined with the policies of her parents, had allowed her to focus more on her creativity. It wasn't quite her favorite pastime—it came in as a close second—but it was definitely one that was more widely accepted and appreciated, and wouldn't land her in jail for the rest of her life if she were caught.

Soon the gin and tonics Lyla and her date had been knocking back led Alex to excuse himself to the restroom. As he wound his way through the patrons, he flagged down the waitress—reticent from having been bumped earlier—and ordered two more cocktails. Lyla watched him, then brought her cell phone screen to life with a tap to look at the time. While her date was away, she called the waitress over before the girl could retrieve Alex's order.

"Sweetie, you can bring my date's drink, but I'll take a simple glass of seltzer with a twist of lime, but in the exact same type of glass. Thanks. And the same for any rounds we have from here on out. Make sure they look like the same drink, okay?" She wadded up a fifty-dollar bill and curled the waitress's fingers around it. She eagerly nodded. Lyla was done drinking for the night. She needed to maintain her focus, but, at the same time, she needed to appear as though she were still having a good ol' time drinking it up.

When Alex returned, they chatted for an hour or so more before he suggested they head out in search of something quieter. *Finally*, she thought as they split the cost of the tab and hurriedly exited the club.

"You know, if you're still interested in my artwork," Lyla began when they reached the parking lot, "I was gonna stop by my studio tonight after our date. We can go now. Together? It's quiet, and we'd have the place to ourselves. What do you say?"

"Of course. That'd be great. Should we take my car or yours?"

"I'd prefer to drive, if you don't mind?" *So I don't leave any evidence of myself in your car . . .*

Moments later they hopped in Lyla's SUV so she could show him her latest fixation, all the while knowing that her latest fixation was sitting right beside her. Her purse was between them, slumped on the center console, and she reached over and patted it gently, thinking of the tortoise-shell eyeglass case and the row of syringes concealed inside.

2
Lie There and Die.

OUTSIDE, THE HOOD of the SUV consumed the lines of I-95 beneath it. Lyla watched as each one disappeared, bringing them closer to their destination, bringing Alex closer to his fate, and bringing Lyla closer to her vengeance. She glanced down at his hand tapping anxiously in his lap and noticed a conspicuous tan-line on Alex's left ring finger; somehow she'd missed it while they were inside the club. *He opted to do without his wedding band tonight. How clever*, she thought sarcastically.

With both hands on the steering wheel, Lyla nodded down at his never idle hands. "Something you want to tell me, Alex?" she asked, knowing he wouldn't have a chance to explain it later.

He cleared his throat, caught off guard. "I was hoping you wouldn't notice," he said, wincing. Sheepishly, he rubbed at the pale ring of skin. "I knew I shouldn't wear it, but I also knew the tan-line would give me away. I wasn't sure if you noticed at the park . . ." Alex dropped his attention to the passing road beyond his window, his voice trailing off into his shoulder.

"I did notice at the park," Lyla said flatly.

Earlier in the week, Lyla had sought inspiration for her next piece while having lunch in the breezy tranquility of Rittenhouse Square. That afternoon, she sat cross-legged on a red and white Phillies blanket. She didn't care much for baseball, but somewhere in her travels it had been a free giveaway. She sat facing up toward the sun, her skin glowing and her glossy, black hair blowing. The balmy breeze rustled the leaves above her, as well as the blades of grass around her. She'd been quietly absorbing the sights, sounds, and smells of summer when she noticed him, probably also taking advantage of the unusually comfortable August weather.

He was walking two bushy Akitas. Lyla remembered being impressed with their coloring and stature. She had flipped past dog shows on television before, and these two almost certainly demonstrated show-quality attributes. One of the dogs had knocked over Lyla's latté while chasing an elusive squirrel when Alex approached to apologize.

"Hi, I'm so sorry about that. It's their first time out today, so they're acting a little stir crazy. Was that from Starbucks? I could buy you another," he'd said, peering past Lyla to try to get a glimpse of the logo on the cardboard cup.

"Oh, yeah, but no, that's quite all right. Totally unnecessary. I'm awake now, anyway," Lyla had teased. She'd brushed a few strands of hair from her eyes and smiled coquettishly at him from her blanket, squinting against the sun that shone behind the man's head like a glowing corona. She'd shielded her eyes with her arm. Glaring sun or not, she hadn't been able to ignore his deep-set dark hazel eyes. They complimented his complexion, which was the sandy color of ginger root. "Would you like to join me? You seem rather awake yourself, so maybe we could be awake together?" She was just plain flirting with him now, but he didn't seem to mind.

"I would love to, but I gotta get home and get back to work."

"Oh, you work from home? So do I! Although, right now, I guess I'm working from here."

He'd given her a quizzical look as he scanned her blanket, probably searching for a laptop, a notebook, a folder or anything that could possibly be indicative of "work" being done. "Really?" he asked, after he hadn't found so much as a pen.

Lyla had giggled again. "Yes. I'm an artist. I'll be starting a new piece soon, nature-inspired, interspersed with chess pieces," Lyla gestured to the park's many chess tables, "and I felt I needed a little more inspiration to get myself motivated today. Plus, it's just too beautiful out here to stay inside."

"I see. Well it was great meeting you . . .?"

"Lyla."

"Lyla. That's a beautiful name. I'm Alex, by the way."

"Alex, huh? That's funny. You don't look like an Alex," she'd said with a raised brow.

"Okay, what do I look like?"

"You look like a guy who's gonna call me later this week to ask me out." Lyla had reached into her bulky bag and pulled a business card from a zippered side compartment. She'd handed it to Alex, batting her eyes. Even then she'd known he would use it, but he wouldn't dare hold on to it. "What do you say?"

Stunned by her forwardness, the smile that had been growing across his face had faltered for just a second before spreading to a grin. "I . . . I say . . . I'll give you a call later, and maybe we could set something up for Friday."

"Sounds great, but you should probably get going. Your dogs look like they're licking their chops at that cotton ball of a Pomeranian over there."

"Good eye." Alex had whistled and clapped sharply for his dogs. "I should probably let you get back to 'work' anyway." He'd laughed lightheartedly. "I'll call you soon. It was great meeting you."

"Likewise," she had said.

So, of course, during that brief encounter, Lyla had noticed Alex's wedding band, but dared not mention it; she didn't want to risk flustering her prey and possibly missing a delightfully unexpected opportunity. Besides, she enjoyed her little hobby most when the unsuspecting targets simply fell in her lap.

"And . . ." Alex prodded. Lyla hadn't noticed he had been staring wide-eyed at the side of her head as she drove, waiting for an answer.

"I figured you might have had an explanation." Lyla concealed the fact that that ring was the only reason she had agreed to get together in the first place. Yet she was still curious. She had to ask. "Well, do you? Have an explanation?"

Once again, he began to stumble over his words. Lyla knew that even if their evening together had been a real date, she would have been turned off by Alex's severe lack of confidence. At least, she presumed as much—she hadn't been on a real date in a decade.

"Not exactly," Alex continued. "She's a terrific woman, but we married kind of young, and sometimes I wonder, 'what if?'"

"Uh-huh. I see." Lyla forced the words through clenched teeth and tight lips. Now she was having a hard time disguising her true emotions, and they both fell silent. She recalled her own mother using that same empty excuse years ago to justify her father's actions.

Beside her, Alex sat with hunched shoulders, silently staring out the window. He seemed genuinely disappointed in himself, but Lyla didn't care. He was trying to be honest with her, when the person he should be trying to be honest with was his wife. Lyla was disgusted, but took solace in the fact that justice would soon be served.

They were almost there, the SUV curling around the exit. They weren't headed to any art studio, however—at least, not technically. They were headed to a self-storage facility on the outskirts of South Philadelphia. Lyla did, in fact, store some of her completed pieces there, but it was also the depository of her more *personal* collectibles.

The SUV crept to a stop in the darkened parking lot. The pair hopped out, and the neon sign above them flashed intermittently. By its sickly light, Lyla could see Alex's face twisted in confusion. "*This* is where your art studio is?" he asked, gesturing to the flickering letters of the EZ Extra Space self-storage sign.

Lyla hurried him along. "Well, it isn't much, but the rent's cheap, and I can concentrate without interruption," she said with a casual shrug.

"Do you have adequate lighting in these things?" he asked, rapping his knuckles against the corrugated metal sides of one of the units as they turned a corner. So far, he seemed utterly unimpressed.

"Oh, you have no idea," she said cryptically. Alex frowned.

He followed closely at Lyla's heels, the echo of his footsteps joining the melodic tiny bells on her anklet. He paused several times, glancing around the dark, dismal facility. "Should we even be here this late?" he asked. "It's almost one in the morning."

"This place allows twenty-four-hour access to the outer units. Don't worry."

"Then why are we heading through the center aisle?" Alex asked, his voice unsteady.

"Shortcut." *And the cameras here are just for show, unlike the ones watching the perimeter.*

Their walk down the stale smelling, dimly lit alley came to an end at unit number forty-three. Lyla's heart danced, giddy. She was engrossed with everything around her: the pale fluorescent lights of the hall, the cold steel door to the unit, even the sound of her own breathing, which she had to consciously control, lest she give away her excitement.

Lyla reached into her seemingly bottomless purse to find the keys to the unit. She also felt around for the tortoise-shell eyeglass case while Alex looked around curiously, shuffling his feet. He was still pretty fidgety for someone who had no idea what his night was about to become.

Lyla's long, slender fingers discretely pried open the eyeglass case she'd been visiting in her purse all night and fondled the syringes. While she exaggerated the jangling noise of the keys—pretending they were entangled within the contents of her purse—she grabbed a syringe and gripped it firmly between her index and middle fingers, positioning her thumb on the plunger. She completed this expertly, all without looking, her hands still concealed within the depths of her purse while Alex waited behind her, softly tapping his foot. Finally, with her left hand, she placed the key in the lock, opened the door, and ushered Alex inside.

He stepped in front of her. She hit a switch. Lights flooded the room like a late night Phillies game at Citizen's Bank Park. Compared with the blue-black dark of the night outside, Alex's eyes couldn't quite handle the adjustment; he squinted and raised an arm to shield his face. Dropping her purse with a thud, Lyla moved in. She lunged toward him in one swift motion, plunging the syringe into Alex's neck. She aimed for his jugular vein, but knew, even with her medical background, the immediacy of the moment didn't allow for such specificity. It was more likely the needle had entered the thick muscle of Alex's neck, taking minutes instead of seconds to take effect. As the chemical burned its way into his body and through his system, Lyla forcefully kicked his legs out from under him, and he hit the cold cement floor, landing on his back. His arms and legs were bent in conflicting directions. He struggled to lift himself up several times but, like an insect that had fallen backward into a puddle of glue, he failed. By now, the drug was beginning to take effect. Alex's breathing slowed. His eyes widened as he feverishly tried to comprehend what was going on around him—Lyla knew the expression well.

She knelt beside her immobilized captive and glared into his expanding pupils; like a solar eclipse, the hazel hue of his beautiful eyes slowly disappeared. She could see her own reflection: the strong seriousness of her face highlighted only by the excitement in her own eyes. As she stared at her reflection, framed within Alex's eyes, she saw her mother's vindication. She didn't look anything like her mother, but she saw it.

Now, Lyla took a deep breath and prepared to speak slowly. Her voice would be the last thing Alex would ever hear.

"Do you know why you're here, Alex?" He was incapable of responding, of course, since he was completely paralyzed, so she continued, her voice stern but barely above a whisper. "You're here because I despise you, and others like you. You're here because you should be at home with your wife, not out trying to get lucky with some pretty girl you met in the park. You're here, Alex, because I empathize with your wife, and I want to help her." She watched as he silently suffocated; his heart and respiratory muscles were paralyzed, like the rest of his body. As he slowly slipped into cardiac arrest, Lyla leaned in even closer. Hovering just above his ear, she whispered, "I'm helping her by freeing her—from you."

Lyla stood up. Alex couldn't respond. He couldn't stutter and stumble over pathetic excuses and meaningless justifications. All he could do was lie there and die.

***

Lyla stood up, stepped over Alex, and snatched her purse from the floor. She pulled out a travel-sized package of Kleenex and used one as a barrier between her fingers and Alex's eyelids as she eased them shut; she didn't want to leave any trace of herself on his beautiful face, and she couldn't have him staring at her, drawing up guilt from her gut like bitter bile. He looked peaceful, and he was handsome even in death. She forced herself to look away; her smile slowly fading along with her excitement. It was time to wrap this evening up—considering her next set of actions; she chuckled at the unintentional pun.

In the corner of the storage unit stood a spool of unstretched canvas—the type used for paintings—next to an oversized dolly. Lyla rolled the dolly in Alex's direction and unfolded the canvas. After she laid the canvas flat out on the floor, she rolled Alex's body onto it and then up *into* it. She then stood him up, tussling with the dead weight, the sack rolling and lolling this way and that as she wrestled to place him on the platform of the dolly. Her anklet's bells jangled furiously with her every struggle. Finally, Lyla leaned him up against the handle and, using a length of heavy-duty twine, she secured him to the backbone of the dolly in order to roll him out to her car.

Oops, I almost forgot. Out of breath, Lyla reached back into her purse and searched again for the eyeglass case. Fingering through the syringes, this time, she grabbed an empty one. She tugged a few of the canvas folds down and loosened some of the twine—she needed a blood sample. Expertly, with fingers seasoned by years of practice, Lyla inserted the syringe between two of Alex's fingers—where the ME would be less likely to see the puncture mark—and withdrew a few CCs of his blood while it was still warm. She replaced the syringe back into the eyeglass case and re-secured the twine and the canvas.

Before she gathered her things and headed out of the storage unit, she rolled a scrunchie off of her wrist, reaching up to secure her hair in a ponytail. The elastic snapped, harshly popping her hand with a sting of pain. Lyla cursed under her breath as she left, locking the door behind her. After toiling with the deadweight, her arms felt like liquid and her legs like lead, but she had to hurry.

Lyla was hardly concerned about moving Alex's body in this manner, since she used the exact same method to transport her larger, more cumbersome art pieces. Most, if not all of the security guards and staff knew her by name and were quite used to the sight of her rolling oddly-shaped objects covered in bleached-white burlap in and out of the facility.

Before she could reach her car, she was met by one of the facility's security guards. From the looks of him, he was a new hire. *Of course.*

"Kinda late to be moving, isn't it, lady?" he huffed, out of breath, though he had no reason to be. He was young, and not particularly attractive, with reddish-brown hair and a freckled face. He resembled the kid in the *Mad Magazine* logo, but all grown up. His squinted eyes glanced curiously at Lyla; she noticed his pupils were constricted.

"Yeah, well, I'm sort of a night owl," Lyla said. She flashed a charming smile while toying with a lock of her hair.

"Okay, but I've seen my share of night owls around here, and they're never dressed like that," he said, nodding at her snug plum-colored dress and heels.

She smiled slyly. "This trip was an afterthought."

The guard continued to eye her with one eyebrow raised, seemingly unconvinced. *It's like he's impervious to my charm.* What if he tried to help with her *package*? It would be fairly easy for him to ascertain that something that *feels* soft and fleshy is probably made of flesh. She needed to think quickly while simultaneously trying to maneuver her way around him. But she couldn't think. She thought it was the guard's goofy, distracting grin—until a sound registered behind her. *Footsteps.* She whipped her head around, doubting it was another patron of the facility at that hour. Sure enough, it was another damn security guard. Just as she was beginning to think the place was way too over-staffed for two o'clock in the morning, she recognized the man walking briskly toward them.

"Willis, oh, thank God." Giggling, the uneasiness, trailed from her voice. "Tell your buddy here that I troll around here so often I should collect the same pay as you two."

Willis laughed as he approached. "What do you need with our pay? You do well enough selling those masterpieces of yours."

Lyla blushed. Willis was her favorite, and he'd been there when she first began leasing a unit several years ago. With brown skin speckled with moles and thick hair that had probably started to turn gray decades ago, he had a Southern grandfatherly charm that put her at ease. He was friendly, polite, and never meddlesome—unlike the new guy. Willis reminded Lyla of Morgan Freeman, and who didn't like Morgan Freeman?

As much as Lyla adored Willis and his compliments about her work, she really needed to get back to the club, to Alex's car. Although the body wouldn't be completely stiff from rigor mortis for another twelve hours, it would soon begin to exhibit the early signs, and she couldn't take any chances; not to mention the postmortem lividity had to be consistent with the body's positioning. A discrepancy involving the time of Alex's death could lead to an unwelcome investigation. Following the deaths of her parents and husband, Lyla had endured enough investigation. She had been nothing but lucky back then. Now she had to be careful, calculating.

"Well, you boys have fun and stay awake. Next time I'll bring coffee." She smiled brightly and waved goodnight as she lowered her head and hurried toward her truck with earnest. She could hear them calling behind her, offering to help load her 'artwork' into the back of her car, but, without looking back, she dismissed them with a flick of her hand. She reached the parking lot, loaded Alex's body into the back of her Xterra, and then tossed the dolly into the back seat. Lyla was relieved to be on the road, though her skin itched with the moisture from her exertion.

Earlier that night, Lyla, had watched Alex pull up to the club from her own car, so she found his sedan, a charcoal-gray Lexus, with ease. Plus, Philadelphia bars and nightclubs closed at two a.m., so there weren't many cars left in the parking lot. Lyla parked next to the Lexus, but facing the opposite direction, popped the trunk, and climbed over her front and back seats and into the area where Alex's body lay. She was glad for the extra give that her dress afforded her. Unfortunately, her hair was in her face and waving all around the body. Frustrated, Lyla, threw her curls over her shoulder and carefully unwrapped Alex's body.

She glanced outside, and when she was sure there was no one around, she pushed open the back hatch and rolled him out. Lyla struggled once again with the deadweight, as she stood Alex's body up near his driver-side door and let him drop naturally to the ground. She pulled his keys from his pants pocket, wiped them clean of her fingerprints with a Kleenex, and placed them in his right hand. Of course, they slipped slightly out of his grasp, but that was for the better. The whole point of her elaborate scheme was to make it appear as though Alex had simply dropped dead while approaching his car door. Finally, she stepped back into her SUV and pulled a small lint roller from her purse. Within minutes, after removing traces of her hair and other fibers from Alex's lifeless body, the staging was complete, and Lyla returned to her Xterra and drove off.

Alex was now someone else's problem: the problem of the passerby who squealed into the night when he or she discovered the lifeless body; the problem of the police officer, working the graveyard shift; the problem of the medical examiner, baffled by the circumstances surrounding Alex's death . . . But, most importantly, Alex would *not* be the problem of his wife. Not anymore. His life of lies and betrayal was over. Lyla's mother would be proud.

3
A Lighthouse Among the Darkness.

A SCRATCHY VOICE on the radio broke through the urban static of outside car horns and idling engines, its own static in competition. "Bike patrol officer flagged. Parking lot on the corner of 9th and South. Witness found a subject unresponsive. Requesting back-up units to check location and subject."

Officer Brighthouse's empty can of Red Bull made a hollow, tinny sound, clattering against the cup holder, as he threw it down to reach for the radio. "X-2-3, we're in the area; we're en route."

"2-3-Copy."

Brighthouse replaced the receiver on its cradle and started humming. Meanwhile, Brighthouse's partner for the shift, Byron Blakely, sighed. "What are you whistling about?"

"I'm humming."

"Whatever. I'm sensing a suspicious circs call at best. I woulda thought you'd be bummed."

"Relax. You never know; it could get interesting." Brighthouse's voice was boyish and playful, just like his appearance. His eyes housed an infinite innocence, and light brown curls framed his clean-shaven face, furthering his young, fresh, frat-boy look. The only thing betraying his youth was the jagged pink scar that wrapped around a third of his scalp, beginning above his right ear and ending just over his left shoulder. Whenever Brighthouse tried to grow his hair, tried to hide it, tried to be normal, their captain ordered him to trim it. With the scar once again freshly exposed, it itched and burned, a psychosomatic reminder that he wasn't a boy.

Despite his grim past, he was ever the optimist in the present. He turned on the flashers and hoped they had drawn a killer case—pun definitely intended. Brighthouse always assumed there was foul play.

There could be some poor soul swinging from a rope, suicide note taped to his forehead, and Brighthouse would still want to investigate "all possible avenues." Of course that was protocol, but Brighthouse would be the only one at the scene actually willing to investigate—hungry to, in fact. Everyone else did so because they had to. For that reason, his colleagues teased him, calling him Officer "Lighthouse," since he was always searching for something, like a beam of light, methodically rotating among the darkness. According to them, he was disillusioned to the point of delusion, and it frustrated the hell out of everyone.

Slightly more seasoned than Brighthouse, Officer Blakely's years on the force showed. A peppering of gray was starting to crop up around his hairline of dark, close-cut hair, his once broad shoulders had shrunk with each passing year of service, and he was slightly round in the middle. In addition, he was much more content with leaving well enough alone than Jason Brighthouse. That was his way of putting it. Brighthouse thought he'd lost his ambition, had simply become lazy, complacent. Blakely's days of over-zealous investigating were behind him, and his years in the Philadelphia Police Department had created a cynicism that clashed earnestly with Brighthouse's fanaticism. As far as Blakely was concerned, if you heard hoof beats, you thought horses. Brighthouse, on the other hand, would like nothing more than to be absolutely sure that he didn't hear zebras or water buffalo.

The cruiser slowly rounded the corner and pulled up next to the medical examiner's van. Earlier uniforms had already taped off the scene with streamers of yellow crime scene tape. Although their color was sunny, the occasion was somber—a sad party indeed. A few of the officers could be seen controlling the crowd of a dozen or so onlookers: stragglers whose shifts at nearby clubs and bars had ended; nosy local residents risen from their slumber by the sirens and flashing lights cascading across their bedrooms. The detective on scene wore a rumpled shirt and a crooked tie. His fly was down. He sipped from his coffee, disinterested, which was somewhat to be expected; Philly homicide detectives had hefty caseloads, and being called out in the early morning hours on a suspicious circs case tore them from the stacks of active cases on their desks.

A man wearing navy blue cargo shorts, a sweaty polo shirt, and a helmet motioned to them. Flailing his arms furiously, he beckoned for them to follow him, eagerly pointing ahead to the scene before Brighthouse and Blakely could fully get out of the car. As they approached, Brighthouse realized he wasn't summoning them, but rather gesturing wildly to the uninterested detective as he shouted the relevant details over his shoulder. By the time Brighthouse and Blakely reached him, they'd missed half of what he'd said. Luckily, so had the detective, who dryly asked him to start from the top—and speak slower.

"I was riding by—you know, patrolling my beat and all—when this drunk chick, uh witness, comes running up to me," the officer said in one of those thick, South Philly Italian accents. It fascinated Brighthouse; the intonations reminded him of any number of characters from *The Sopranos*. Unsurprisingly, given his accent, the name on the bike cop's badge read CAPARRELLI. "She almost made me ride right into a storefront! Anyway, she started babbling on about a dead guy, but I could barely understand her, so I just told her to show me what the hell she was talking about. She led me out here, and when I saw the body I radioed dispatch and secured the area."

Brighthouse jotted down everything Officer Caparrelli was saying for his own record, even though the detective held a digital recorder in his non-coffee-bearing hand.

A crime scene tech Brighthouse hadn't previously noticed interrupted Caparrelli's report. "Did you touch anything? Check for a pulse, disturb the scene in any way?"

"No, no, not at all," he said, assuredly. "I know better. I could tell the guy was dead." He swirled a finger around his lips. "Blue around the mouth. I mean, I felt for a pulse at the neck, but that was it. So, like I said, I secured the scene and the witness, that's all. By the way, she's right over there. Her name's Megan Rimes."

"Okay, thanks." The detective jutted his chin toward an officer holding a clipboard on the other side of the parking lot. "Make sure you sign the entry log, but I'm pretty sure you can go ahead and get back to your route."

Officer Caparrelli grabbed his bike and rode off in that direction. The detective shuffled away without a word, and Blakely turned to Brighthouse. "Shouldn't we see what's left for us to do?" Brighthouse nodded, frowning at the crew of officers already busy at work.

They followed after the detective. Brighthouse was surprised to find how much ground he'd covered before they caught up with him. The bedraggled detective had tracked down a Danish. He ate it sloppily as he spoke. Crumbs spilled down his chest, some of them finding the nooks of his crooked tie and nesting there.

"Listen fellas, I already sent units to assist the crime scene guys in a grid-search of the area, and a couple more went to canvass the neighborhood for anyone who saw anything or recognizes the vic. Not likely, since, according to his license, his name is Alexander Livanos, and he's not from around here; he's from Manayunk. Bottom line, there's nothing really to do here until the autopsy report comes back with the determined cause of death. I don't think the witness has been interviewed yet. Either of you ever take a statement?"

Brighthouse and Blakely just stood there. Detectives were supposed to take witness statements if there was a body involved. Blakely spoke up first. "I have, sir, but—"

"It's okay, have at it." He winked, handing him the digital recorder. Danish crumbs that had been stuck to his cheek fell to his shoulder. Brighthouse, out of respect for the dead man mere yards away, stifled a snort.

"What do you want?" Blakely asked as they edged away from the detective, leaving him to his crumbs and coffee. "To poke around the scene, or help me interview the drunken witness?"

To Brighthouse this was pretty much a rhetorical question: he wanted the scene. He also wanted to question the medical examiner about what she had found. Brighthouse, already walking toward the body, called over his shoulder. "I'll take a look at the scene. You're much more of a people person."

Blakely grumbled, discreetly gave him the finger by pretending to itch his eyebrow, and headed toward the witness.

Officer Blakely shook his head as he took in the sight of the young girl leaning against the ME's van, shivering in her tiny silver top and short denim skirt. Her feet were bare, coated in filth, and adorned with chipped blue nail polish. She was holding a pair of strappy, matching silver heels in her left hand and a lit cigarette in her right. Her long blonde hair seemed like it may have looked flawless earlier in the evening, but the sweaty, sticky clubs she'd visited throughout the night had definitely gotten the better of it. Surely, the cool August breeze wasn't helping either.

"Megan Rimes?"

The young girl responded blandly. "Yeah?"

"I'm Officer Byron Blakely." He turned on the digital recorder and got his notepad ready. "You wanna tell me what happened, what you saw, or uh, found?"

The girl stumbled before she spoke, even though movement hadn't been necessary. "I left Club 32 at last call and headed over to the South Street Diner with a couple of my girls." The bike cop was right: this chick was barely coherent. She spoke quickly, but with an intoxicated slur that made it almost impossible for Officer Blakely to keep up. "After we left they hopped a cab, but I don't live too far away from here, so I decided to walk. I started to cut through this parking lot when I saw that guy just lying on the ground by that car. Something about the way he was lying there, not curled up, not leaned up against anything . . . It just didn't seem intentional, you know? And his keys were basically in his hand. He made it that far only to pass out right outside his car? Couldn't even get inside and sleep it off? That's what I woulda done, nice car like that, probably has heated seats and everything. I called to him. He didn't say anything. I nudged him with my foot a little. Nothing. So I ran back out to the sidewalk to find a cop. South Street's always crawling with them on weekends." She rolled her eyes and huffed as she spoke those last words, visibly annoyed.

"Yeah, sorry about that," Blakely quipped sarcastically.

Ms. Rimes took a short drag of her cigarette. "Anyway, I ran into that other cop, the one on the bike, and told him what happened."

Blakely shot her a quizzical look, "Why didn't you just call 9-1-1?"

Another pull on the cigarette. "My phone was dead." She rolled her eyes again and turned her head to the side, exhaling the smoke slowly. As if Blakely had questioned the validity of that statement, she added, "I was texting on it all day, okay? And me and my girls were taking all kinds of pictures and videos all night, and that really drains my battery. Look, can I go now?" She crossed her arms, her high heels clunking against her narrow abdomen. "I just wanna get to bed." She yawned, and her breath reeked of cigarettes and licorice, suggesting one too many shots of Jägermeister.

"Yeah, in a minute. Just a few more questions," Blakely said, growing impatient himself. "You said you were at Club 32. Is it possible the victim's in any of the pictures or videos you shot?"

"I doubt it. You know, you cops are always trolling around down here. Don't you ever look around? Club 32 is way on the other end of South Street. We weren't anywhere near here."

"Still, we might have to take a look. Anyway, did you see anyone else around the parking lot when you found the body? Or anything that seemed strange to you?"

"Nope. The parking lot was empty. Just me and the dead guy. After the bars close, South Street becomes a ghost town." She tapped her cigarette, then shuffled her feet to avoid the falling ash.

"Yeah, all right. Thank you, Miss Rimes. Do us a favor and call if you remember anything else. Hey, and jot down your cell phone number for me in case I need to ask you anything else pertaining to tonight."

While Megan struggled to write down her contact information, refusing to put down either her shoes or her cigarette, Blakely searched for the detective to inquire about the witness's cell phone. His glance happened upon Brighthouse. He was carefully circling the victim's body, every now and then stooping down low to examine it more closely. Blakely shook his head as he watched his partner, missing only a magnifying glass and a tweed cap to complete the image of Sherlock Holmes.

Unaware that Blakely's judgmental gaze shadowed him, mockingly comparing him to the famous Sir Arthur Conan Doyle character, Brighthouse orbited the body sprawled on the pavement next to the smoky gray Lexus. In the dark of the night, the old oil stains of cars long gone could be mistaken for blood—but there was no blood. There was nothing. Something just didn't seem right, yet Brighthouse couldn't quite figure out what. The body appeared to have just fallen to the ground. *A man, in seemingly perfect health, prepared to enter his car, and just fell over?*

He approached the medical examiner, Dr. DiCicco, whom he'd only seen, but never spoken to. She was signaling her assistants to prepare to transport the body. "Does anything about this seem strange to you, Doc?"

At first, the diminutive woman didn't even look up at the officer. When she did, it was as if she peered up and through him. Her piercing eyes were probably used to dealing with detectives, not patrol officers. Brighthouse simply pointed to the victim again.

"Well, not at the moment," she said in a hurried voice, watching as the assistants carefully enveloped the dead man into a crisp white body bag. "He could have died from cardiac arrest or stroke, possibly even drug overdose, though I doubt the latter, given the lack of pulmonary edema around the mouth or vomitus at the scene. Speaking of the scene, would you mind stepping back from it?" Brighthouse backed away from the prone body using the path already cleared by crime scene techs. "Anyway, officer, I prefer not to speculate before I get him on the table."

"He's kind of young to have suffered something like that, don't you think? A heart attack, or a stroke? Are you sure you don't see any other kind of trauma?"

"Are you questioning my abilities, young man? Or do you just not know how this works?" She was looking at him fully now. Brighthouse didn't like it, but he tried not to squirm. His scar itched. He wondered if scratching it was the same as squirming. But the burning scar also reminded him that he wasn't just a young patrol officer. He knew something didn't feel right and deep down he felt he had his father's intuition.

"No," he said firmly. "I just don't believe for one second that a thirty-year-old man in good shape and I'm guessing, good health, could just fall down dead from a heart attack or a stroke. You can't tell me that's normal."

"Not normal per se, but it's definitely not unheard of," she said matter-of-factly.

"All right, well, perhaps I'll see you at the autopsy."

"Only detectives observe during the post. If there's anything probative, I'm sure you'll have access to my report. Why are you so interested, anyway?" Her last words came tumbling over her shoulder as she walked away, obviously a rhetorical question. She had no intention of sticking around for an answer.

Despite the ME's slight stature, Brighthouse had heard she boldly said what she meant and meant what she said; he knew better than to jog after her and press her any further. Instead, he thanked her coolly and watched her hoist herself into the passenger seat of the ME's van before it pulled off.

He walked back toward the site where the body had lain. There were no yellow evidence flags. There was no evidence. There was nothing. Until he spotted something.

Fluttering—more like struggling for motion in the thick late-August air—there was a single, long, dark hair, held fast in the crook of the driver-side side-view mirror. Brighthouse couldn't explain it, but he knew it was significant, and enthusiastically called for Blakely to come over and take a look.

Blakely dragged his feet on his way over. "What is it now?"

"A hair," Brighthouse said excitedly, summoning one of the crime scene techs from across the parking lot.

"So what? It's probably from the witness."

"No." Brighthouse's tone reciprocated his partner's irritation. "Seriously? The witness was a blonde. This hair is damn-near black."

"Maybe it's his girlfriend's. Or his wife's. Or any random woman's who walked through this parking lot and pulled a brush out of her purse. For the love of Christ, Lighthouse, the guy's time was just up." Through clenched teeth, Blakely's words were rushing into one another, but Brighthouse could tell his partner was mercifully struggling to keep his frustration at bay. "We were called out here to take statements and help out. We've helped out. There's nothing more for us to do here." He swallowed, and his features fell into a soft expression before he added in an equally soft voice, "Let it go."

Brighthouse knew he couldn't do that, so he said nothing.

Blakely just shook his head sadly. "I'll be in the car, bro."

4
Blood for Blood.

LYLA SAT UP with a start, her lavender satin nightgown glued to her frame from sweat. It was Wednesday morning, 4:30 a.m., and she'd had *the* nightmare again. For the past few months, as the ten year anniversary of her mother's death grew nearer, she'd been experiencing terrifyingly realistic dreams where she woke up to find that the floors in her house were saturated with fresh blood. In the dreams, she made her way through the hallway to investigate, where she found her mother, wandering around and bleeding profusely from one of her wrists. The most frightening aspect of the dreams was their realism: she heard her mother's muffled cries; she saw her mother's lifeless, glazed-over eyes; she felt the soggy, blood-soaked carpet beneath her feet; she even detected her mother's perfume, sourly tainted by the metallic smell of blood. Regrettably, each and every time she experienced the torturous dream, just when she thought she'd be able to reach out to her mother, hold her, help her, save her—Lyla woke up.

Much too rattled to fall back asleep, Lyla pulled her sweat-soaked nightgown up over her head and tossed it into a nearby hamper. She slipped into her robe and headed to the second bedroom down the hall. A custom-made, beech wood easel stood in the corner, propping up her latest canvas. Lyla took a few minutes to look over her work while she readied her palette with fresh paint. She sat on the plush, leather-cushioned stool that let out a familiar sigh under her weight, and began fluttering her brush across the unfinished painting. Adding feathery strokes of lashes to frame the terrified pair of eyes staring back at her, she recreated in her mind the final, fateful moments of Alex's pathetic life—and how invigorating it had felt to extinguish that life with a push of her thumb.

Sometimes Lyla chose to paint their lips, or maybe a hand, or some other singular part of their body. Using just black, white, and red paint—as always—Lyla worked on the abstract rendering of Alex's eyes at the time of his death. The emphasis was on the word *abstract*, which she did consciously so the artwork could not be directly associated to any individual victim. Conceptually, Lyla was able to capture the severity of Alex's fright and desperation, as well as her own liberation, represented by the reflection of the satisfaction in her own eyes within each of Alex's pupils. She carried out the formality following the demise of each of her victims, ritually mixing a syringe full of their blood with the red paint to add a personal, yet unseen, touch.

She kept the finished pieces in a locked antique trunk at the self-storage facility. Her only distant concern was DNA analysis, but honestly, not even the most astute investigator would stop to consider genetically testing the paint used in an assortment of random paintings. Besides, Lyla cherished her personal collection, which far out-weighed the risks of their existence. Each of the paintings afforded Lyla another piece in the puzzle of closure she so desperately sought.

Eventually Lyla's wrist grew stiff and her eyelids loose, falling at will with welcome exhaustion. With the painting complete, she felt she could finally catch a few more hours of sleep before her late morning appointment with her psychologist. Ever since the unrelenting nightmares had begun, she'd thought it might be a good idea to see a professional. She had only seen the woman a few times so far, but each of the sessions had consisted of seemingly insignificant background information—age, occupation, hobbies—thus nothing of substance had been explored. It wasn't for the woman's lack of trying; Lyla had been reticent. Yet now she found herself anxious to share her innermost secrets, especially with someone bound by confidentiality. Her murderous habits would have to remain private, of course, but she longed to explore certain aspects of her childhood. Besides, maybe the good doctor would prove to be a godsend; maybe she could vindicate some of the demons that burrowed deep inside Lyla's psyche. And maybe, just maybe, she would no longer seek out her own twisted ideals of justice. Maybe she'd finally be able to live a normal life? Lyla tried to picture herself as a domesticated soccer mom, packing lunches and cooking dinners. The thought of it was warming, even somewhat tickling, helping to lull her back to sleep amid a flurry of maybes.

When Lyla awoke, it was a little after nine in the morning and her eyes felt bright and her head clear. The sun was radiant, the sky blue, and what few birds Philadelphia had to offer were chirping over the urban din. *Today will be a good day.* She dressed and grabbed her oversized purse, complete with fresh syringes and other necessary materials—she didn't know *how* good her day would be—and headed out the door. Her plan was to drive out to the storage facility, admire her latest work one final time, lock it up, and head over to the psychologist's office. A good, simple day, indeed.

Parked outside her unit at the storage facility, Lyla hadn't even flicked off her engine before she heard a voice through the open windows. She could almost see his foolish grin and his too-inquisitive-for-his-own-good stare before the guard rounded the vehicle.

"Hey there, Miss. I didn't think I'd see you back here so soon. I guess you were right. You really are here enough to command a salary." He chuckled as he approached and began to peer inside Lyla's SUV with cupped hands. "Whatcha got for us today?"

Lyla hopped out and quickly slammed the door, hoping to emphasize her irritation. She didn't have anything in there of consequence, but she didn't need this guy becoming accustomed to poking his nose around. "Nothing much. Just finished up a painting. Wanted to drop it off."

"My wife works security at the Art Museum. You know, the one with the *Rocky* steps? Once a week I meet her on those steps for lunch, and I run towards her, humming the theme song from the movie." Lyla tried not to roll her eyes as he demonstrated this for her, jogging in place. "Anyway, I guess security is a family business." He laughed heartily. "She works there for the art, though. Are you shopping for a buyer? For the new piece you're dropping off?"

"No, this one's not for sale. I'm sorry." Lyla snatched the wrapped canvas from her back seat, slammed the door again, and tried to brush past the guard for a second time. He sidestepped her.

"Well, maybe I could bring her by here and you could show her some of your other pieces. I know she would really be interested in buying something for the house. You know, we're actually remodeling our living room and were looking for something to go right over the—"

"Listen, forgive me, but I really just need to get this in there," she interrupted, in the sweetest way possible. She held up the parcel and gestured in the direction of her unit up ahead, "I have to be on my way. I have an appointment that I cannot be late for. I'm sorry. Perhaps we could discuss this next time? And I promise to remember the coffee." Lyla restrained herself from tapping her foot as she waited for his response; she was on a time schedule and could do without the guard's small talk. She found herself on the verge of asking him for his work schedule just so she could avoid these little chats and intrusions altogether.

"Okay, sure. And I'm holding you to it! There isn't a Starbucks or Dunkin' Donuts for miles."

Lyla offered a curt smile and rushed off; the meddling guard already forgotten. With her most recent painting in tow, Lyla's mind wandered to Alex. Something about him, about his death, had seemed different, like a turning point in her life. As she pondered the meaning of these meandering feelings, she accidentally passed her unit, ending up instead at unit forty-six—the age her mother had been when she'd died. *Eerie*. She shrugged it off, and spun around, arriving at the familiar steel door of unit forty-three.

Safely inside its confines, she removed the padlock from the antique trunk using the key hidden between the bells on her anklet and slowly thumbed through the other paintings. There were dozens of them, drops of blood added to all but one: that of her father, her very first victim. His wasn't the first painting she'd done, but it was the one she'd often wanted to destroy. It was a portrait, done in red, black, and white like the others, and it was the only image that was recognizable, able to be tied to one specific victim.

Following his death, a visit to her mother's grave had cleared her head, had shown her a path. Infidelity had caused her mother's death, had caused her mother to bleed herself dry. Killing her father had not been enough, so Lyla promised her mother she'd find more like him. And she'd take their blood—their blood for her mother's blood. So simple. Just like an eye for an eye, this was blood for blood. It was only right; it was only just.

Finished shuffling through the many canvases in the trunk, she returned to the most recent painting of Alex's eyes, the eyes that had seemed so intuitive that evening. The drab interior of the storage facility may have tipped Alex off, but Lyla remembered his unease even earlier that evening: his questions, and the way he had been unable to stand still as she fumbled through her purse for her keys. *Somehow he knew*. That would explain why his eyes were filled with such ghastly terror, whereas her other victims had appeared genuinely surprised, an emotion that gave way to terror. *Too bad I can't discuss this particular conundrum with my new psychologist*, she mused half-jokingly. The thought made her conscious of the time, and she shot up, locked the trunk, and left.

Lyla exited the highway onto Callowhill Street, making several turns toward the tormenting hustle and bustle of the Center City section of Philadelphia. It reminded her of the never-ending chaos of Manhattan, but with far fewer lanes and slightly fewer one-way streets. It unnerved her to drive down the heavily trafficked streets, especially in her bulky Xterra, but she had no choice, so she tried her best to stay calm. The last thing she needed was to arrive at the psychologist's office with wide eyes and sweaty palms, appearing as though she had something to hide—even if she did.

Ahead, a yellow cab picked up its fare and veered recklessly back into the stream of traffic, right in front of Lyla. She almost didn't hit her brakes in time, coming within a second of sending shattered taillights and headlights splashing into the air. A cacophony of car horns and squealing tires surrounded her. Lyla decided then to pull into the parking garage up ahead and walk the rest of the way.

With their dark shadows and anonymity, parking garages excited Lyla. They seemed like the perfect venue to engage in her dark little hobby, and she wished she could have one all to herself. The dank and shady spaces that undoubtedly caused others to cringe made Lyla's mind race with inspiration. All she needed was a target. She eyed a man in a navy blue suit, his wedding ring visible as he lifted his key fob to lock his shiny sedan, but first Lyla needed to tend to some emotional unloading.

Passing throngs of business people buzzing around on early lunch breaks, Lyla, casually strolled toward City Hall. Her psychologist operated a private practice around the corner from the historic Philadelphia landmark. Despite the fact that it was located on the seventeenth floor of an impressive metropolitan building, once you stepped off the elevator, the down-home décor of the practice made one feel right at home. Lyla's shoulders fell at ease as she approached the young female receptionist. She let out a deep breath and announced herself. "Hi, I'm Lyla Kyle and I have an eleven o'clock appointment to see Dr. Jillian Atford.

5
A Fancy Shoulder Shrug.

BRIGHTHOUSE SAT IN solitude at one of the many desks at the station; the click clacking of the keyboard clashed with the tick tocking of the clock on the wall behind him. It was just about six a.m. and his graveyard shift was finally coming to an end, just as the day was beginning. He finished up some paperwork, tossed it aside, and stood to leave when the desk phone rang. He shuffled the papers aside, in the process knocking over what remained inside his open can of Red Bull. Yelling and cursing as he tried to salvage what was left of the last hour's work, he picked up the phone and angrily answered. It was Dr. DiCicco. Brighthouse's scowl slowly upturned into a broad, callow grin.

"I knew you wouldn't let me down."

Like the last time they'd spoken, her voice was flat and unyielding. "Yeah, yeah, yeah, relax. I don't have very much for you to go on. And you should be getting this from the lead detective on the case, but calling you is my good deed for the day."

Feeling somewhat deflated, Brighthouse's voice became quieter, "Thank you. What do you have?"

"The prelim didn't reveal anything more than what we already knew, but after I performed the autopsy—"

Elated, he cut her off. "You're kidding? And you already have the results? It's Wednesday. It's only been *days*! It usually takes *weeks* to get back to us with autopsy reports."

"I know, but this particular case was bothering me . . . for a number of reasons. It actually kept me up at night. So I conducted the autopsy and—"

"Wait—"

"Officer Brighthouse! Will you let me speak?"

"Sorry to interrupt, but are you at your office now?"

"No, I'm in Cancun. Can't you smell the coconuts? Please don't make me hang up on you." Her voice was still dry, despite what may have been her best attempt at humor.

"Go ahead. Hang up. I'm on my way over. Just have to stop and grab a Red Bull. You need anything?"

Sighing, and without answering, Dr. DiCicco hung up the phone.

The medical examiner was sitting cross-legged behind a large, L-shaped, metal desk. The lifeless gray paint that covered the walls and ceiling was chipped and peeling in a few places. The windows bore the same thick frosting as the door, prohibiting the late summer sunlight from shining through. The artificial, fluorescent lighting cast harsh shadows across her face; it was unfortunate, for she was rather attractive for an older woman, despite her sharp bone structure and permanent glower. She reminded Brighthouse of an archetypal librarian or a schoolteacher, especially with her dark, shoulder-length hair pulled back, and her reading glasses perched on the tip of her nose. Just as she looked up to greet him, he interrupted her for the third time that day. "Okay Doc, start with the prelim, and explain everything to me . . . like I'm a four-year-old."

She gave him a queer look: her eyebrows crooked, and her lips pursed to one side.

"Sorry, I was up watching *Philadelphia* before shift last night." She continued to stare at him, so Brighthouse continued. "You know, Denzel Washington? Tom Hanks? Denzel is a lawyer defending Tom Hanks, who has AIDS. I'm sure you've seen it, where—"

"Officer Brighthouse, if you're done playing Siskel and Ebert, I have an autopsy report to review. I rushed these results, and I'm doing you a courtesy by even discussing them with you."

"You're right. Of course. I'm sorry. It must be all the Red Bull." He held up the can and gave it a wiggle. "I gotta do something to get through these graveyard shifts." He fought not to touch the scar on his scalp, and smiled hesitantly. "I had an accident . . . a traumatic brain injury a while back. The location . . . one of the side effects was increased fatigue. Anyway, please, continue."

The medical examiner's face softened for the scantest of seconds before she continued. "The preliminary examination is basically an external examination. In the case of Alex Livanos—"

"Who?"

"That was his name. He did have a name, you know."

"Yeah, I have a tiny little memory problem, too." He held the thumb and forefinger of his free hand an inch apart. "Another side effect. No big deal. Please go on."

"Anyway, the prelim yielded no new information, just like I presumed at the scene and told you over the phone. Based on the lack of rigor mortis and the victim's unfixed postmortem lividity, he died between one and two a.m. on Saturday. There were no visible bruises or marks of any kind. No trace elements, either."

"Wait, you said, between, one and two a.m.?" Brighthouse took out a pen and a small notepad from his left breast pocket and began taking vigorous notes. *If the victim died in the parking lot at that time, why didn't anyone discover him until a couple hours later?*

"That's correct. Is that significant?" The ME peered up at him over her dark-rimmed reading glasses.

"Might be. And lividity is when the blood pools toward the surface that the body is lying on, right?"

Dr. DiCicco nodded. "Right. Gravity acts on the heavier red blood cells because they are no longer being circulated throughout the body."

"And how long does that usually take? I mean, since that's what hinted toward time of death."

"It usually takes about six hours for the blood pooling to become completely fixed. In Mr. Livanos' case, the blood had begun to settle; however, it wasn't entirely fixed. As for the rigor that begins somewhere between thirty minutes and three hours after, and is completed somewhere between six and twelve hours. The victim's body had barely begun to stiffen."

Brighthouse had finally become serious and subdued, certain the medical examiner's findings were probative. There was no way Alex

Livanos died in a full parking lot and no way had no one seen him when the clubs emptied out. Brighthouse was sure of it, as he drew arrows and asterisks throughout his notes.

"Ante mortem bruises developed on the backs of the lower legs," Dr. DiCicco continued, "which, in my professional opinion, were not a result of his collapse. X-rays and fluoroscopy were both negative."

"Wait, go back. You said a few minutes ago that there were no signs of bruising. I don't understand."

"Yes. Not at first, but, like I said, they developed over time since they occurred right around the time of death."

"Now, I'm not doubting you, but how can you tell the difference between those bruises, and any bruises he may have sustained just falling to the ground?"

Dr. DiCicco eyed him with one brow raised and Brighthouse immediately regretted his question, but he was genuinely curious. He loved this kind of stuff. "For one, the location. The victim fell forward and on his left. He wouldn't have bruised the backs of his calves during such a collapse. More importantly, in the areas bruised by the fall, there was no coagulation of the tissue's blood. That in itself is probative—it means he was dead before he hit the ground."

Brighthouse's pen hadn't stopped recording the medical examiner's every word. "What else?"

"Next came the full autopsy. Unfortunately, it was just as baffling."

Brighthouse dropped his arms to his sides and his chin to his chest, exhaling in frustration, his body language matching the ME's discouraged tone. "Okay, lay it on me," he grumbled.

"Well, after I cut him open, I examined the heart and lungs. There was no evidence of a myocardial infarction–"

"You mean a 'heart attack.' Why couldn't you just say 'heart attack?'"

She dropped the report to her lap to shoot him a piercing glare before reading further. "The victim's lungs and airways were also clear. His brain yielded no sign of a cerebrovascular accident—I'm sorry—a *stroke*. So my official COD is cardiac arrest."

Brighthouse looked up from his tiny notepad, clearly confused. "But you just said he didn't have a heart attack."

"Exactly. Heart attack is not the same as heart failure. You can have one without necessarily having the other. Basically, 'cardiac arrest' is medical-examiner-speak for 'I don't know how or why, but this person's heart just stopped beating.'"

"I see, so 'cardiac arrest' is basically just a fancy shoulder shrug. And there was no indication at all as to why his heart would have stopped beating?"

"No, that's what's so troubling. His BNP levels—brain natriuretic peptide, secreted by the ventricles when the heart is excessively overworked—were too low to indicate conclusively any cardiac etiology. Regardless, Mr. Livanos exhibited none of the usual risk factors: no cardiovascular disease, no high cholesterol, no diabetes, zero nicotine or narcotics in his system. He did have a BAC of 0.076, but that's below the legal limit, therefore, not really worth mentioning."

"Damn." Brighthouse shook his head. He was sure this case was going to lead somewhere.

"I also conducted a full toxicological panel. I tested samples of blood, urine, and stomach contents. Histological samples of the liver, both kidneys, the brain, and other tissues were tested as well."

"Okay, and what did you test for?"

"Everything. Mineral acids and organic acids. Heavy metal poisoning. Alkaloids and non-alkaloids. Gas poisoning. Food poisoning. It's all listed in the report. I made you a copy."

"And?" Brighthouse wheeled his hands around one another, urging her on, hoping for a lead to run with.

"There was nothing. Tox was clean, too. I'm sorry. If I think of anything else, I'll call you." Her tightened frown showed she was every bit as embittered as Brighthouse.

"Thanks, Doc. I appreciate you taking the time to contact me and go over the results. I know you didn't have to." Brighthouse wasn't sure, but he thought he saw a hint of kindness wash over her face, if just for a second.

"Truth be told, the detective assigned to the case didn't even show up to the autopsy. And when I called him with the results, he resented the fact that I'd rushed this report and no others. I do what I can, you know? And I suppose a small part of me decided to assist you because, in some ways, you remind me of my brother."

She fell quiet, rolled her chair over to the other side of the desk, and proceeded to gather what Brighthouse assumed was the second copy of the report. As she did so, he meandered around her office, picking up specimens and teaching models and tapping the sides of jars containing preserved organs. Dr. DiCicco was stapling the report together when a glass jar containing fetal conjoined twins in formaldehyde almost slipped from the officer's hands. "Officer Brighthouse!"

"Yes?" he replied. His eyes were round and innocent, his voice high-pitched and boyish as he placed the jar back on the shelf with care.

"Here is your copy. Now, please—and I don't say this with affection—get out of my office."

Brighthouse took the papers and bowed. "Thank you very much. Don't forget, if you think of anything else, please call me on my cell."

"You have to leave first for me to be able to think."

"Fair enough, Doc."

Byron Blakely was pulling his beat-up, blue Mitsubishi Montero into the driveway of his modest two-story Northeast Philadelphia home when his cell phone vibrated. A quick glance at the screen and he saw it was Brighthouse, calling him at 7:30 a.m.—well after their shift was over—and he knew he didn't want to hear what his friend had to say, but he answered the call anyway. "This better be good, Lighthouse."

"It is. You remember that DB in the parking lot last week?"

"The suspicious circs case? Christ, man. Do you have any idea how tired I am? Couldn't you at least let me take a nap before you drop a load of crap on me?" He hoped the intonation of his voice hinted that he was about thirty seconds from full-blown anger, because that would at least give Brighthouse a head start.

Brighthouse, however, didn't seem to care. He persisted, and Blakely was forced to listen. "Shut up and pay attention. Anyway, I just left the ME's office—I'm actually still in my car—she rushed the results of the autopsy and found *nothing*."

"Great. Case closed." Blakely pulled the phone away from his ear to hang up, but heard his partner still talking and resigned himself to the conversation for a little longer.

"Seriously, shut up. She may have found nothing, but she did say the bruising on the back of the guy's lower legs seemed to be inconsistent with his fall. And his TOD didn't quite add up, either."

"Okay, I'll bite." In a mocking tone, complete with a bobbling of his head that he knew Brighthouse couldn't see, he asked, "How didn't his TOD add up?"

"Because Dr. DiCicco estimated his time of death was around one or two a.m. The parking lot would have been *full* of cars at that time on a Friday night. There would have been plenty of witnesses strolling about. How come no one saw him keel over? How come no one discovered his body until hours later? Unless . . ."

"Please tell me you're about to get to the point." Brighthouse, becoming squeakier with excitement by the minute, had precious few seconds before Blakely got sick of sitting in his SUV.

"Unless the victim didn't die in the parking lot. Maybe he was placed there." Before Blakely could respond, Brighthouse exclaimed in his ear, "It was a body dump!"

Officer Blakely dropped the phone to his lap, took in a deep breath, and exhaled slowly before lifting the phone to his ear again. "I'm hanging up now. I'm going inside to kiss my wife and help my children get packed for their camping trip. Then I'm going to sleep. I'm sure my dreams won't be as ridiculous as this phone call, but that's another story. Then I'm going to take a shower, get dressed and go grab a few beers at Mickey's with the guys. Then, and only then, will I be well rested enough, and perhaps drunk enough, to even try to listen to your rambling. Okay?"

"I'll take it." Brighthouse must have had Blakely on speaker phone because he could hear his partner clapping and rubbing his hands together in excitement. "I'm gonna grab a Red Bull and head back to the precinct. I need to look into something. I'll see you tonight."

Blakely finally exited his car and, on the other side of Philadelphia, Brighthouse started his.

6
Lionesses.

DR. ATFORD SMILED BRIGHTLY. She held the door open for her patient and watched as Lyla timidly entered the office. "I almost thought you weren't gonna show," she said sweetly.

"I know. I'm sorry I'm late, Dr. Atford. I was trapped in that god-awful traffic, almost rear-ended a cab, and ended up parking in a garage a few blocks away just to get away from it all. Forgive me."

"First of all, Lyla, I keep telling you that you can just call me Jillian; you don't have to be so formal. 'Dr. Atford' makes me seem so pretentious. Second, I'm glad you made it. I was looking forward to exploring the depths of your troubles this time—you know, finding out why you've chosen to seek therapy and to see if we can get to the heart of a few things that may be disrupting you internally. Especially since our last few meetings have been pretty superficial, right?"

Jillian nodded reassuringly at her client, and the soft brown, shoulder-length twists in her hair flounced gently. Her voice was thick, slow, and sweet, like honey or maple syrup, the latter of which was coincidentally the exact color of her skin. With each buttery syllable she spoke; she exuded a warmness that instantly put her patients at ease, each of them feeling like they had known her for years.

Dr. Atford kept her office as inviting as her demeanor. Instead of basic drab colors like eggshell, taupe, and beige, she employed bold, rich tones: brown, mahogany, and burgundy. A few cultural masks and sculptures adorned the space, interspersed among bookshelves of reference texts and leather-bound first editions of classic novels. Just over her desk she'd hung a large, oil painting of the African Savannah, complete with tall, wispy grass captured in mid-sway and a pride of lions amid herds of water buffalo, gazelles, and zebras. The painting was meant to reel clients in, not unlike Dr. Atford's personality, but Jillian had chosen it because the hunters were sitting so amicably among their prey, fitting in because they had to, because they shared the same habitat. That fascinated Dr. Atford.

She had been doing this work for a long time. After receiving her Master's degree from Temple University, she'd taken some time off before taking a position in the Center City practice. She hadn't cared for the head psychologist, so she ended up counseling incarcerated females for a couple of years. In those women she'd seen so much of herself, so many orphans, so many abandoned to their own devices and their own fates that she could only stomach the work for so long, grateful that she hadn't ended up like them. Not entirely anyway—she simply hadn't been caught.

Although she still retained a few rehabilitating females as clients, Dr. Atford had broadened her client base and quickly became a highly regarded and frequently recommended psychologist. In fact, she'd recently renewed her contract with the Philadelphia Police Department as Stress Manager and Chief Psychologist, providing psychological support and evaluations to the officers, as well as modifying and overseeing their own in-house counseling services. She enjoyed working with the officers, but oftentimes treating them meant fighting back feelings she had buried long ago, feelings from a darker time in her life that she preferred to bury rather than resurrect.

Lyla's case roused Jillian's interest on several levels. For one, she was beautiful and a successful artist, yet she had chosen to seek therapy. *Why?* It wasn't that Jillian's other patients weren't attractive or successful, but that Lyla was on the extreme end of both of those spectrums. She was certainly nothing like the women Jillian had visited in prison for years, fighting addiction, abuse, and poverty. Lyla seemed outwardly personable, but at the same time like she was hiding something unfathomable, damnable, and dark, a puzzle Jillian was determined to solve. Possibly the most unnerving part of Lyla's sessions was her nagging familiarity. She wasn't sure why or from where, but somehow Jillian recognized or even *knew* Lyla, and that was one more riddle Jillian needed to decipher. The name *Lyla Kyle* gave Jillian pause, but how small could the world be?

Jillian motioned for Lyla to have a seat on the chocolate brown leather couch across from the office's impressive bay window. Perpendicular to the couch was a matching armchair. Jillian settled into it, crossed her bare legs, her complexion melting away into that of the leather. She turned on a small, digital voice-recorder. Lyla was seated at this point; Dr. Atford observed her quietly looking around as if this were her first visit, though her surroundings should have been as familiar to her as her face was to Jillian.

During her last few appointments, with the topic of conversation lighter, Lyla's mind had been on auto-pilot, allowing her to answer questions without much forethought. She'd spent the sessions staring out of the window, watching the hubbub of the world below, and getting lost in the African Savannah above Jillian's desk. She admired the way the lionesses were just waiting for the right time to pick their prey. Each time she stared at the painting; she tried to spot the weakest gazelle or the weakest zebra, the one the lionesses would target next. Lyla knew it was the females that did the hunting.

"So, Lyla, how have you been since our last meeting?" Jillian asked. Her twinkling eyes filled the room as brilliantly as the sun's reflection off of her sterling silver bracelets.

Startled, snapped back into the office from wherever her mind had been wandering, Lyla's muscles tightened briefly, but she recovered without revealing herself. "I've been well, I guess. Just working on my artwork. I've been finishing up that sculpture I was telling you about last time, as well as working on my private collection . . ." Her words trailed off and arrived at a smile. "Speaking of which, I went on a date. It ended . . . abruptly, though. Turned out the guy was married," she feigned a frown, "as they always are, with my luck."

"I'm sorry to hear that. How did you find out that he was married?" Jillian's voice was smothered in concern, yet her facial expression contradicted this. She sucked her upper lip inward, as if she were trying to figure something out. This seemed odd to Lyla;

especially since they hadn't yet discussed anything substantial enough to warrant perplexity.

"It's almost as if I seek them out or something," Lyla said, skipping over Dr. Atford's question. "It's strange. They're *always* married. And then I *always* have to just," Lyla paused, "get rid of them."

Jillian squirmed a bit in the leather chair, which elicited a sound reminiscent of a twisted balloon. Lyla wondered if she'd chosen that particular hue of leather so she could blend into the chair on purpose. Was she trying to make her patients more comfortable or was she simply more comfortable when she, herself, was hiding?

"Do you want to tell me about your private collection?"

"No." Lyla's response was firm and startlingly unforeseen. It annoyed Lyla that Dr. Atford had tried to change the subject, even if it was to something she'd probably assumed would be more agreeable.

"Okay. What would you like to talk about?"

"To be honest, I was hoping I could discuss with you some nightmares I've been having as of late. They're the reason I sought your services in the first place . . . I guess I've just been hesitant to mention them. Seemed silly, a grown woman seeking help about her nightmares, you know?"

"Absolutely, we can talk about that. That's not silly at all. A lot of people struggle with night terrors. When did they begin?" Jillian exhaled, visibly relieved.

"Well, my mom died ten years and eleven days ago. They began right around then: the ten-year anniversary, that is. They're awful and vivid, and I know they mean something because they keep recurring." Lyla went on to explain the dreams to Dr. Atford, making sure to mention the inclusion of all five of her senses, which added to the dreams' frightening tangibility.

"Well it sounds to me like there's an obvious childhood link," Jillian said, her voice quivering, her eyes avoiding those of her patient's. "Maybe some unresolved feelings toward the circumstances surrounding your mother's death."

Lyla frowned. "What's there to resolve? I know how she died. I found her. And I wasn't a child, I was an adult."

Jillian leaned forward. "So, she did, in fact, take her own life?" she asked, her voice vacillating.

"Yes. It's not like an unsolved murder or anything like that. Then the nightmares would make sense. But I know everything. I was there . . . I mean, like I said . . . I found her. Plus, it's been ten years. I don't understand it." Now, Lyla's words wavered as well, and her eyes were becoming glassy with tears.

"All right, let's not think about that day. Tell me about your mother. What was she like? Did you get along well? Were you close?" The doctor had fired her previous questions in such rapid succession, so out of character for her, that the pause preceding her next question was pronounced. "What did she look like?"

Lyla raised an eyebrow at Jillian's last, rather peculiar, inquiry, but ultimately ignored it. "We got along great. We were very close, although not as close as my dad and I. You know because I was Daddy's little girl, but yes, we were close." Lyla sat back, settling further into the cushions of the couch, letting them hug her and help her through this more difficult session. "She was a great woman. Always there for me. She was also a stay-at-home mom, so she had all the time in the world for home-cooked meals, pep talks, helping with homework, getting me ready for the prom. You know, all the things you see on TV."

"Okay, good. Very good. Can you tell me . . . more . . . about your mother? I mean anything else you want to share about her, some of her strengths maybe?"

"Um, strengths. Hmm . . ." Lyla sat up again, and began fidgeting with her purse strap. "Well, the first thing that comes to mind is how much she sacrificed for the sake of family."

"What do you mean?"

"My mother was the sort of person who excelled at everything she did, everything she tried. She could have been anything in this world. She was good with numbers, with literature, amazing with art, with people, with animals—just about any and everything. But she gave up trying to pursue any of her own goals so that she could raise me and be a good wife to my dad."

"Did you admire that quality in her?"

"I'm sure a lot of people would." Lyla sighed and began to stare out of the window.

"But you didn't," Jillian said.

"I would have admired her more if she'd stood up for herself."

"What do you mean? It doesn't sound like your father forced her to give up her dreams. Unless I'm misunderstanding what you're telling me," Jillian said, almost defensively.

"No, I suppose not." Hearing Jillian's tone, Lyla stole her gaze from the window and focused her attention on her psychologist, who was leaning so far forward she would soon be poised to fall from her chair. All the while, the doctor wrung her hands and picked at her fingernails.

"So, let's delve into the meaning behind that particular comment. What did you mean by 'if she stood up for herself?'"

"She was just naïve about certain things, that's all."

"Such as?"

Lyla was becoming increasingly apprehensive. Speaking about her mother was difficult enough but Jillian's body language was unsettling.

"Just things with my dad. She let a lot of things happen that shouldn't have happened. She should have stood up for herself, but she didn't, choosing instead to keep the family together." Jillian didn't say anything, so Lyla added, "Maybe if she had just done *something*, she wouldn't have died that day, alone on the floor, and I wouldn't have had to find her like that, and we wouldn't be here."

Jillian knew these questions were upsetting Lyla, but she also knew she needed to continue to press her patient—not because they were close to a breakthrough, but because Jillian was close to answers. She couldn't ignore certain coincidences, like Lyla's name. How many Lyla Kyles could there be? And then there were the circumstances of her mother's death. It was all starting to add up.

Jillian refrained from biting her lip, but couldn't help scraping the undersides of each of her nails, one by one, in succession—first her left hand, then the right, then back to the left. She turned her attention from her fingers to her patient and found Lyla had been watching her fidget with her hands just as intently, observing her every nervous movement.

Jillian recovered quickly, her tone as sugary as ever. "Lyla, what kinds of things? What was going on with your dad that your mother shouldn't have put up with? You can tell me. It's okay. That's what you're here for."

Lyla was silent for several minutes. She simply sat there, staring blankly out of the window. Jillian stood up slowly from the chair and sat down next to her on the couch, wanting to reach out and touch her, inspect her, look for hints of her own past within the other woman. Instead, Jillian reached her hand out and placed it on Lyla's knee, gently rubbing it, trying desperately to steady her patient's uneasiness, hoping she could coax a few more details from her before their hour was up. Although she was certain she knew the answer, she had to know for sure. Very softly she asked, "Lyla, did your father's actions have anything to do with your mother's death?"

Without saying a word Lyla immediately knocked the doctor's hand away and stood up. Her purse fell to the floor with a thud, and as she hurried to collect it. "This session is over," she said in a quiet, chilling tone.

"Lyla, it's okay. This is good. We need to explore the things in your past that still upset you. That's why we're here." Jillian stood up and reached out, trying to calm her down, trying to stop her.

Her efforts were in vain. Lyla flung open the door, turned around briefly, and said, "Next time," before slamming the door behind her. Jillian could hear her patient's heels stomping through the waiting area towards the elevators.

Dumbfounded, Jillian stood in the center of her office. It would have been an understatement to say that she had hit a nerve with Lyla; her question had either offended her or been completely on target. If Lyla was whom Jillian thought she was, it was probably the latter. If not, why else would Lyla have agreed to talk more "next time?" Coupled with everything Jillian had learned—and remembered—during the session, Lyla's reaction only furthered Jillian's fears about who her new patient really was.

7
Should Something Ever Go Awry.

LYLA HADN'T QUITE composed herself yet; her hands still trembled, and her index finger was sore from jamming the elevator call button at the psychologist's office moments before. As soon as the doors had opened, she'd rushed in, her body electrified with raw emotion. She'd barely been able to press the lobby floor button that would bring her one step closer to the garage down the street, to her SUV, and to her home.

Lyla breathed in and out deeply, focusing on the driver's seat where she sat in the depths of the parking garage, far removed from the dreadful demons of her youth. The long breaths, meant to be calming, were futile and soon became shallow. Lyla's anger and hatred for her father percolated beneath her skin, and she needed to release it. She pounded on the steering wheel, wishing for such a release, wishing she had a date planned that night.

A car alarm on another level of the garage went off, and Lyla couldn't bear to listen to its rhythmic honking. She scrambled around, searching for the keys she'd laid in her lap; she knew exactly where she would head next to relieve a little tension.

Lyla's SUV eased to a stop in front of the fitness club, at which she was a long-time member. She was in remarkable shape: aside from belonging to a gym, disposing of grown men on a somewhat regular basis didn't hurt either.

She kept a duffel bag full of gym necessities in her back seat, which she reached for and lugged up into her lap before hopping out.

Lyla enjoyed Tae Bo and kick-boxing classes most, figuring not only could she rely on her skills should something ever go awry with one of her victims, but the unbridled aggression that came with every jab and roundhouse kick kept her from having to dispose of a new victim every other day.

As she strolled through the lobby towards the locker rooms, she could feel every head turn to admire her, specifically two men who were stretching near the treadmills on the other side of the gym. Even though she was emotionally distressed, her radar was functioning just fine—so Lyla paused before entering the locker room and smiled at the pair of them, noticing the subtle shimmer of their wedding bands. She emerged a few minutes later and made her way over to the mats—as close to the two married men as she could get without appearing obvious.

Before Lyla had arrived within earshot of them, she observed them peering and stealing glances at her: they were talking about her. She muted her music, but continued to wear the earphones, hoping to hear something she could use.

Both men were now jogging briskly on their treadmills. Positioned on the floor mat, each leg extended, Lyla stretched as far forward as possible, struggling to make out their conversation. It seemed they were currently preoccupied with a gym regular they had nicknamed Sonny Short Shorts. Lyla had to stifle a giggle; she was familiar with that particular gentleman. He never actually worked out, except for an occasional ride on the stationary bike. Instead, he preferred to mill about aimlessly, always wearing a sleeveless white shirt and the tiniest pair of blue shorts. He was well over six feet tall, making the shorts appear even shorter, and he always seemed to unintentionally end up squatting or straddling a piece of equipment exactly opposite Lyla. As he did so, he'd expose far more of himself than she wished to see—which is why, at that exact moment, Lyla had to stand up, turn her back to 'Sonny,' and stretch her quads. She could now focus solely on the conversation at hand. Thankfully, the subject had changed its course—back to her.

"Have you ever seen her in here before?" The cuter of the two asked.

"Yeah, a bunch of times. She doesn't seem to have a regular schedule though. Lord knows I've tried to find out, so I could make sure I'm here when she is."

"You ever try to talk to her?"

"Nah, I just like to watch her. I'm married, remember?"

"So what? So am I. You can't have a little fun? A little chat? Just go over there and talk to her. If you don't, I will."

Lyla silently choked down her contempt. *A little fun. Yeah, because a little fun never hurt anybody, right boys?*

"Yeah, right. You will?"

"Watch me." The first guy's voice was growing louder. Had her music been on, Lyla would have still heard him.

"Will you please keep it down? What if she hears us talking about her?"

"Women like that sort of thing," the cute one boasted. "It's a compliment to them. Relax." He nudged his friend hard with his elbow. "Now watch. I'm gonna get her while she's alone."

"What are you gonna say?" his friend asked, slack-jawed.

"Are you serious? Is this junior high or something? You don't know how to talk to girls?" He laughed as he waved off his friend's remarks and stepped off the treadmill.

Content in the knowledge that wherever she went at least one of the men would follow, Lyla gathered her towel and water bottle and headed for the empty aerobics room across the gym. There, she practiced a few yoga positions while she patiently laid in wait. Watching her prey through the glass, she was reminded of the lionesses in Dr. Atford's painting, surrounded by temptation, but biding their time in the tall grasses of the plains.

His reflection appeared in the mirror in front of her. He was standing right behind her, admiring her downward-facing dog with bright brown eyes. Through the mirror, she admired him right back. His height and broad back and shoulders cast a shadow over her, and his thick arms twisted and bulged like tree branches. Lyla disengaged from her stance and turned gracefully around before lowering herself to a cross-legged sitting position, resisting the urge to reach out and touch his smooth caramel skin.

"I'm impressed a big guy like you was able to sneak up on me," she lied. "Is there something I can do for you? Do you need this room for something?"

In a slightly Southern accent, Lyla hadn't noticed before; he politely responded, "Actually, do you work here? I'm new here, and was wondering if you could give me some advice on classes to sign up for and whatnot."

Now, why did he have to lie? Lyla asked herself. First of all, she obviously didn't work there. Everyone who worked there wore those stupid yellow T-shirts. Second, she'd just overheard him exclaiming to his buddy that he knew how to talk to girls. Apparently not, if that was his way of approaching her. Still, Lyla decided to play along, since it meant potentially acquiring a new target. "What makes you think I work here?" she asked, smiling kindly.

"Well, you're in here alone . . . and I just figured you were an instructor or something."

"I'm not an instructor, but I could probably teach you a few things." She winked at him, still smiling. She hated that she couldn't stop staring at his body. He was blushing.

"I see."

Lyla giggled. "Don't get all bashful on me. Come, sit over here with me." She patted the mat. "You can help me stretch."

Sitting with her legs wide and outstretched, she motioned for him to sit across from her in the same position. "Now just put your feet where my ankles are, grab my arms like this, and pull me close to you." She grabbed each of his arms near the crook of his elbows while he awkwardly grasped the underside of each of her forearms.

"Umm . . ."

"Relax, I won't hurt you." *Not yet, anyway*. "What's your name?"

"Derrick."

"Big strong name for a big strong guy. I like it," she tittered. "My name is Lyla." As he pulled her forward, their faces became close. The warmth of his breath hit her lips and traveled rhythmically down the front of her tank top. She leaned in even more, so that her lips almost caressed his ear, and whispered, "So what do you say we get all sweaty together again tomorrow night?"

"Just like that?" he asked, pulling back, one eyebrow raised. Like all the others before him, he was stunned by her presumptuousness.

"Just like that," Lyla breathed into Derrick's ear, one syllable at a time. "Yes or no? I can meet you at Blue Martini around ten."

"Umm, definitely, absolutely. I mean, yes, I'll see you then." Lyla wasn't sure which was hotter: his buttery drawl, or his bold, burly body. He even had two darling dimples etched into each side of his smile. Not quite understanding what just happened; Derrick stood up to rejoin his friend. He paused at the door of the studio and waved a diffident goodbye.

Derrick coolly crossed the gym to meet his friend near the free weights before showing any signs of bluster. Lyla obviously couldn't hear them, but she gathered from their gestures and facial expressions that Derrick's friend couldn't believe he'd never tried to talk to her himself. The poor guy even seemed envious and disappointed. *If only he knew.*

8
Chasing After the Ghost.

MICKEY'S WAS A small Irish pub, tucked away down one of Center City's many side streets. The street itself was narrow and bubbled with the cobblestone of history never paved over.

The stench of garbage, urine, and fried food was particularly pungent on the last day of August. Despite its apparent lack of charm, the city's finest flocked to the little bar and grill for respite after their shifts to trade stories and theories, and to let the hops of their favorite beers relax the pressures of being a Philadelphia cop out of their muscles. Mickey's was one of the few places they could go where they felt respected and appreciated. That, and Mickey's crew made excellent French fries.

Officer Brighthouse hopped through the alley on his tiptoes to avoid the murky puddles and random trash that festered in the path in front of him. Full of energy, he was psyched to present his theories to Blakely. He sensed there was something important about this case. Day in and day out, the only calls they ever caught were gang shootings and robberies, drug deals and break-ins. Even that hostage situation at Family Dollar didn't amount to anything but a whole lot of paperwork, just like everything else. For once, he longed to explore the death of an ordinary citizen who was just out trying to have an ordinary life. He wanted it to mean something to the victim, and he'd be lying if he said he hadn't wanted to advance his career. If this case, the case of Alex Livanos' untimely death, turned out to be as significant as Brighthouse felt it was deep in the core of his gut, then it was all worth it; otherwise, the overtime and sleepless nights he'd most likely endure, not to mention the ridicule from his colleagues, would be nothing but empty sacrifices. He couldn't have it all be for nothing. He couldn't squander his second chance at life.

The heavy wooden door creaked as Brighthouse opened it, and the bells hanging from the inside doorknob jingled loudly as it slammed shut behind him. Mickey's was a typical hole-in-the-wall Philly bar, adorned with torn banners for house specials, praise for the local sports teams, and neon signs that winked at Brighthouse, suggesting he order a Corona. Faded yellow newspaper clippings paying tribute to fallen officers also lined the walls—including one paying tribute to Brighthouse's own father. He tried not to look at it, lest he deflate his mood as he searched for his partner around the bar.

Officer Blakely was seated in front of a touch-screen computer game in the far left corner of the room. His left hand clutched a tall, frosty mug of Yuengling—the only brand he bothered with—and his right hand busily attended to the puzzle on the monitor in front of him. He turned when Brighthouse approached, but made no attempt to interrupt the computerized challenge, which was timed, to properly greet his partner. Brighthouse understood, and quietly took a stool to the right of Blakely as Mickey wordlessly fashioned him a J&B scotch on the rocks.

"A J&B for JB. How the hell are ya, Junior?" Mickey asked, slamming the drink down in front of Brighthouse. This was his usual greeting, ever since Mickey had realized Brighthouse's drink of choice could be remembered quite easily since his name, Jason Brighthouse, bore the same initials. Luckily for Mickey, the familiar salutation never felt stale or overused to the officer. He also didn't mind when the bar owner called him "Junior," just like his father had whenever he'd spoken about his son to friends and colleagues, which is probably why Mickey had fallen accustomed to using the moniker himself.

"I'd be better if Blakely weren't glued to that stupid screen."

His partner grunted while Mickey let out a bellyful of laughter he seemed to have been storing up all night.

"You know, you look more and more like your old man every day." The neon signs overhead colored Mickey's head of fluffy white hair an assortment of hues as he poured himself a finger of scotch and raised it

Brighthouse nodded and did the same. “So I’ve heard. I think I’ve got his instincts, too. At least, I hope so.” Brighthouse took another swig.

“I’m sure you do,” Mickey said before meandering off to tend to other patrons.

When Blakely finally finished his game, he acknowledged his partner, though it wasn’t a friendly greeting.

“I’m not drunk enough yet. Can you come back in an hour?” he grumbled.

Brighthouse grinned as he sipped his scotch. “Nope. I want you somewhat coherent.”

Blakely let out a long, beer-saturated breath. “Okay. Whatcha got?”

“Do you remember what I said about Dr. DiCicco’s autopsy?”

“Maybe. Something about bruises and time of death, I think.”

“Fine, I’ll start there. The short version is that she found some bruising on the back of the victim’s legs that were inconsistent with his fall, and occurred around the time of his death. Speaking of which, she put the TOD around one a.m., when the parking lot would have been full, which leads me to believe that he didn’t die there.”

Blakely raised his mug, which was almost empty, in salute. “All rational inferences.” He was starting to slur. “I’m with you so far, bro.”

“Good. So, after I spoke to you, I went back down to the precinct and contacted the vic’s widow—”

“Brighthouse, you didn’t. She’s grieving, man. C’mon . . .”

“I know, but it was necessary to our investigation.”

“*Our* investigation? You mean *your* wild goose chase?”

Brighthouse’s face colored and he slammed his drink down on the bar top. “Hey, we’re partners. *My* wild goose chase is *your* wild goose chase.” Brighthouse was fed up with the constant mockery.

“Whatever.” Turning away from Brighthouse, he shouted, “Hey, can I get another beer over here please, Mick? I’m gonna need it.”

“Anyway,” Brighthouse continued through gritted teeth, “she was very helpful in answering a few random lingering questions that I had. For starters, she's a natural blonde."

"So?" Mickey set down another frothy Yuengling—a pint this time—and Blakely quickly scooped it up and gulped it down. Brighthouse wondered how many his friend had consumed before he'd arrived.

"So that means the hair that I found at the scene wasn't hers."

Blakely raised his mug again. "Fine, what else?"

"The victim was left-handed. His car keys were found in his right hand. His body was most likely posed, which fits with my theory that he didn't die in that parking lot." He was in such exaltation that he barely noticed that Blakely was still taunting him quietly, moving his arms in imitation of Brighthouse. "Plus, Mrs. Livanos says that her husband claimed he was heading to Atlantic City for the night to play poker with a few clients. What was he doing on South Street, then? Which brings me to the parking lot. I went there tonight before I came here. The attendant that was working that night says he remembers a hot *brunette* in a black SUV that used the lot earlier that night and left around eleven p.m. with a guy. He wasn't sure if the guy he saw was the victim, but he said they looked similar."

"So you're saying we should put out a BOLO for hot brunette girls? Wait, isn't there a hot girl database we could use? Or maybe we should just drive around in our patrol cars, and any chicks we see that we'd like to fuck, we haul in for questioning. Hmm . . ." Blakely stroked his chin as he continued. "Then we could cross-check the DMV database for black SUVs registered in Philadelphia. I'm sure there's only a couple thousand. Piece of cake."

Behind them, both men heard the creak of the door followed by the clamor of its bells. Together they turned and stared at the woman that entered. She sashayed in, and their heads turned, slowly tracking her across the room. It seemed an angelic chiming followed her, as well. It wasn't coming from the jarring pub door's bells, but from her silvery anklet. As she leaned against the bar to order a six-pack of beer, their gazes traveled over every curve of her impeccable physique: from the anklet of bells below one of her firm calves to the small of her back, and from around her tiny waist to her shapely breasts. She was breathtaking. Brighthouse and Blakely completely forgot what they had been arguing about before she entered. She completed her purchase and headed back out into the night, the sweet fragrance of pears and vanilla briefly replacing that of the stale-aired pub she'd left behind.

"Now we should definitely bring her sweet ass in for questioning," Blakely slurred as he held up his mug toward the door in yet another toasting gesture.

The two of them composed themselves, and Blakely looked at Brighthouse with a hearty laugh. "What are you staring at her for? Emma still looks good. When are you gonna knock her up, so I don't have to envy you anymore?"

"Man, not you, too. That's been her problem as of late. We've been arguing because she wants to have kids now, and I wanna wait a couple more years. She's even been talking about separating, because 'we don't have the same goals,' or whatever."

"Sounds rough, man. I'm sorry." There was a long pause as they both tipped serious faces into their glasses and took labored sips of their drinks. Then, Blakely continued, "Well, maybe, and this is just a friendly suggestion, you should spend a little less of your time and energy chasing phony cases and more time at home with your wife. That might help ease the tension a little, you know?"

"So, you're saying that it's entirely my fault that my wife wants to leave me?"

"No, but—"

"You know what? I'll explain it to you the way I've tried to explain it to Emma I don't know how many times. The way I feel is, if I see something in a case that the detectives don't, maybe the captain will see something in me, and I'll make detective myself. With a bigger paycheck and less reckless on-the-street hours, then we can start a fucking family, if that's okay with everybody. But you know what? I didn't come here for this. I'll see you on shift tomorrow night."

Brighthouse stood up abruptly, reached into his pocket, and pulled out a crinkled twenty-dollar bill, which he angrily threw onto the bar for Mickey. He sulked on his way out the door and slammed it behind him. As his feet shuffled sadly through the alley, he stomped angrily into every puddle that he had been so careful to avoid earlier. *Maybe Blakely is right*, he thought to himself, as he turned the corner and headed toward the multilevel garage up the street. Not only was he a running joke on the force, but his increased efforts to prove himself were also driving a searing hot stake right through the heart of his marriage. Brighthouse reached the entrance of the garage wondering if his childhood dream, if the dream that kept him simultaneously cowering in the shadow of his father's success and chasing after the ghost of his father's approval, was ruining his life.

Five minutes later, Brighthouse left the somber solitude of the parking garage elevator and stared in disbelief at the scene before him. Shattered glass littered the ground surrounding his dusty Maxima with the rusted out panel. A pale figure with skin stretched too tightly over his bones was settled in the driver's seat, hunched over, completely preoccupied with hot-wiring Jason's car. Brighthouse crouched down low to the ground, low to the shadows, and crept toward his vehicle. With concentrated movements, he retrieved the .38 caliber Beretta from the ankle holster beneath his right pants leg—his off-duty weapon. As Brighthouse approached his car, he inadvertently stepped on the scattered dirty diamonds of broken glass, which crunched loudly under his weight and movement. The strung-out thief turned his head sharply. His eyes were drooping, yet alert at the same time, sickly and bloodshot, but wide with appreciation of his situation as he reached for something behind his back—presumably something tucked into his waistband. Brighthouse immediately stood and took aim.

"Police! Step out of the vehicle slowly with your hands up. Now!" The man ignored him. The pale yellow fluorescent lighting of the garage highlighted the object the junkie had reached for: a gun, just as Brighthouse had suspected. It was a small caliber revolver, probably a .22. The man exited the car unsteadily, aiming at Brighthouse and mumbling unintelligibly. Brighthouse warned him again, “Drop the weapon, now.”

The man with a crazed look in his eyes took one shaky step forward, and a frenzy of shots rang out, exploding and echoing through the garage in a shower of fractured glass, adding hundreds more of the uncut gems to the ground.

Unscathed, Brighthouse, scurried to the man lying beside his open car door. The man’s blood had spattered into its open interior and onto the half dozen empty Red Bull cans inside. He kicked the revolver out of reach, and it skittered under the front end of the Maxima. Kneeling, he checked for a pulse. Nothing. He backed away slowly and reached for his cell phone.

A scratchy female voice answered, “9-1-1. What’s your emergency?”

“This is Officer Jason Brighthouse. There’s been a shooting.”

9
Her Coveted Soliloquy.

LYLA SAT OUTSIDE of the Blue Martini Lounge, hazard lights flashing, drumming her fingers on the dashboard while she waited to spot her most recent quarry. Realizing she was early, she tilted her head back against the headrest, her eyes closed. She lightly tapped her foot to the music while the engine idled, and the air flowing from the vents caused her bangs to flutter, every so often intermingling them with her long eyelashes. Lyla wondered if she was tired of this, tired of the constant vengeance, tired of chasing closure, tired of the dead-end dates that literally ended with death at her feet. Despite the six-pack of beer she'd purchased to dull her thoughts the previous evening—since driving around for hours without a destination had no effect—she had again gotten very little sleep due to the nightmares; maybe that was the only reason for her exhaustion.

A few songs and several minutes later, Lyla was startled by a loud and unexpected knocking on the passenger-side window. Derrick's warm smile greeted her behind the glass. She had felt an attraction to him yesterday when he was all sweaty and sticky, but boy, did he clean up nicely. He was freshly shaven, and his hair was cut particularly close to the scalp, as if he had just left the barber's chair. Lyla lowered the window and the spiced and woodsy scent of his cologne wafted into the interior of her SUV. He smelled almost as good as he looked, and Lyla hated him for it, and wondered if he put this much effort into his dates with his wife. Before Lyla could speak, Derrick reached in through the open passenger-side window, unlocked the door, and let himself in.

Slightly discomposed by his gesture, Lyla failed to come up with a clever salutation, so she went with something more generic. "Hello, handsome."

"Hi, beautiful. Long time, no see." Lyla fought the effects of his sultry Southern accent, which made her want to melt right there in her seat. "Hey, I have an idea," he said. "Since nightclubs are so loud and everything, what do you say we go out for a bite to eat? My friend told me about a nice little Mexican restaurant around here. And I heard they have a great margarita selection, too. What do you think?"

"Umm . . ." Lyla was dumbfounded. She couldn't believe what was happening.

He must have sensed her uneasiness toward his proposal, as he continued to try to persuade her. "I just thought that it would be nice to be able to sit across from each other and talk, that's all. Plus, I'm not much of a dancer," he said with a bit of laughter. He placed his hand on her leg and his palm eclipsed her knee. "Oh, and I sort of already made a reservation."

Lyla tried to gather her thoughts; Derrick was preemptively striking her usual plan. Instead of deciding that clubs weren't conducive to conversation while they were there, allowing her to invite him to her "studio," he had been smart enough to figure it out beforehand. She couldn't go to a restaurant with a soon-to-be victim. *What if we're remembered? What if he uses a credit card to pay for our meal?* The police would surely check his records to map out his final movements. Too many what ifs. Too many risks. Lyla wasn't in control . . .

"Okay, sure, but it would have to be my treat." She turned to give him an endearing puppy-dog glance.

He guffawed, and it echoed within the SUV's cabin. "Absolutely not! I don't know how gentlemen do things up here, but down South, a lady never takes the check. Anyway, it was my idea, so it will be my treat."

Damn. She should have seen that coming. "Okay, if you say so. But next time is on me."

"Don't push me, little lady. Besides, how do you know there's gonna be a 'next time?'"

Exactly. There won't be a next time. You'll never do this to your wife again. "Why wouldn't there be a next time?" she lied sweetly, winking. "Now where is this place?"

"It's in Center City. On 13th and Sansom. It's just a block or so up from a parking garage. And, don't worry, I plan on paying for that, too."

At the mention of a parking garage, the cogs of Lyla's mind began to toil and turn. Lyla's original plans may have been stymied, but her overall goal was still within sight. *Improvisation can be a beautiful thing.* She switched off her hazard lights, went around the block, and headed east on South Street.

They rolled past block upon block of late evening revelers, their tipsy reverie spilling in through the cracked windows, exacerbating the couple's silence.

"Are you always this quiet on first dates, Ms. Lyla?" Derrick finally asked as they turned onto Lombard Street.

The sound of his voice slicing through the stillness caused Lyla to jump slightly. She was trying so hard to reconfigure her plans that she had hardly remembered that she wasn't riding alone. "No, you just kind of threw me off with your change of plans. I'm one of those people that keeps a mental itinerary." She giggled to disguise her constraint. "So, I'm just trying to compose myself. Now tell me something, where did you get that adorable accent?"

"Well, believe it or not, I was actually born here in Philadelphia, but when I was younger, my family moved down to Georgia. I just came back about a year and a half ago." He paused. "You like my accent?"

"Of course, who wouldn't?"

"Umm, let's see. Just about everyone." He let out a hardy laugh and continued, "People up here seem to think I sound like a redneck or something. That's the only thing they can associate the accent with, unfortunately." He placed his hand on her thigh, once again engulfing her leg, giving it a squeeze. "I'm glad you like it, though.

At the mercy of one-way streets, they turned the corner on 13th Street in order to loop around to the garage near the restaurant, and Lyla decided it was time to know something, time to hear something.

"Can I ask you a personal question?"

"Anything." His fingertips embraced her thigh. Lyla's eyes remained on the road.

"Aren't you married?"

"Yes, ma'am. I hope that's not a problem?"

She couldn't believe his candor and nonchalance. *I hope that's not a problem?* All the appeal he'd held in her eyes—his caramel complexion, his dimples, his scent, his body, that accent—all of it dissipated, evaporated. She answered him frankly. "It might be for you."

Derrick changed the subject, as though he was certain Lyla was joking. "You're going to love this restaurant. From what I hear, they have the best Mexican food in the city. Homemade tortilla chips. You do like Mexican food, right? I'm sorry, I didn't even ask."

"Umm, to be honest, I've never really had authentic Mexican food before." *And I'm not going to start tonight, either.* She turned her head to hide a smirk as they pulled into the garage.

There seemed to be more going on in the garage than usual, and it didn't escape Derrick's notice. "What's going on in here?" he asked. "What's with the commotion?"

"Yeah, didn't you hear? Some guy got shot in here last night trying to steal an off-duty cop's car. His bad luck, I guess. It was on the news this morning."

"Oh, no, I had no idea. I don't watch the news. But I see *you* do."

Of course she did. Lyla watched the news four times a day—on the lookout for herself. She turned toward him, mirthless. "I guess death just interests me, Derrick."

Derrick's face fell with confusion. He probably didn't quite know what Lyla meant, especially since her voice had become a little brash with the thought of possibly showing him just how much death interested her. She parked the car a few floors up—though they had passed plenty of available parking spaces—and headed for the elevator. Once confined within the grimy, steel walls, the elevator lurched—and so did her date. He moved in on her, catching her by surprise for the second or third time that evening—she'd lost count.

He grabbed her waist and, kissing her vigorously, he pushed her into the back right corner of the elevator. He was reaching backward to press a button, probably to delay the elevator, but Lyla shoved him away and spun herself out of his clutches and into the front left corner, diagonally across from him.

"What are you doing?" Lyla's voice was heightened with confusion. Her eyes were wide and she could feel her face pulsing in tune with her thumping heartbeat.

Derrick appeared just as baffled in his corner of the elevator, the two of them facing each other like opposing fighters in wildly different weight classes. "What? You said you wanted to get 'hot and steamy?' Who says we have to wait 'til after dinner?" His head was cocked to the side, and he was smiling slyly at her. "Don't worry." He glanced around toward the ceiling. "I don't see any cameras in here."

He lunged for her again, but couldn't have expected what came next. The heel of Lyla's hand drove directly into his throat. Because she was shorter than him, the force of the blow was directed upward, which not only left him gasping for air, but also caused his jaw to snap shut and severely lacerate his tongue. Derrick's hands immediately flew up to his face, where blood was streaming from his mouth, only to be quickly absorbed by his snug, black shirt. Completely taken aback, Derrick was unable to react, standing frozen instead, with his hands cupped under his chin.

Lyla, despite being equally stunned, sprang into action. She reached into her purse and removed her precious eyeglass case. While Derrick was still struggling in the corner to compose himself, Lyla swiftly kicked him in the side of his left knee, bringing him to the ground, to a height she could more easily work with. His eyes were wild with fear as he cowered on the floor in front of her. She had to get this over with soon, which meant denying herself her coveted soliloquy, and denying Derrick any shred of an explanation. Without saying a word, she moved forward and yanked Derrick's head toward the core of her body with her left hand. He reached up with both arms to fend her off, and she jabbed the needle into his left armpit, hoping his underarm hair would be enough to disguise the puncture mark.

She could feel his body jerk under the pain of the injection. Then, something happened that had never happened to Lyla before: the syringe snapped, leaving the tip of the needle protruding from the crook under Derrick's arm like a single porcupine quill. Stepping back in horror, Lyla frantically jammed her hand against the elevator buttons in order to open the doors and make her escape. The elevator finally opened, was finally willing to part with her. She felt a strong, manly hand on her ankle. Derrick was a massive man. Whatever partial dosage had entered his system had not been enough to take him down, and certainly had not been enough to kill him.

With her left hand, she clutched the outside of the elevator and pulled herself beyond the open doors. Once free, Lyla again searched inside her purse, which was dangling from her right arm, for the eyeglass case. As she gripped her last remaining syringe, Derrick continued to tug on her leg, the elevator doors systematically trying to chomp down on him, momentarily throwing her off balance. The eyeglass case dropped to the floor, and she whipped her head around to watch it bounce out of reach behind his expansive body. With one last desperate thrust, Lyla injected him a second time, that time between the fingers that clung to her ankle, again hoping to hide the needle mark. Lyla stood, still gripping the outside of the doors to keep Derrick from dragging her within his grasp with his last waning energy. She watched as one by one his fingers eased their hold on her.

Finally subdued, Derrick seemed to slump back, to retreat into the recesses of the elevator like a defeated dragon—but Lyla was the monster. She snatched her leg free from his lifeless fingers and stepped over his listless body. She had one last thing to do. Reclaiming her mother's eyeglass case from under him, she retrieved an empty syringe, and withdrew some of Derrick's blood before heaving aside his paralyzed body to grope under his arm for the broken needle tip. Not feeling it, she assumed it had fallen loose and sprinted off to disappear into the darkness of a nearby stairwell.

***

Trembling, Lyla started the engine of her SUV, tires screeching twice as she reversed from the parking space and once again as she rushed down the spiral tiers of the garage. As she emerged from the parking lot, she dropped her head in despair as she realized just how careless she had been. She should have called the whole plan off, or postponed it, even. Instead, she put herself, her freedom, in danger. She didn't have time to remove all traces of herself from the scene, from Derrick's body, or from the elevator. Not to mention the fact that there were already cops throughout the garage, investigating last night's shooting. What if she'd left evidence behind? What if she had been seen with him in the garage? Too many what ifs. Too many risks. Lyla was spiraling. She had to pull it together; she needed to focus. She was losing control . . .

Her mind was spinning as fast as her tires as she inadvertently ran the red light in front of her. Seconds later, red and blue lights pulsed behind her, accompanied by the ear-piercing whir of sirens. Lyla braked and hugged the curb. Considering her recklessness, she prayed for a traffic ticket and nothing more.

Still quivering, her license and proof of registration and insurance in her lap, Lyla kept her eyes transfixed on the rearview mirror above her. The officer was fairly young with a serious brow, like her fathers had been. She wondered about the women her father had stopped, how those stops may have gone. Lyla supposed it was probably quite easy to get away with murder if you were beautiful and Officer Kyle pulled you over.

During the officer's stride up to her door, Lyla continued to watch him in the rearview mirror as he clutched the clip mic attached to his left shoulder. His brow furrowed; he stared intently at the ground, appearing to listen to something compelling. He responded back before jogging up to her window. Lyla lowered it.

"Good evening, ma'am. Listen, I actually have a more pressing situation to attend to, so you're off the hook on running that red light. But do us all a favor, and be more careful." He nodded and tipped his hat before hurrying back to his patrol car. Lyla's relief was short-lived, however, because the officer's urgency could only mean one thing—Derrick's body had already been found.

10
Daddy Had Lots of Girls.

MINUTES PAST MIDNIGHT, Lyla's hands were still quaking with the weight of her keys and her foolhardiness as she unlocked her front door. She'd only narrowly escaped. She couldn't believe how near she'd come to being ticketed so close to the crime scene. Despite how sloppily she had conducted herself, the last thing she needed was official documentation that connected her with the area.

Following a brief shower, her wet hair dampening her faded violet shirt and sending a shiver down her back, Lyla sat in front of her easel and stared blankly at the canvas in front of her. She was too rattled to paint. Derrick's death didn't count. She'd never connected with him. She'd been too occupied with fending him off to see the terror unfold in his eyes. There was no resolution, no purposefulness, and no explanation. All in all, his death was highly unsatisfying. Lyla sighed, exasperated, but the tension and anxiety was overwhelming, and at its pinnacle, she lashed out with both feet and kicked over her easel, splintering one of its slender legs. A small tin of red paint—spiked with Derrick's blood—also crashed to the floor, seeping into the hardwood panels.

Lyla rushed from the studio, creating her own wind in her wake, stirring charcoal drawings behind her as she left for the sanctuary of her bedroom. She flopped herself across the bed and glanced at her cell phone, but soon realized that she had no one to call to unburden herself on. Lyla reeled at the thought that something she had turned to for years for comfort and control had left her anxious and alone. For the second time in a short while, Lyla entertained a brief urge for normalcy.

Perhaps opening up to Dr. Atford might be the best thing for her.

And so it was settled: she would visit the psychologist's office first thing Monday morning.

After moping through the hours until Monday, Lyla clawed herself out of the house at dawn. Arriving at the Center City Starbucks at six a.m., she'd never had a fresher latte. For hours, she sat in the corner, vacillating between patiently waiting while gathering her thoughts and staring at the café's clock. Her gaze wandered from the back table where she sat, through the café, and out the window, to watch the number of hurried passersby increase with each hour. Lyla started to wonder if one of the married men rushing past on this very morning might cross her path at a later date, but she quickly forced the thought from her mind. How could she daydream about a 'later date' when she was still careening from last night's date?

At nine a.m., Lyla headed into Dr. Atford's office building. She didn't have an appointment, but she had to be seen. She had to talk to someone before her impulses destroyed her. The elevator ride up to the seventeenth floor felt uncomfortably familiar, and Lyla's fingers trembled with the overwhelming urge to lash out. In a way that was a good thing, because she really needed to face her past, and her only motivation to do so was the immediate present.

Lyla exited the elevator, approached the petite, young receptionist, and began to state her name, but was instantly cut off. "Good morning, Ms. Kyle. How may we help you today?"

Lyla wasn't surprised. She realized that a woman like herself was probably not easily forgotten, by men or women. "Actually, sweetie, I was hoping to see Dr. Atford today. I know I don't have an appointment, but . . ."

"Well, I'm terribly sorry, Ms. Kyle," she said, with a forced smile meant to ease Lyla's urgency, "she is currently with a patient. In fact, she's booked solid the entire day." She started clicking something on her computer screen. "You'd be better off waiting until your next scheduled appointment . . . on Wednesday."

"No." Lyla leaned on the counter. "Listen, Suzie, or whatever your little name is—"

"Sharon—"

"I think, rather, I know, I would be better off if I saw Dr. Atford right now."

Lyla strolled off toward Jillian's office door, glancing behind her. Sharon had picked up the phone, presumably to call building security, but must have immediately realized there was no time for that because she dropped the receiver and shot up from her desk. She tried to make her way out from behind it, tried to chase after Lyla, but her skirt snagged on an open desk drawer. This gave Lyla the extra twenty seconds she needed to open Jillian's door and slink inside. She closed the door behind her and leaned on it heavily, although she could feel the door handle turning, repeatedly jutting into her ass. Lyla could hear Sharon's shouts on the other side, but she didn't care.

"Dr. Atford I'm really sorry, but I need to see you. It's an emergency."

Jillian's features were still, her voice calm as she tried to diffuse the situation. "Lyla, whatever it is, I'm sure it can wait. We'll have plenty of time to explore it during our next session."

"No." Lyla was shouting in desperation now. "I am a threat to myself and others. Surely that merits an emergency session?" She nodded to the other patient and snickered. "I mean, what's her biggest problem? She's sick of car-pooling all her bratty kids to soccer practice?" Lyla knelt down in front of the patient, who was rendered speechless at the scene unfolding around her. "What's the matter? Would you rather be snack-mom?" Lyla asked, her tone condescending, her head cocked to one side.

Sharon entered the room, now that Lyla was no longer blocking the door. She stood in the middle of the office, mouth agape with a mixture of fear and confusion. Jillian stood up. "Lyla, I need you to leave. If you'd like, we can talk during my lunch hour at two o'clock, but I'm afraid that's the best I can do."

Lyla straightened also, the patient in front of her frozen in a state of mortified shock. "Maybe you didn't hear me, Dr. Atford. I AM A THREAT TO MYSELF AND OTHERS!" She turned back toward the soccer mom. "Now get out of here. Go! Buy yourself some new clothes, and maybe your husband's wandering eyes might wander back to you for once. Go. GET THE FUCK OUT!"

Jillian swallowed audibly, approached her patient, and softly asked if they could continue next week. Meanwhile, Lyla took a seat right next to the woman on the couch, and stared at her until she gathered her belongings, snatched part of her skirt from under Lyla's thigh, and left in a huff. Jillian closed the office door behind the poor woman, and Sharon could be heard on the other side working on damage control: apologizing profusely and offering a free session.

Dr. Atford made her way back to her armchair. She sighed loudly and studied Lyla. "Okay. You have my undivided attention. What's troubling you? Are the nightmares getting worse? I must say, after that performance, they'd better be so bad you're suffering from sleep-deprivation induced psychosis."

"No. The nightmares have stayed the same. I'm here to talk to you about why I get them. I think it has something to do with my youth. With what happened between my parents that I've never told anyone. I've kept it inside so long . . . and . . . I need to confront it, I think, in order to get past it. Does that make sense?"

"It makes perfect sense. Where would you like to begin?"

"I would like to begin with my dad."

The office fell silent; just the tapping of Jillian's pen against her notepad filled the room while she waited for Lyla to work up the nerve to begin speaking. Mostly Jillian tried to mask the sound of her heart rate, certain it was perceptible to her patient. She hadn't been in the center of such a volatile situation since a day she'd long since buried. A day where only she had survived. A day not far removed from her patient's past. Jillian took a deep breath and sat back, the leather couch sounding almost as if it were exhaling with her. Meanwhile, Lyla also seemed ready to begin.

"I was Daddy's little girl. But Daddy had lots of *girls*, if you know what I mean. And given his profession—he was a cop, you know—it was easy for him to get away with it. He would tell us he was working late. Or meeting with informants. Or on a stakeout. And we had no reason not to believe him."

Jillian leaned forward, her softly twisted hair falling gently over the front of her shoulders. She fought to split her attention, knowing Lyla's revelations were important, but also looking and listening for something to confirm her suspicions about Lyla's identity. It was Jillian's job to want to help her, but she couldn't focus entirely on Lyla's words. Instead, she also focused on Lyla's mouth as she spoke. Rather, the way her mouth moved; it was so familiar. In fact, all of her facial expressions reminded Jillian of *him*. It couldn't be a coincidence.

"At first I didn't even notice it," Lyla continued. "I was young, and I idealized my dad. He was brave. He caught bad guys and still had time to call me at bedtime, just to tell me goodnight." Her voice deteriorated from slightly jovial to somber. "Then one day I saw him. Kissing her. He didn't see me. It was my last year of residency, and I was meeting a friend downtown to help her shop for a gown for her college's Father-Daughter Gala." Lyla snickered. "The irony, right?"

Jillian's pen dropped. It rolled down her notepad and into her lap. She never made a move to grab it. She no longer needed to take notes—and she no longer had trouble focusing on her patient's words.

"I remember seeing a squad car parked down the alley near Mickey's," Lyla continued, "my dad and his cop friends used to hang out there. Cops still go there, I think. Anyway, the car was parked kinda cock-eyed, so the ID number on the passenger side, near the gas gauge, was visible. I recognized it as the car he drove. I was all set to skip up the length of the alley to greet him when I noticed a woman. She was leaning into the driver-side window. She wore a low-cut, white tank top, and was obviously using her arms to press her breasts together." Lyla's upper lip snarled with disgust at the memory. "I remember her brown skin glistening, in spite of the shadows. I remember the way she played with her hair, twirled it with her fingers. Then she did the unthinkable."

Jillian was listening intently now. She swallowed hard, though she hadn't wanted to display her discomfort.

"The woman leaned completely into my dad's squad car and kissed him. On the lips. Passionately." Lyla's voice was shaky. "I could see his hand—his left hand that bore his wedding ring, for God's sake—stroking the side of her face."

Oh, God . . . Dr. Atford felt her heart race and a muscle in her right forearm began to twitch; she felt its pulse all the way down to her fingertips. She picked at her fingernails, couldn't keep her hands still.

Lyla may have had a breakthrough, but Jillian was about to have a breakdown.

She was the young woman who had leaned into the squad car and kissed Lyla's father all those years ago, in the flickering shadows of a Philadelphia alleyway.

11
Piecing Everything Together.

OFFICER BRIGHTHOUSE INHALED a deep breath of stale, coffee-drenched air. He sat at one of the communal desks, twisting an already-kinked telephone cord, engrossed by the information streaming through the other end of the phone. He let out his breath, but its hot moisture and coffee-tinged odor offended him; he preferred Red Bull. The nearest store had been all sold out, probably because of him.

Earlier, Brighthouse had searched the National Center for the Analysis of Violent Crime, or NCAVC's databases for suspicious deaths similar to his current obsession: the mysterious death of Alex Livanos. Normally, it would seem counterintuitive to look for suspicious circumstances in a database known for detailing violent crimes and spree killings, however, Brighthouse was well aware that occasionally law enforcement personnel added cases which could not be conclusively ruled homicides—but definitely indicated foul play—to its Unit IV, better known as the Violent Criminal Apprehension Program, or VICAP. So far, he had spoken with the Delaware County ME and the Montgomery County Coroner. At the moment, he was on the phone with the Chester County Coroner. Each official had confirmed Brighthouse's suspicions: there was a strange epidemic affecting young men in the greater Philadelphia area—an epidemic his instincts told him was the clever handiwork of a cunning serial killer. Brighthouse just needed to prove it.

"Yep, that sounds just like the report on our victim," Brighthouse replied to the coroner. "No health problems, good-looking, found near a nightclub, in a parking lot. Tell me, was your guy also married?"

"Umm, I believe so, yes." The voice on the other end was the complete opposite of Dr. DiCicco's, surprisingly upbeat for a woman who had her hands wrist-deep in human innards all day; then again, Brighthouse was probably the most cheerful cop anyone had ever met.

"And he was wearing his wedding ring?"

"Yes, I remember having to cut it off because it was so snug. I was told the wife was very upset about that."

"Okay, thank you, Doctor . . . ?"

"Oh, just call me Alex."

"Just like our victim." *Oops, not a coincidence I should have pointed out.*

The coroner didn't seem to mind though, as she chimed in, "Yes, but I'm a woman. And alive, so . . ." She giggled like a coed.

"Right, of course. Well, thank you again. I'll call you if I have any other questions."

"Sounds great, and good luck with your case."

Brighthouse bid the chirpy coroner good day and briskly hung up the phone. He needed to find Blakely. Right now.

It was ten minutes before roll call for shift change, and Blakely was nowhere in sight, that meant he was probably yakking with the other officers in the locker room. Brighthouse crossed the squad room, weaving between the rows of desks, the pins on his uniform glinting and gleaming under the fluorescent lights. Aware of the time, he jogged down the hallway and into the locker room. Sure enough, Blakely was posed in the center of two rows of dull, blue-gray, metal lockers, one leg up on a bench. He was hunched over, tightening his bootlaces and rambling on about the Eagles' last preseason game.

"Hey Byron, can we grab a cup of coffee or something? I wanna run something by you." Jason Brighthouse, being the butt of all jokes around the department, preferred, no, *needed*, to get Blakely out of there and away from their colleagues in order to talk safely about his findings.

"Jason, shift starts in a few minutes, can't it wait?" As usual, Blakely's voice was fraught with irritation.

"Well, no, it can't. I have to head to Center City to start my mandatory psych sessions, you know, because of my shooting? So I definitely won't be partnered with you this afternoon. Please?" Brighthouse was trying not to sound desperate as all eyes in the locker room were on him, waiting for an opportunity to break out his much despised nickname. "I just want to pick your brain about something."

Blakely slammed his locker shut, stood up tall, and sighed heavily. "Please don't tell me this is still about that DB from the parking lot." Blakely sounded exhausted with his friend's antics.

Hurt, Brighthouse opened his own locker. He didn't need anything from it, but he used the door to shield himself from his colleagues, to hide the sudden wash of pink embarrassment that had come over his face.

"Yes, but I did some research, called around, and. . ." The cops who had stuck around to hear their exchange before heading to roll call burst into laughter. Brighthouse couldn't stand it. His scar bristled, and he left before the heat he felt in that soft, striated tissue became even more visible in his cheeks.

Blakely caught up with him in the hallway. Beneath his steely, sarcastic exterior, Brighthouse knew he sometimes had an indulgent spot for Jason. His friend flicked up his left wrist to check his watch. "You have less than five minutes. Go. And may I suggest you use abbreviations and small words."

In one breath, Brighthouse spilled what he knew. "I came in this morning, off the clock of course, and used the NCAVC database to search for other cases like ours. Found four, pretty local, over the last couple of years. Clifton Heights, Plymouth Meeting, Tredyffrin, and UPENN. I spoke to the MEs and county coroners, and in all, except the UPENN case, all the victims were young, married men, not a single health problem or obvious COD. And not a single fiber or hair or piece of lint. On any of them. I still have to track down Dr. DiCicco about the UPENN victim, since that one was right in her backyard. I'm surprised she didn't remember it on her own—"

"Wait, why do we care about lint?" Blakely asked dryly, waving his hands around to force Brighthouse's story backward.

"Because Alex Livanos owned two Akitas. Two, furry, fluffy-ass dogs. Yet not a single dog hair was found on his body. Not one."

"Maybe he brushed himself off before he went out. Lots of people do that."

"That's what I thought, too, but every seat in his car was covered in dog hair. There's no possible way none of it transferred to his clothes while he was driving." Looking at his partner's face, Brighthouse could tell he was scratching the surface. "I'm telling you, it's like someone *cleaned him off* before his body was found."

"Okay, that actually is a bit strange." Blakely looked down, obviously thinking. "Okay, I have to run or I'll be late for roll call. We'll talk about this tonight, after shift, at Mickey's."

Without a second thought or another word, Blakely jogged up the hall to make roll call on time, leaving Brighthouse elated to have someone's support for once.

Despite his progressive conversation with Blakely, it was with sluggish steps that Brighthouse headed to his mandated session with the department's outsourced psychologist. The officer-involved shooting was starting to take a toll on him. All he wanted to do was focus on this case, and not his failing marriage. Throughout the past several weeks, he only intermittently wore his wedding band, and he couldn't even say the same for Emma. In fact, he wouldn't be surprised if his marital issues were a factor in his captain pushing so hard for the shrink sessions in the first place. Especially since it was most definitely a clean shoot—caught on the only operational security camera on that level of the parking garage. *If only there had been eyes on what happened to that man they found unconscious in the elevator last Thursday night.* Brighthouse rushed the thought from his mind. Though the idea fought to persist, it wasn't his case.

The afternoon sun shone off the leering buildings of Center City as they swallowed Brighthouse's sedan. He passed the very garage where the fatal confrontation with the gaunt, thieving junkie took place, an incident that was proving a most unwelcome distraction.

Just then, another distraction filled the car with the simplified instrumental version of "Who Are You," the theme song to Brighthouse's favorite TV show; his cell phone was ringing.

Tugging it from his belt clip with a *click*, he answered, "Brighthouse here."

"Hi . . . Officer Brighthouse?" The female voice on the other end was drab, tired, and vaguely familiar with its subtle Greek accent. Before Brighthouse could identify it, she beat him to it. "It's Mrs. Livanos. I don't know if you remember me, my husband was found almost two weeks ago."

"Yes, of course. I'm sorry again for your loss." Brighthouse hated uttering such a robotic mantra, but mostly he hated how easily it slipped from his lips, so he tried something more personal. "How are you holding up?"

"As well as can be expected. Listen, I was just wondering," her voice cracked, "where is my husband's wedding band? It wasn't among his personal effects and, as you could imagine, I would really like to have it."

"Yes, yes, of course," he also wished he didn't repeat himself when he was nervous. *But why am I nervous?* "I understand, Mrs. Livanos, but there was no ring found with the body, uh, his body, I mean, your husband's body. I'm terribly sorry." There was an awkward pseudo-silence as neither party spoke, but the poor woman wept. Brighthouse tried to comfort her, tried to offer a rational, innocent explanation as he parallel-parked his car near City Hall. "Are you sure he hadn't taken it off to have it cleaned or resized?"

"No." Her voice was cold beneath the sobs. "He said he was meeting some clients for a poker night in Atlantic City . . . and look where you found him. The only obvious explanation . . ." She was fully bawling now. Brighthouse's heart twisted like a wrung sponge.

"Ma'am, you don't know . . . that, or anything, for certain, and there's no need to get yourself even more upset. I'm sure it will turn up, and there will be a perfectly innocent explanation." Brighthouse realized that he might have just lied to a grieving widow and winced. "If it doesn't, maybe some passerby thought it was worth something, and lifted it. You never know. Now, I really do apologize, but I have to go. I promise to call you if we come across your husband's ring. I will deliver it to you personally." An empty promise was the least he could do after trying to convince a grieving widow her husband's infidelity hadn't cost him his life.

The shattered driver-side window had been replaced, and it was noticeably newer looking than the others. That bothered Brighthouse, reminded him of the shiny pink skin scar on his scalp, a constant souvenir of his second chance. He shrugged it off and started walking the short distance toward the high-rise that housed the psychologist's office.

After a lengthy elevator ride to the seventeenth floor, Brighthouse just wanted to get the appointment over with; he knew exactly what to do. He was ready to regurgitate every possible cliché in order to prove that he was capable of continuing active duty. You had to be comfortable taking a life, but you couldn't be too comfortable, like some kind of renegade psycho-cop. But you also couldn't act traumatized at having dispensed your weapon. Brighthouse knew exactly what to do. Yep, he was ready. *Bring it on, Shrink.*

The elevator doors parted, and Brighthouse approached the receptionist. She seemed rattled. He watched as she attempted, with shaky hands, to refill a mug with a dozen pens, the pens spilling all over the desk after each try. She hadn't even noticed him standing there. "Sorry I'm late, I got held up at the precinct. I'm Jason Brighthouse, here to see Dr. Jillian Atford."

"Yes, Yes. She's just finishing up with an, um, emergency session." She picked up the telephone. "I'll let her know you're here."

Brighthouse was so focused on the receptionist's intentional whispering into the receiver that he almost didn't notice the emergency patient leaving Dr. Atford's office. *Almost.*

She brushed past him just as he inhaled, as if she'd timed it. She smelled like pears and something else, probably some flower he'd only seen for sale in the nursery section of Home Depot and couldn't pronounce, like gardenias or hydrangeas. He smiled, watching her walk past, the soft sound of bells tickling his ears as she strode by. The way she glided across the room was as mesmerizing as her scent—and just as familiar. She stooped down, and leaned over the counter to speak to the receptionist. Her long, dark hair cascaded into her face. She turned, facing him, as she brushed the hair behind her ear with a slender, dainty finger. He recognized her. Instantly. She was the striking woman that had come into the bar the night he had argued with Blakely about the Alex Livanos case. The night he had stomped through the alley. The night he had shot a junkie in a dark, damp parking garage. Just as he finished piecing everything together, a buttery, yet slightly shaky, voice called out from the open office door.

"See you soon, Lyla." Then she turned to him. "Officer Brighthouse? I'm ready for you now."

12
Drifting and Bobbing.

LYLA HELD THE young man's gaze, even though Dr. Atford beckoned him to his appointment. She enjoyed the way his eyes sparkled with boyish wonderment. He was quite handsome, and Lyla found herself curious, wondering why he sought the help of a psychologist. *He looks so normal*. Then again, so did she.

"Ms. Kyle?" The receptionist was trying to keep Lyla's attention, trying to confirm Lyla's next visit, her voice filled with agitation. "Does next Wednesday work for you?"

"Um, next week?" Lyla faced the young girl in front of her, equally annoyed, her expression far less inviting than it had been when she was glancing at Dr. Atford's next patient. "No. I'll take something sooner, Stacy."

"It's *Sha-ron*." The receptionist enunciated each syllable sternly, trying to drill the name into Lyla's brain, seemingly unaware that Lyla was calling her by the wrong name on purpose. "Fine," she exhaled markedly. "When would *you* like to come in?"

"Hmm, sometime sooner than next week," Lyla quipped sarcastically.

"Okay. Dr. Atford is still available the day after tomorrow. You could keep your originally scheduled appointment at two p.m.?"

"Great. Thanks, Sheila." Lyla paused, grinning while the receptionist appeared to be biting the tip of her tongue clean off. "Listen, I'm sorry about earlier. I didn't mean to be so maniacal."

Sharon frowned, clearly uncertain whether Lyla was being sincere or not, so she just nodded and curled her mouth into an unsure half smile.

***

Lyla's drive home was a blur, filled with thoughts of her father and all of his fateful deceit. Mostly, she harped on all of the implicative nuances that had grown painfully obvious as she passed from childhood to young adulthood. Oftentimes, her dad would receive phone calls during dinner, and then he'd excuse himself. It was not suspicious in itself, but when he returned to the table, the stories that followed were always just a tad too detailed, as though he'd rehearsed them in his head before the phone even rang. She remembered hugging him close, and sometimes he didn't quite smell like his manly self; there were times he smelled faintly of women's perfume, yet she hadn't seen him embrace her mother in years. Mostly this was after he had worked late, but strangely, returned home in civilian clothes instead of his dress blues, or the cheap suits he wore once he became a detective. If she or her mother had questioned him, he would make up something about being on a stakeout, or meeting with informants, which, more often than not, were females.

Like Lyla had told Dr. Atford, she was Daddy's little girl, but Daddy had lots of girls. And one of those girls had ruined her family. Ruined her life. Her father's favorite girl had no shame. She'd called the house. She'd driven up and down the block, just to see if Lyla's father was home. She'd mailed him gifts and charming little letters, sealed faintly with her lip print. Then, there was the awful sight in the alley. That had to have been her. And Lyla's poor mother never said a word. She'd taken his messages, handed him his packages, all the while setting a place for him at the dinner table, waiting for the day he would truly occupy it. Every night she did that, until the last night. The last night Lyla remembered seeing her mother. She had looked so beautiful. The next day she was dead in Lyla's arms.

Through a misty veil of tears, plagued by the thought of discovering her mom, dead and covered in her own blood, just as she was in her nightmares, Lyla drove right past her street. After circling around the block, she pulled up, went inside, and changed into something comfortable. Lyla wanted nothing more than to settle onto the stool in the second bedroom down the hall, her converted studio—her actual studio—but she knew she would only stare at the blank canvas in front of her, at the small canister on the table, an amalgam of red paint mixed with Derrick's blood. She had been looking forward to painting his massive, muscular shoulders. Instead, Lyla decided she could make the afternoon kickboxing class if she left right then.

Lyla drove the short distance to the gym; her mood already lightened. She was pleased with herself for finding something to do with her time, other than replay her failed assault of Derrick in her mind—until she pulled into the gym's parking lot. A flimsy card table, rocking on rickety legs from the hubbub surrounding it, was set up outside the double doors of the gym. The banner that hung from the front of the table immediately caught Lyla's attention, as it read: *DONATIONS FOR DERRICK.* On the tabletop sat two large plastic jugs, stripped of their product labels, and replaced by hand-drawn signs bearing the same words. Drifting from ribbons and bobbing above the man and woman standing behind the table were various balloons reading: *GET WELL SOON!*

Get Well Soon? Oh no . . .

With each thought sliding into place, each clue, Lyla gripped the stirring wheel tighter, but not tighter than her chest felt.

Lyla squeezed her eyes shut, and when she opened them, she realized she recognized the man behind the table: Derrick's friend, who had been working out with him the day he had approached her. *Okay, I have to think fast.* She breathed in deeply through her mouth, hoping the air-conditioned breeze would cool her core. One last breath and she grabbed her duffel bag from the back seat. She thought about putting her head down and rushing past the table of do-gooders, but she needed more information. Derrick could be dead, but perhaps his family couldn't pay for the funeral arrangements. Maybe he'd taken a few days in the hospital to die, so there were lingering hospital bills. These were perfectly plausible explanations that didn't affect her in any way, but—and she hated to have to correct her own thoughts—if Derrick were, in fact, dead, why did the damn balloons say "Get Well Soon"?

She struggled to quiet her thoughts as she approached the table. The woman was petite and attractive. If she were Derrick's wife, he should have been ashamed of himself for even thinking of cheating on her. She smiled sweetly as Lyla put a few crumpled up dollar bills and a handful of coins into one of the large, plastic jugs. "I'm sorry, this is all I had in my car. I don't usually bring my purse—"

The woman cut her off, "Oh, no, it's fine. We appreciate every cent. My husband's medical bills are really becoming a bit more than I can handle."

Okay, so she is his wife. And, from the sound of it, Derrick was still alive. Lyla wished she could speak to his friend, but he was standing a few feet away, engaged in a conversation with another gym member.

"I understand." Lyla paused, trying to figure out a clever way to manipulate the young woman into giving up the information she needed. "Yeah, several years ago, before my husband passed away, it was hard dealing with all of the bills and arrangements right away, until the life insurance paid out. I'm guessing you and your husband didn't. . . ?" Her voice rose higher to pose the question she wasn't sure how to ask.

"No, we didn't think we needed it. We're so young, you know?" The woman sniffed, as Lyla felt relief at the revelation that maybe Derrick was not going to be an issue. Unfortunately, she was just pausing to blow her nose. She continued, "But, we don't have to worry about that right now. The doctors are optimistic that Derrick will recover from his coma. I just wish someone could tell me what . . . never mind."

Lyla felt her heart beat against its own constriction, but on the outside she kept her composure. She nodded absentmindedly as the woman went on about Derrick's condition, presumably skipping the part where she wondered what her husband had been doing in Center City, or what had happened to him in that elevator. Lyla's ears perked up when she heard the woman mention West Philly General Hospital. She knew she needed to devise a plan to tie up a handsome, muscular loose-end with a Southern drawl.

"I'm Ellie, by the way. Ellie Warner." The woman's hand was outstretched in front of her.

"Lyla Kyle, nice to meet you." *I'm sorry I'll have to make you a widow.*

Lyla only made it as far as the breezeway when she felt a tap on her shoulder. Startled, she whipped around and her ponytail slapped the man behind her across his tired-looking face. Derrick's friend removed one of her long dark hairs from his mouth.

With her eyebrows raised in confusion, Lyla pretended she didn't recognize him. "Can I help you?"

"You're Lyla, right?"

"Yes?"

"I'm Jeremy. Derrick called me 'Jerry,' but he was the only one. He had a way about him that—"

"I'm sorry, how exactly can I help you?"

"My friend, Derrick, who's in the hospital," he gestured toward the table outside, "he told me he had a date with you. I think it was the night he ended up in the hospital. I didn't want to say anything in front of El . . ."

"Oh, right. We had planned to meet up in Center City. Later, I ended up feeling uncomfortable about the whole thing, since I had noticed his wedding band. We hadn't exchanged numbers, which I understood, but I didn't know how to reach him, and I hate to say it, but I just stood him up. I'm so sorry to hear about what happened to him, though. Really."

"So, you didn't see him at all? Outside of here?" He gave her a sideways glance, almost like he was interrogating her. *Who does he think he is?* For a second, Lyla wondered what the friend did for a living, and hoped he wasn't a cop.

"No, and I don't really remember seeing him here, to be honest. I mean, besides the day he asked me out."

"Asked you out? He told me you were the one who asked him out?"

"Well, of course he told you that. That's the macho thing to say, right?" Lyla needed to shake this guy within the next thirty seconds. She could feel her wall of cool composure beginning to crumble.

Jeremy cleared his throat. "Yeah. Yeah, I, uh, I guess you're right."

"Listen, I really am trying to make it to this kickboxing class, so . . . I hope Derrick pulls through." With a terse nod, Lyla spun on her heels and threw open the door in front of her. She walked confidently to the locker room, right past Sonny Short Shorts, who was squatting down to examine the chest press machine. She was disappointed that she could see the doors to the kickboxing class were closed, and the session was already underway. Lyla would once again have to settle for cardio to calm her rattled nerves, though she hated how the treadmill was becoming a metaphor for her life: running, not going anywhere, and longing to be doing something else.

13
Frantic Desperation.

"I GUESS I JUST always dreamed of being a cop, but never of being a husband. Maybe that's why I don't really know how to be a husband . . . I mean, like, she wants to have kids. Now! Kids. Can you believe it? I can't fathom it. God forbid something happens to me in the line of duty . . . or off-duty. You know, because I was off-duty when that shit went down in the garage? Anyway, I can't even bear the thought of leaving Emma alone and pregnant, or alone to raise our children by herself. And now she wants to separate because of it. Why can't she just wait a few years? I could put in for a transfer and we could move to a safer city or something. What's the rush? It's not like her 'lady clock' is winding down or anything. For God's sake, she's only twenty-seven." Brighthouse shook his head back and forth as though he were trying to rid it of all thoughts. "I just don't know how to process it all. But that has no bearing on me firing my weapon that night. None whatsoever. That was a clean shoot! You just write *that* down, Dr. Atford."

Jillian's office was filled with the rise and fall of Officer Brighthouse's animated voice and nothing more. Jillian didn't ask questions, or encourage his diatribe. She didn't probe. She didn't take notes. She really wasn't even listening to the cadence of his voice until Brighthouse addressed her directly. When she looked up, he was pointing at the notepad on her lap, with frantic desperation in his eyes. She snapped back to the present just long enough to stare at Brighthouse inquisitively, to give the impression that she'd been listening the whole time and was simply pondering his musings. She held this look as long as she could, as she feverishly searched her subconscious memory for the officer's last words. She then remembered that he was defending his shooting—she should have known—and managed to utter a contrived, "Of course," before scribbling a few lines of gibberish on the otherwise blank note pad.

"It's not up to me to decide whether or not it was a legitimate shooting, Jason. But it is up to me to decide whether you are of the soundest mindset to continue your position on the force. I have to be sure before turning in my report, you understand? Now, tell me more about your home life. Do you honestly think . . . ?" Jillian hesitated, probing her memory again. *What the hell did he say his wife's name was?*

"Emma." Brighthouse prodded, presumably deducing the reasoning behind her prolonged pause.

"Yes, do you honestly think Emma is serious about leaving, or is it possible she's bluffing? Do you really think she's offering you such a concrete ultimatum?"

Jason looked down at his lap. "Ya know, I don't really know anymore. I know she wants to have a baby, but I'm not sure starting a family is such a good idea, with me being a beat cop, and all. I had originally said I would start out in Philly, and then transfer to a suburban precinct, but now I'm kinda comfortable, and I want to stay here. She's fine with staying, but still wants to have a baby." Still focused downward, he shook his head again, sadly now, seeming torn over his options.

What Officer Brighthouse didn't know was she was barely listening. Jillian had drifted a decade backward, to the forbidden love story between a young graduate student and a handsome, albeit married, Philadelphia police officer.

One night, on their way home from their evening classes, Jillian and her roommate, Mel, were mugged at gunpoint on a deserted subway platform. Two officers came to take their statements: one was Calvin Kyle. If she hadn't known otherwise—and if he hadn't been almost twenty years her senior—she would have figured him for one of those strippers that arrive at the door of a bachelorette party dressed as a sexy cop. Tall and tan, and armed with a smile, Jillian could have ripped the description from any cheesy romance novel. As Jillian recalled these memories, she sighed ever so slightly, but managed to nod toward her patient before returning to the tugs of her nostalgia.

That summer was bittersweet for Jillian. She fell in love with a married man, torn between the overwhelming guilt and the underlying feeling that she was more entitled to be with Calvin than his own wife. Especially after the life she'd had: abandoned at birth and tumbled through an endless line of foster homes like flotsam in the sewer. She'd led a life of rejection, abuse, and things being taken from her. She'd deserved one thing, even if ill gotten. Hadn't she?

One day that feeling she'd tried so desperately to keep in a dark corner of her mind crept to the surface of Jillian's being with a vengeance. She'd driven to Calvin's house and confronted Mrs. Kyle. Jillian recalled her surprise that such a seemingly meek woman put up such a ferocious fight, and not just physically. Calvin's wife had told Jillian how naïve she was and that her husband had several girlfriends but always came home. She began spouting off names, and Jillian had wanted to slam her hands over her ears like a little kid trying to ward off the ill-will of a bully, trying not to hear the verbal assault on her innocent little feelings.

When Mrs. Kyle had headed upstairs and instructed Jillian to let herself out, she had instead let herself into the Kyles' kitchen—and grabbed a paring knife.

Preoccupied with the memory of the struggle that ensued and the bountiful pool of blood she'd stepped over to exit the house, Jillian barely noticed Officer Brighthouse had risen to leave. He seemed calmer, so maybe their session had made a difference. Jillian slyly glanced at the clock on the wall behind him and saw that their time had indeed come to an end. She stood with him, smoothed her skirt, and casually walked him to the door. Feigning interest in their farewell, she hurried through assuring him they shouldn't require many more sessions before he was officially cleared.

Throughout their final exchange, Jillian was on autopilot. She couldn't believe she had dredged up memories of her tryst with Calvin Kyle—and her subsequent encounter with his wife—but treating officers often evoked memories of him. Now, much to

Jillian's dismay, her mind had inevitably wandered to the devastating event that had followed: Calvin's death, three days later.

14
Thoroughly Piqued.

THE DOOR SWUNG OPEN. A chubby woman in a stiff blue uniform sat behind bulletproof glass. A young man walked briskly to the counter, the door banging shut behind him. The incoming draft carried with it the smells of a nearby food truck: sausage, eggs, cheese, and toasted Kaiser Rolls. It was still morning. Later in the afternoon, the same draft would bring the aroma of greasy cheese steaks and shoestring fries smothered in salt, pepper, and ketchup.

"I need to speak to someone. I want to report a possible assault." He paused. "I mean; I don't know if I can even report someone else's assault, or if there even was an assault, for that matter, but I need to speak to someone." Unfortunately, he had failed to extract so much as a look of concern from the female officer in front of him.

He resumed pleading with her: asking to speak to a cop, any cop, about the attack on his friend. The taciturn lady behind the glass didn't even bother to calm the man down. Instead, she continued to stare at him, blinking slowly, looking bored. Jeremy's one-sided arguing only grew louder.

"Are you hearing me, lady? That woman was supposed to hook up with my friend. Now my friend is in the hospital. Please! You gotta listen to what I'm saying."

Brighthouse was supposed to be on his way to lunch after putting together a few notes about what he had learned from VICAP yesterday. He'd overheard a few words of the man's accusations and was admittedly interested. "Umm, sir? I might be able to help. What do you say we grab a cup of coffee?"

Brighthouse gently guided him to an unoccupied desk and pulled over a chair from a nearby desk. Waving his hand over it, he indicated that the troubled man should have a seat. "Wait right here a sec, I'll go score us that coffee."

Within minutes, Brighthouse was stooped over, a frosty can of Red Bull in one hand for himself, the other arm outstretched, offering a piping hot disposable cup of coffee to his guest. Jeremy grasped the cup firmly as Brighthouse sat behind the desk, and shifted some papers out of the way to make room for the beverages.

"So, my name's Brighthouse. Is there anything else I can get for you? Are you hungry? We've got a vending machine."

"No thanks, man. I just want someone to listen to me about my friend, that's all."

"I understand. What's your name, and who's your friend?"

"My name is Jeremy. Jeremy Sanders. My friend, Derrick, was found unconscious in a parking garage elevator in Center City."

"Yes, yes, not our precinct, but I heard about that." Of course Brighthouse remembered him: he was only found because law enforcement personnel had still been trickling in and out of that particular parking garage due to his shooting the previous evening. In fact, he was almost sure he'd heard the guy was only alive because of Brighthouse's incident. *At least some good came from it.*

"What makes you think he was attacked in any way?" he asked. "He was found without much of a scratch on him." Brighthouse instantly thought of the Alex Livanos case.

"I know . . . I can't explain that part. The doctors said he lacerated his tongue, but that could have been caused by a seizure prior to his collapse or something, they don't know. But I do know that he was supposed to have a date that night. With a girl from our gym."

The sounds of Mrs. Livanos's sobs over his cell phone echoed in Brighthouse's mind. "I thought your friend was married?"

"He was, I mean, he *is*. But there's something about this girl. You know, something that just sucks you in and makes you forget everything around you, and act like you don't care about anything else in the world. She's gorgeous and mysterious and just—I dunno—has something about her that draws you in. I almost asked her out myself, and I've been married for eight years. Have you ever met a girl like that?"

Officer Brighthouse immediately thought of the woman he had seen at Mickey's and again later at the shrink's office. "I suppose, maybe once or twice." He cleared his throat. "And why exactly do you think she's involved?"

"I have no idea. I just feel uneasy about her. What if *I* was the one that asked her out? What if *I* was the one lying in the hospital right now?"

"Okay, okay, I'll look into it." He reached for a small, white notepad, nearly knocking over his coffee in the process. "At which hospital is your friend staying?"

"West Philly Gen. He's in a coma."

Brighthouse scribbled, frowned for a second, and then looked up. "I'm sorry, did you already mention his last name?"

"I don't think so. It's Warner."

He scribbled some more. "Great, I'll see if there was a case file started, take a look at all this, and if there's something to be found I'll work it. You have my word. Even if it's on my own time. Is there anything else you can tell me? Anything else that you think might help?"

"Actually, yeah. I saw her at the gym. I confronted her. Her name is Lyla; I don't know her last name. The gym would have it though, right? Anyway, she said she didn't see Derrick that night. She also said that Derrick asked *her* out." He shook his head adamantly. "That's just not true."

"And how can you be sure? Were you there?"

"Not really, no. But I was talking to him right before he went up to her. It took a little ribbing from me, you know? He tried to act, I dunno, you know how guys are. But there's no way he just walked in there and asked her out. No way."

Hmm, why would she lie? Brighthouse's interest was thoroughly piqued. He almost didn't remember he was headed to lunch, until his stomach let out a grumbling bellow. It was worth missing lunch, though, if this young stranger's hunch provided him with a new case.

Brighthouse couldn't ignore the similarities between this case and the Alex Livanos case. Two married men. No obvious cause of death for one, or injury for the other. And an unknown pretty woman possibly tied to both men?

Brighthouse showed Jeremy out of the precinct, but was left with little time for lunch. Reluctantly, he decided to visit the vending machine for a high-calorie, low-nutrient meal to eat at one of the communal desks while he contemplated his next move. As he walked past the kitchenette that housed the coffee maker, he spotted Blakely, smirking. He knew without asking that his friend had probably overheard at least part of his conversation with Jeremy. He looked forward to the verbal tug of war it would take to convince him he might be onto something, especially if this business with Derrick Warner and the pretty gym girl ended up being related to their current case.

As Brighthouse stood in front of the vending machine, trying to decide between a Big Texas Cheese Danish and Tastykake Butterscotch Krimpets, he heard footsteps behind him. Blakely's reflection appeared in the glass. Going against the grain of his Philadelphia upbringing, Brighthouse hastily chose the Danish, and, after it had descended into the compartment below, he retrieved it and turned on his heel to greet his partner's cynical sneer.

"I have a feeling you've added another wild goose chase to the list. Don't you value your free time at all, Lighthouse?"

"Actually, if we're lucky, I think it might be connected to *our* current wild goose chase, as you so thoughtfully describe it."

"Is that right? This should be good . . ."

"Well, of course, it's only a slight possibility, but if I'm right, then it just strengthens my hunch that we have some kind of silent serial killer on the loose."

"Right, you were blabbering about that yesterday. You said you called around, right? All I remember is some crap about lint. I guess I never did make it over to Mickey's last night. My fault. What else ya got?"

"I didn't make it, either. Anyway, every single victim was married. Every single victim seems to have died naturally." Brighthouse struggled to count out each point on his fingers while also juggling his Danish. "But none of the MEs can figure out why, because every single victim was perfectly healthy."

"Hmm. And how does that tie in with whoever that was you were talking to this morning?"

"That was Jeremy Sanders. He's good friends with the guy they found in the elevator the day after my shooting. Said the docs can't figure out what happened to him. Sanders swears the guy was attacked somehow, and he thinks the girl he was supposed to have a date with that night had something to do with it."

"I heard that guy was pretty big, like WWE-wrestler-big. Took multiple EMTs to load him onto the stretcher. And you're saying a girl incapacitated him? I don't buy it."

"Well, he didn't say the girl attacked him, just that she might have something to do with it."

"Okay, I guess that makes sense. Maybe she has a male accomplice. So, I guess our next step is to find the girl. Any idea where?"

"Jeremy said she's a regular at his gym, and her first name is Lyla. Shouldn't be too hard to track her down so you can interrogate her."

"Me?" Blakely rolled his eyes, but his face soon broke out into a sly smile. "Why me? And since when do we interrogate people? How many times do I have to remind you that we're patrol cops, Jason?"

"Because you're the people-person, Byron." Brighthouse winked a boyish wink as he took an eager bite of his Danish and headed back toward the desks. "And we can't be patrol cops forever," he called back over his shoulder.

15
Straight as a Stone Wall.

THE SUV's ENGINE GRUMBLED. Parked a couple of blocks from Gen Tower, Lyla prepared to go inside West Philadelphia General Hospital, organizing her thoughts as questions danced, and schemes swirled inside her head. Deliberately slowing the pace of her breath to calm herself, Lyla flicked the key in the ignition and the engine fell silent. In an instant, the whizzing of passing cars and the murmur of the pedestrians around University City felt almost ear-splitting as Lyla opened her car door and slinked out onto the sidewalk.

Lyla passed through the wide-mouthed, revolving doors to the hospital. The sunlight shone on the golden metal and accentuated the matching threads in the marble floor, the clapping of her heels echoing throughout the lobby. The ladies at the front desk, who were normally so rigid and crotchety towards visitors, knew Lyla from her residency years ago. Not only were they glad to see her, but they also offered her a visitor's pass, with an abundance of fanfare and without a second thought.

When their desk phone rang, however, momentarily stealing their attention, Lyla headed for the elevators. She needed to find CJ.

Lyla spotted CJ pushing a cart of supplies down the hallway. Even from behind, his shaggy, mousy hair was unmistakable. She sneaked up behind him and playfully tapped him on his right shoulder, then dodged to his left. His hair ruffled as he whipped his head to the right, just to see no one there. Worked every time. Lyla's giggle gave her away, though. He abandoned his cart momentarily and found her to his left, hugging her immediately. Lyla felt her feet lift slightly into the air. When they separated, his gap-toothed smile took up half his face, and reminded Lyla that she really was fond of him.

Lyla met CJ in medical school, where their paths crossed frequently. He was now one of the hospital's head pharmacists. His full name was Cristoph James Lahm. She used to tease him that it sounded like the name of a German Calvin Klein underwear model. In reality, CJ was anything but. He was shorter than Lyla by at least a couple of inches. His shaggy hair framed a pie-shaped face that had remained acne-infested well past their college days. His eyes were a beautiful shade of blue, but they were round and cartoonish, and protruded from his face as though his head were being stepped on. His gums were large, and his teeth were small, spread out like two rows of picket fencing. But he was sweet, he loved her, and most importantly, Lyla needed him.

After Lyla had dropped out of her residency, she had only stepped foot inside the hospital to acquire materials: hypodermic needles and vials of succinylcholine. CJ had unwittingly assisted her over the years. Having fallen for her deceit, he believed that she worked in a veterinary clinic in an impoverished West Philly neighborhood that couldn't always afford to order materials. His affection for Lyla dulled his common sense, which is probably why he never questioned the items Lyla asked for—which happened to be deadly weapons.

"Long time, no visit, Ly-dye!"

"I know, I've been so busy with my work, I haven't really had a chance to steal a moment."

"You're still doing that artsy-fartsy stuff?" CJ showed Lyla the whites of his eyes, rolling them upward toward the ceiling. "When are you gonna return to your true calling? You know you belong in a hospital." He lightly punched her in the shoulder, wearing a playful grin.

"No, I don't. And you know better. I don't belong here anymore." She caught his gaze and held it firm, returning a coldness that she hoped conveyed she didn't want to discuss the subject any further.

CJ nodded, conceding her point. "Okay, okay. So what brings you through the doors today? You need more supplies for the kitties and the cockatoos?"

Her pouty mouth grew into a smile. “I don’t see many cockatoos in West Philly,” she said with a giggle that cleared the previous moment’s coarseness. “As a matter of fact, I could use a few things, but I’m actually here to see a friend of mine.”

“No kidding? Who?”

“Just a guy from the gym. He’s in a coma, and I met his wife yesterday and thought I would come pay my respects.”

“Pay your respects? That bleak a prognosis, huh?”

“Well, maybe I shouldn’t have phrased it that way. The wife is holding out hope, but I don’t think it looks good.” She paused and placed her finger on her chin. “You know . . .” Lyla’s voice increased in pitch, and her eyebrows arched, running toward her forehead as if they knew they wouldn’t agree with the next words out of her mouth.

“What?”

She knew she didn’t need to, but Lyla closed the gap between herself and CJ. She even touched his arm gently, and, though it was just a brief graze, she could almost feel the energy of his heart fluttering. “I could get a better idea about my friend if you could get me his chart.”

“I dunno Ly, I could get in a lot of trouble for that.”

“Yeah, but maybe I could offer some insight to his wife. She’s really torn up, and who knows what the doctors are filling her head with?”

He leaned forward and, in a loud whisper, he asked, “Is the wife hot?”

Lyla punched him in the arm. “Cristoph!”

“All right, all right. I was just asking because you’re making it seem like she might be a widow soon.” He pretended to elbow her the way he would a drinking buddy, but Lyla shot him a look that prompted him to clear his throat loudly before he could make physical contact. “Anyway, I’ll see what I can do. What’s his name?”

“Derrick Warner.”

CJ raised one questioning eyebrow, “You know the *last name* of a guy from the gym? Impressive. Do you know what room he's in?"

"How else would I find him? And no, everyone at the front desk was so happy to see me, I forgot to ask them about the room number." In reality, Lyla couldn't have her name in the visitor's log; not with what she was planning to do once she found Derrick.

"Okay, so I'll go look into that. And while I'm at it, what supplies do you need?"

"Huh?"

"For the clinic?"

"Oh, yes, um, of course. Uh, some sux, needles, bandages . . . you know, the usual."

"No problem. I'll round that up for you." He took both her hands in his warm, stubby fingers and looked into her eyes. "It really is good to see you, Lyla."

"Always a pleasure, Calvin-Klein-Cristoph," she replied, jerking her head back and forth with each word of the nickname.

"Good, wait here." He gave her hands a squeeze and disappeared down the hall with his cart.

Lyla didn't want to wait there. She was anxious to act. She shifted her weight from one long leg to the other as she surveyed the doctors and nurses hustling about in their dark blue scrubs. They looked more like prisoners than people trained to save lives. She supposed, in a way, a hospital was like a prison. The rigidity of the schedule, the illusion of control, had felt like nothing short of a prison to Lyla ten years ago. Especially when, distracted by the deaths of her parents, she'd almost killed a young girl. But she needed to focus on the present, focus on dealing with Derrick—and yielding more permanent results this time.

The thought of disposing of the inconvenience that was Derrick's will to live began to soothe Lyla like hot tea on a cold morning. While she waited for CJ in the window-lined hallway, gazing at the sun's darting reflections off the glass sky-walk across the way, she lost herself, once again wondering how long she could continue this lifestyle. Her consciousness only came crawling back when her friend popped up from around the corner, sans supplies cart. He must have locked it up in order to find out about Derrick.

"Do you have something for me?" Lyla said cheerily.

CJ's nose twitched. "Yes, your guy is on the eighth floor, room 817." Lyla found it peculiar that he was avoiding eye contact with her.

"What?" Her friend studied his shoes, and at that moment Lyla knew what had prompted his mood change. "Like I said, I just saw him around the gym from time to time. I met his wife when she was taking donations outside of the gym . . ." Her voice trailed off, and a fist formed in her stomach, reminding her of the agony she'd felt when she'd spotted the collections table.

"Is there something you're not telling me?" CJ asked in a small voice.

Now Lyla was the one with the raised eyebrow. "Such as?"

"Were you sleeping with this guy? I'm just sayin', he's a married man." Christoph shook his shaggy-haired head. "That's fucked up."

"I can assure you of two things," Lyla's face was as straight as a stone wall and just as hard, "I was not sleeping with him, and if I were, it wouldn't be any of your business."

"Fine. Fair enough. The dude's chart is in place outside of his room, take a quick peek, and if anyone says anything, I'm sure you'll use your feminine charms to your benefit."

"Hey! Or my former residency."

"Right." CJ gave her an exaggerated wink. "About your supplies, meet me by the gift shop in the lobby across the street at one o'clock, we'll do lunch. That is, if you don't mind being seen with me in my scrubs."

"Okay, no problem." Lyla plunged her hand into her over-sized purse and retrieved her cell phone, tapping a button to activate the screen. "What is it now? Eleven? Okay, yeah, I can do that. By the way, scrubs are sexy, Christoph."

"They were on *you*, Ly-dye."

On the eighth floor, Lyla strode casually down the hall to Derrick's room. As expected, Ellie was sitting quietly on a hard plastic chair next to his bed, reading aloud. Lyla wasn't sure, but it sounded like *Moby Dick*. Odd choice, if you wanted someone to come *out* of a coma. Then again, for all Lyla knew, it was his favorite literary classic; it wasn't like she'd gotten to know Derrick. A smile crept across her lips at the thought, and she had to quickly shoo it away as she sneaked into the sunny room. Ellie turned her head to the door, but continued reading until she had finished the passage. She turned off the e-reader, set it softly on the bed next to her husband, and stood to face Lyla. Her face was drawn from more than exhaustion; it was tight with anger. The friendliness of their first encounter was gone. Confused, Lyla decided against grabbing Derrick's chart under the guise of reviewing it with Ellie. Instead, she introduced herself.

"Mrs. Warner? Hello again. Remember me? Lyla? We met at the gym yesterday when you were taking collections, and—?

"I know who you are," Ellie said, each word splashing out, foul, like vinegar. "You're the woman who was sleeping with my husband."

"Excuse me?" Taken aback, Lyla actually took an unconscious step toward the door. "No, I don't think you understand. I only saw your husband around the gym."

"Jeremy says otherwise, Lyla."

Having been stabbed with the icy sound of her own name and feeling completely blindsided, Lyla stood tall in defiance. "Listen, I don't even know Jeremy, and whatever he said—"

"He said you were supposed to go out with my husband the night he was attacked. What I can't quite figure out is how a pretty little thing like you was able to take him down."

"Okay, okay, I *was* supposed to go out with Derrick that night, but I stood him up. It didn't sit well with me that he was married . . . but you should know something."

Ellie folded her arms across her chest. "What's that?"

"It was Jeremy's idea that Derrick ask me out. So maybe you shouldn't take what he says at face value. For all you know, *he* attacked your husband."

"That's ridiculous."

"But it's not impossible. It's more likely that he 'took him down' than I did, right? Listen, I came here as a courtesy. Maybe you should go get some coffee or something. Clear your head. Call Jeremy, even."

"Why should I listen to you?"

"Because I'm not the one physically and emotionally drained because the man I love is in a coma. You need to think about things rationally, Ellie." Lyla stepped forward, reaching her hand out to touch Ellie's arm, not unlike how she had done to CJ just moments prior.

"I am Mrs. Warner to you," Ellie said sternly as she dodged Lyla's gesture. "And I will go get a cup of coffee, but if you know what's good for you, you'll leave *my* husband's room. Now."

Lyla's mouth fell slack with the realization that she hadn't been able to disable the woman's anger.

"You don't think I'd leave you alone with him, do you? I don't care what you have to say about Jeremy."

"Yes ma'am. Again, I'm sorry—"

"Don't." Ellie Warner held up a hand, as if to stop the traffic of Lyla's words dead in their tracks. She passed by her rival with such frostiness that even the floor beneath their feet felt like it'd turned to permafrost. Ellie moved slowly and with purpose, glaring at Lyla the entire time. She said nothing with words, but plenty with silence, holding the hospital room door open for her. After Ellie had followed her out, Lyla watched her move down the hall and pass around the corner.

She wished Derrick's wife hadn't been there, hadn't seen her. Lyla knew she was taking a risk, going forward with her plan to eliminate a loose end, even after she'd been spotted by such a suspicious witness. Unfortunately, the risk of Derrick awakening from his coma before Lyla could return at a later date was far greater—and one she was loathe to take.

Reentering the hospital room, Lyla tried to figure out how best to do away with Derrick. She was out of succinylcholine, but even if she had one last vial, the monitors would alert the hospital staff, and

Derrick would be quickly placed on a respirator. Fast-acting first responders and their artificial ventilation had saved him the first time, and Lyla couldn't allow that to happen again.

She only had a few minutes to act, so she grabbed an extra pillow from the bay window on the other side of the bed. *Three minutes. I just need three minutes. Five to be safe.* She would smother him and slip out unnoticed before the staff responded to the monitors, and hopefully before Ellie returned.

Lyla loomed over Derrick, pillow hovering over his handsome brown face, sun beaming through the bay window behind her like an ironic halo. Then she heard footsteps stop just outside the hospital room door—right before it squealed open.

16
The Anchor in His Stomach.

BRIGHTHOUSE RODE IN the police cruiser alone, hummed along with the radio, and occasionally puckered his boyish lips to whistle out of tune. Running down a possible lead enlivened the officer, and that morning he had busied himself with trying to track down the pretty girl from Jeremy's suspicions. All he had was her first name, and that wouldn't get him anywhere, so he had stopped by their gym. He'd puffed his chest out and injected an unnatural sternness into his voice, attempting to intimidate by way of an authoritative tone. The kid behind the counter was more orange than tan, with spiky hair and biceps that bulged out of the cut-off sleeves of his yellow uniform. Although his stuttering replies were filled with stops and starts, he'd held his position, unconvinced that he should provide a gym member's personal information, even to the police. Brighthouse threw around words like "obstruction," "accessory," and "liability," and in fifteen minutes he had spun a web of words so sinewy that they must have dizzied the poor guy. The kid still refused to give up Lyla's address without a court order, but eventually a last name had seemed harmless enough.

Armed with a full name, Brighthouse could make some progress in the search for the mysterious Lyla Kyle. He ran a search for her DMV record, and the license photo shocked him into disbelief. He'd recognized her long, dark hair, even though the photograph had stifled its billowy movement. He'd seen her saunter into Mickey's pub and remembered the sweet smell of her wake. He'd seen the deep, inviting pools of her eyes at Dr. Atford's office. With his eyes never leaving the picture, Brighthouse shook his head slightly, partly because the DMV photo didn't do her features justice, but mostly because he couldn't believe that the fantasy woman he'd hid in the innermost alcoves of his mind could be tangled up in a possible attempted murder case—perhaps more than one. For a second, his balance wavered, but he fought what felt like the weight of an iron anchor in his stomach, and now he navigated the Northeast Philadelphia streets to Lyla Kyle's registered address. He parked the cruiser in the empty driveway and lumbered past the unusual artwork dotting the lawn and lining the front steps.

There was no answer when he knocked at the door, and he could feel the heaviness in his stomach dissipate, if only for the moment.

Having failed in locating Lyla Kyle at her home, Brighthouse decided to explore another avenue of inquiry. He wanted to talk with Derrick Warner's doctors, but first, he would have a little chat with the medical examiner. He knocked on Dr. DiCicco's frosted glass door. As she approached the door from the opposite side, the glass distorted her face into milky splashes of blacks, grays, and flesh tones. When she opened the door and came into focus, the medical examiner was dictating into a small digital recorder. She held up a finger, signaling Brighthouse to keep quiet.

As she finished up, Brighthouse noticed the pale, blue-gray body of a man on the metal table in the morgue beyond her office. The body was nude, of course, so Jason held up his Red Bull to block his view of the man's genitals. He turned to her, face scrunched up, and gestured toward the body with his free hand. "Hey Doc, have a little decency, will ya? Can we get a sheet or something for my man over there?"

Dr. DiCicco let her head fall into the crook between her thumb and forefinger. "And to what do I owe the honor of your immature and unexpected presence today, Officer Brighthouse?"

"I wanted to ask you about a case I came across when looking into the Alex Livanos' death."

"Allow me to venture a guess. The one from nine years ago that happened here on UPENN's campus?"

He moved closer with a sprightly step. "Yeah. How'd you know?"

"Let's just say, you're not the only one that's been preoccupied lately." The ME plopped down into her desk chair and yawned quietly into her hands.

With a high-pitched screech, Brighthouse dragged a stool over from in front of a complex-looking microscopy station. For the next hour, he told Dr. DiCicco everything he had discovered: the four other cases, including the one on UPENN's campus where the victim wasn't married, and the common traits between the victims, including their age, health, marital status, and lack of any definitive ailments found during their autopsies. He also mentioned how her theory on Alex's time of death had led him to conclude that the body had been moved. Also, the victim hadn't been wearing his wedding ring, and he should've been covered in dog hair. Brighthouse even told her Jeremy's suspicions about his friend Derrick Warner.

The two sat in silence for a long while. Finally, she rose from her seat and reached up to a shelf, standing on her toes, raising one leg backward for balance. She came down with a heavy textbook and started flipping pages. She didn't speak, but she uttered the word, "hmm" several times, if that could be considered a word. "I think I might have something," she said at last.

"I'm all ears," Brighthouse said, screeching his stool even closer.

"Well, it's a long shot, but I think these men were poisoned."

"But I thought you said you ran a full toxicology report."

"I did, but it was just the standard one. I didn't check for elevated levels of compounds found naturally in the body. It's possible these men were injected with a substance called succinylcholine. It paralyzes the body, including respiratory function, causing the victim to asphyxiate, to suffocate. Leaves no trace. Except . . ."

"Except what? What?"

"Well, I think I can check for elevated levels of potassium, which would imply a succinylcholine overdose. Then the next step would be, provided there are elevated levels, to reexamine the body for the injection site, excise some tissue, and send that to tox to search for metabolites of the drug. I will tell you this: If *I* missed the puncture mark the first time, whoever's doing this knows what they're doing." She frowned at the thought. "Let me look into it. When is the best time to reach you?"

"Half past any time, Doc," he said with a toothy grin, as she rolled her eyes.

"Okay. I wish I can say I'll look forward to it, but we all know I'm not one for untruths."

Brighthouse chuckled as he stood to leave. As usual, Dr. DiCicco amused him more than she intended. They said their final hurried goodbyes—more like the doctor shooed him out of her office—and he breezed his way down the gray cement stairwell.

Twenty minutes later and he had traded one campus for another, arriving at West Philly General Hospital. Under the shimmering, crystal clear sky-walks, he happened to glance upward. Squinting his eyes against the sun, he could have sworn he spotted the same woman he sought earlier that day in one of the hospital's windows. Her face was the color of sand, her hair the color of crude oil, and even from the ground he was drawn to her eyes. So much so that he bumped into a scrubs-clad man whose heavy shoulder bag struck him in the ribs. Brighthouse grunted, but managed to apologize for his absentmindedness, though the man seemed to barely notice.

The gold revolving door to the hospital was made up of two semicircles, one open for the entering and exiting of pedestrians, and the other closed and full of plants. Brighthouse felt like he was in a spinning terrarium. He exited on the other side into the lobby and approached the desk, hitching up his pants for emphasis; it was something he'd seen his father do. His eyes met with those of a hefty, dark-skinned woman who, though dressed professionally, countered the look with a blue streak of hair in her bangs.

"Hi, ma'am, I'm Jason Brighthouse with the PPD," he flashed his badge and hoped she didn't peer too closely and see he wasn't a detective. "I'm looking to inquire about a patient, Derrick Warner. I believe he's in the ICU. I need to speak with his supervising physician."

She tapped on the keyboard in front of her. "Sure thing, room 817."

"And, I'm sorry, he's in the care of which doctor?"

More tapping. "Right now, the doctor on duty up there is Dr. Rush. I'm sure one of the nurses can point you in the right direction once you get up . . ." Before she could finish, she snapped her fingers toward the elevators. "CJ! Come here, baby. Can you show this nice officer up to the eighth floor and find Dr. Rush for him? He's here about one of the ICU patients."

Brighthouse turned around to find the man who'd been recruited to escort him to the elevators, his round, pimply face and youthful smile rendering him almost kid-like.

17
Bearer of the Plague.

LYLA'S STATELY FIGURE was still folded at the waist, still lingering over Derrick's not quite lifeless body. When she'd heard the footsteps in the hall stop short of the door, the blood in her veins cooled and stiffened like molten lead. Her silent inhalation filled her nostrils with the astringent disinfectant scent of the hospital. After her lungs could hold no longer, she expelled the breath, and it reflected off the pillow she held in front of her and lightly caressed her face. The hard, starched cotton of the pillowcase touched the very tip of Derrick's nose. So close. Lyla turned to replace the pillow to the bay window—just before Jeremy walked in.

His eyes met hers, and she parted her lips to speak, but the silence was broken, not by her voice, but by the sound of the door closing behind him.

"What are you doing here?" he demanded.

"I could ask you the same thing."

"Get away from him." Jeremy traversed the tiny hospital room in three steps to examine his friend more closely. His gaze was just about to settle on the lone pillow sitting on the windowsill when Lyla spoke.

"What is your problem?"

"You did this to him. I know you did," Jeremy said through gritted teeth.

"You know what I think? I think you feel guilty because you were the one who encouraged Derrick to ask me out. I think you feel responsible. You're the reason Derrick is lying in that bed, and it kills you." Lyla's voice was unwavering; she had a plan. "And you know what else? I think you wanted to ask me out yourself, and you feel even guiltier because you didn't, knowing if you had, it might be you lying there—not him."

Having spat out those last words, so laced with venom, a triumphant Lyla crossed her arms and squared her shoulders. With her chin held high, she waited for his response. Realizing she waited in vain, Lyla crept forward inch by inch until she could breathe into the crook of his neck. He stood his ground, but his chest heaved as he seethed with each passing second. She whispered, taunting him now, "Oh, and I had a few words with Ellie, and now she blames you just as much as you blame yourself. Why do you think she's not here? She left. To . . . go . . . find . . . you." For emphasis, she poked him in the chest with each word of her last sentence; each word became softer, but each touch rose higher until she'd jabbed him in the throat.

Lyla retreated from Jeremy's space, but just barely. She watched the muscles in his throat choke down a swallow. His jaw clenched and twitched. Without a word, he opened the door and left, pulling it shut behind him, but Lyla stopped it with the toe of her deep violet sandal and followed, making sure her heels were heard behind him. She needed to see and hear the aftermath of her scheme—and she didn't need him telling people she was alone with his friend after Derrick ended up dead.

Jeremy walked down the hall, weaving between nurses, some of whom spun to avoid shoulder collisions. Ellie appeared in front of him from around the bend, coffee in hand, and Lyla ducked into the doorway of an unoccupied room and peered out to watch the show. Derrick's wife planted her feet to the floor in front of Jeremy, her legs rooting her where she stood. They faced each other toe to toe, and the yelling and gesticulating commenced. Ellie wanted to know why Jeremy would betray her; he was her friend, too. Jeremy wanted to know why she would include Lyla in their affairs. Ellie thought his use of the word "affairs" was timely. Their voices carried throughout the cavernous hallways, rising higher and higher with each syllable. Soon, staff members in dark blue scrubs crowded them from all sides, descending upon them like a swarm of locusts, with Lyla as the bearer of the plague. "Too easy," she sneered to herself.

While every hand on deck was occupied with the altercation between Ellie and Jeremy, Lyla crept back into the room, again, to the bay window. She clutched the pillow and once more poised it over Derrick's peaceful face—but not for long.

Lyla pressed down, locked her elbows, and braced herself. He kicked. She had never smothered anyone before. He spasmed. This was so out of character for her. He twitched. Three minutes elapsed with the quickness of three hours, but she was certain Derrick had passed after five total minutes had gone by. Though the commotion continued down the hall, Lyla fought the instinct to exhale; she still needed to get out of there. The myriad of machines linked to her victim began their cacophony of beeping. The alarms went unheard for the time being, muffled by the shouts beyond the room.

Glancing up the hall, every blue-scrubbed individual in sight, including CJ, encircled the tumult she had created. "Too easy," she mumbled again. Ellie's arms flailed, and Jeremy's were placed in front of his face in a desperate stance of defense. A man Lyla was certain she had seen before was pulling them apart. In fact, she thought she might have seen him when she was looking out of the hallway window earlier. A single spot of metallic flickering burst through the disquiet: the fluorescent light glittering off of the familiar man's badge. He was a cop. She shrugged, ever confident in her plan, and slipped in the opposite direction and disappeared around the corner.

Lyla followed a deserted back stairway down several flights. The air was cooler, less sterile, therefore, less assaulting on the senses. She slowed her pace until the resonating echo of her heels on the steps matched the rhythm of her breathing. She began to relax. Lyla's one messy mistake had finally been corrected. Like a typo whited-out, her page was clean again.

On the fifth floor, she depressed the horizontal bar on the door leading to the pediatric wing. Turning the dial up on her charming nature, she flitted about the department like a hummingbird. Lyla chatted with this nurse, and that, a couple of doctors, even an orderly. She didn't feel like talking, but she concealed her irritation with ease, and made certain to interact with as many people as possible. Some would call it an alibi.

With a little more time to kill before she had to meet CJ for lunch, Lyla spotted a man heading out, car keys chiming in his right hand. It must have been the end of his shift. She'd overheard a few of the nurses refer to him as Dr. Stone. *Never killed a doctor before*. She instinctively searched for—and found—a wedding band. Probably platinum; he *was* a doctor. Lyla suppressed a snort and followed him to the elevators, tossing absentminded goodbyes to acquaintances and old friends along the way. Purposely reaching for the call button at the same time as the handsome doctor, she lowered her eyes and giggled when their fingers brushed against each other. He smiled, and when the elevator doors welcomed them, he politely ushered her in ahead.

In the elevator, they were alone. Lyla noticed wisps of silver in his dark hair. She had to look up to do so; he was tall. She extended the hand he had already grazed and introduced herself. "Lyla Kyle, former medical resident."

He clasped her hand firmly. "Ted Stone. Why 'former?'"

"Oh, long story. May I call you Theodore?"

Lyla imagined Dr. Stone was about to say something like, "May I call you, in general?" Men were predictable like that. Especially the good-looking ones. Before he could say anything, though, the elevator doors opened. They had actually been going up, rather than down to the lobby, and neither had noticed.

Lyla couldn't seem to escape the familiar face that entered from the eighth floor.

18
An Impromptu Centerpiece.

"EXCUSE ME, SIR? You're bleeding." The doctor's voice broke the oddly awkward silence of the space.

Brighthouse stood in the elevator, his stomach lifting against the downward momentum. He tried not to stare at the female deity to his right, the one who'd featured prominently in his thoughts since he'd first spotted her at Mickey's. The one who might also be a silent killer: Lyla Kyle. He barely heard the man's voice behind him, but he wasn't startled by the sudden shoulder tap that followed.

"Sir, your head? It's bleeding." The gentleman pointed in the general direction of the left side of the officer's face.

Jarred from his thoughts, Brighthouse guided his left hand to his forehead after he'd finally turned to address the man's concerns. His fingers touched something warm and sticky, and he felt the need to explain. "There was a bit of a scuffle in the ICU."

Brighthouse didn't need to look at it—he knew it was blood—so he just wiped it on his pants. The man behind him handed him a tissue. Lyla stood to his right. She said nothing and did nothing. He tried several times to catch her eye, but she stared resolutely forward.

"The ICU?" the man asked.

"Yeah, a woman and her husband's friend. I was actually there to interview them and the husband's doctor. Never got a chance. Then a bunch of alarms started going off, everybody was rushing around, and I was pushed aside." Brighthouse thought he glimpsed a flicker of concern in the reflection of Lyla's face in the elevator's metal doors. "I'll have to get in touch with them another day, I guess." He shrugged, never peeling his gaze from his improvised view of her.

"You're a detective?"

"Working toward it. Jason Brighthouse." He turned, and showed the man his badge since he was in civilian clothing. "And you're a doctor?"

"Yes, in pediatrics. Ted Stone." Brighthouse held out the hand he hadn't tainted with blood from his forehead, and they embraced in a firm handshake.

Looking the man up and down as the elevator doors parted, Brighthouse grinned. "Whoa, quite the grip you have there. Could've used you up on the eighth floor."

In the lobby, Brighthouse and the doctor exchanged friendly waves as they strolled in opposite directions, but the officer was still following Lyla's alluring movements. She stopped at the front desk to speak to the blue-haired woman and it reminded him that he needed to return his visitor's badge. Though they were standing a few feet from each other, it wasn't enough—not until she glanced over and smiled at him through the long, dark tendrils of her hair. His heart abated, and he surrendered to the sweet smell of pears that engulfed him. For the second time that day, he didn't hear someone telling him he was bleeding. The object of his affections—but more importantly, his investigation—started to walk off, but the woman behind the desk was handing him a napkin and asking if he needed a doctor. He waved her off. *How badly am I bleeding?* He patted the napkin against the wound. He should have asked for Dr. Rush's schedule, but at that moment he wanted to follow Lyla more than he wanted to find out about Derrick Warner's condition. He felt compelled. He made his choice. The hospital wasn't going anywhere.

Brighthouse tried to keep up with her, but she click-clacked across the lobby floor and through the revolving doors faster than seemed possible in the heels she was wearing. He dashed across the street after her and through yet another revolving door, this one a bit smaller. He caught a glimpse of her shimmering dark hair as she entered the gift shop, and then he saw she was no longer alone; she was talking to a guy in scrubs, which wasn't a helpful observation, since everyone seemed to be wearing scrubs. The guy handed her an arrangement of lilies and a gift bag before they turned to leave. That's when Brighthouse recognized him. He was the pimply-faced guy who'd walked him up to the eighth floor. Was he her boyfriend? *Couldn't be. Look at her and look at him,* he mused. Still, consumed by his need to know more about her, he ducked across the lobby and pretended to talk to the dour-looking female security guard. He made the right choice—she was staring directly at him over her friend's shoulder.

The unlikely couple left a few minutes later, and Brighthouse abruptly ended his conversation. He watched from the revolving doors as they laughed and poked at each other playfully. In a trance, he followed them from afar. Lyla glanced back occasionally, as people tend to do when they feel they are being watched, but he was certain he wasn't seen. He trailed them as he would any person of interest. He even stood in line for a soda at a food truck several down from the crepe truck where they purchased their lunch. The smell was intoxicating. Like her. "What am I doing?" he asked himself under his breath. "Investigating," he justified a moment later.

Brighthouse followed them to a grassy hill peppered with hospital staff and college students from nearby UPENN. Everyone was enjoying the weather. He was enjoying the view. From farther up the hill, he watched her. Her silky hair. Her bright eyes. The way her mouth formed a smile as she spoke. Before he knew it, he had moved closer, within earshot, just as their faces seemed to dampen.

"You know, I'm sorry about your friend," the kid with the unfortunate skin said as he bit into his crepe.

Lyla looked up from arranging her lunch items on the grass, the flowers she'd received acting as an impromptu centerpiece. "Excuse me?"

"That guy, Derrick. He passed away today. I'm sorry, I thought you knew. It was around the time you went to visit him, so I just figured . . ."

Brighthouse's occupation finally took over. *Derrick Warner is dead? Was that what all the alarms were about?* The revelation of Derrick's untimely passing, coupled with the fact that she was there to see him, couldn't be a coincidence.

"No, no, I didn't know," she replied, not looking up from her crepe.

"Yes. Again, I'm sorry."

"It's all right. Like I said, I barely knew him." She sipped from a straw stuck in a Coke can.

"A cop was there to see him."

"That's ridiculous." She pushed his shoulder with her free hand, laughing. If Brighthouse hadn't known any better, he would swear it was nervous laughter. "Why would he want to see an unconscious man?" she asked.

"Well, he wanted to talk to Dr. Rush, and to the guy's family if they were there. Roberta at the front desk asked me to walk him up, but when we got off the elevator two visitors were arguing, and a fight broke out and I kind of left, but then I heard from some of the nurses that the Derrick guy died right after that." He put his food down and looked at her intently with pleading eyes. "Lyla," his face dripped with concern, "what's going on?"

"Nothing."

"Why would a cop want to talk to the family? What happened to your friend? What was he involved in? What are *you* involved in?"

Lyla's face darkened, a red flush overcoming her cheeks. Her eyes bulged at the rapidly fired questions. "What's with your tone?" she asked through tight lips.

"Where were you when that man died?"

"I was in pediatrics, Christoph. You can ask anyone on that floor. I even met Ted Stone, a doctor in that department and—"

"I know who he is."

"Then you can ask him yourself," she said with a huff.

"I'm just worried." He wrung his hands, no longer interested in his crepe. "What if someone asks me something? What if that cop comes back?"

"What do you mean?"

"What do I say?"

The higher CJ's voice pitched, the narrower Lyla's eyes became. "I don't know what you're implying, but I came to the hospital today with the intent of visiting a guy I barely knew out of respect for his wife, whom I also just met. End of story. You know what? I gotta go."

Lyla stood, and her long legs allowed her to tower over CJ; she looked as if she could easily stomp him to death. Snatching her purse from the grass, she went to leave. Before she did, she glanced back over her shoulder, spun, and kicked over the arrangement of lilies—a substitute for stomping on his head until it caved, Brighthouse figured—but there was no emotion in her eyes from where he sat. He watched her disappear down to the sidewalk, melting into the throngs of people.

Brighthouse stood also, stretching and tentatively checking his forehead for blood. Lyla's friend had remained seated, picking at the blades of grass around him and tossing clovers over his shoulder. One of them hit Brighthouse in the shin as he approached. He crouched down beside CJ. As he did so, he noticed a lump slide clumsily down CJ's throat as he eyed Brighthouse's badge. Once again, it struck the officer how child-like Lyla's friend seemed to him though CJ was probably the same age as her, and probably older than Brighthouse himself.

"Remember me? You showed me to the eighth floor? Officer Jason Brighthouse?"

"Yes, I remember." CJ's voice was almost a whisper as he turned his attention from the badge back to the clovers.

"I heard the woman at the desk call you over, but I don't remember your name, I'm sorry," he lied.

"Christoph. Just call me CJ."

Brighthouse pulled something out of his wallet. "CJ, I feel obligated to give you my card. If you remember anything, or learn anything, please don't hesitate to give me a call." The kid's face went green. "You're not in any trouble, but—"

"No, I know. It's just that . . ." He looked back up at Brighthouse. "She's my friend, Officer. Has been for years."

How did he know I was referring to Lyla? Brighthouse was

surprised, yet impressed, at his response, but he tried not to portray any such reaction. “I could see that,” he said calmly. He placed a reassuring hand on CJ’s shoulder. “All I can tell you is to follow your gut.”

Brighthouse stood, his knees cracking. He walked away, trying to quiet the thoughts that were racing to piece themselves together. The whole while, he could feel CJ’s eyes boring into his back. He wasn’t a betting man, but he could almost hear his phone ringing.

19
Extinguish the Image.

DR. JILLIAN ATFORD turned the corner for the fourteenth time. Round and round she'd circled the block, focusing on one particular house, just as she had a decade ago. The neighborhood had changed since then. Houses had grown larger with expensive additions. Cars were sleeker and shinier. Hotter, drier summers, had scorched once plush lawns and gardens. But one thing hadn't changed: Jillian's longing for a man beyond her reach.

She pulled over to the curb, across from a house painted a shade of lilac that reminded her of a summer horizon at dusk. It was beige when she'd frequented the residence years before to steal forbidden glances of her lover. Calvin was hardly ever home then, but his wife was. Jillian didn't learn her name until after she was dead; Calvin didn't speak of her, but the woman knew of Jillian, was aware of his indiscretions. It was no wonder that when Jillian had confronted her it had ended in blows and bloodshed. She remembered sitting on the floor of her bedroom, covered in the woman's crusty, muddy-brown blood for days. *Then it had gotten worse*. She shuddered at the thought as she stepped out of the car and faced the lavender home. It was fairly new, since the previous one had burned to the ground—with Calvin inside.

The last time she'd visited the address was the day of the funeral. She attended Calvin's services and managed to stay hidden, which was easy because his wife was already dead. The police department actually lost two detectives in that fire, Calvin Kyle, and another who happened to be driving past when he was flagged down—by Calvin's daughter, Lyla.

It didn't rain the day of the funeral, like it does in the movies. Jillian remembered feeling as though maybe it should have. The world should have experienced the same pain she felt at having one more thing taken from her. That day, Jillian had arrived at the mound of ashes that resulted from Calvin's unfortunate pyre, the smell of earth and smoke still permeating the air, a dolorous campsite, compounded by the humidity. She recalled creeping around what were the steps to the second floor of the house, kneeling where the bedroom would have been, grinding the ashes between her thumb and forefinger. Tears trailed down her face when she'd tried to picture Calvin asleep by her side. But she could not extinguish the image of his wife, her eyes defying death, piercing through the blood-soaked strands of blonde hair plastered to her face. Jillian would never learn what happened to Calvin, but she shouldered full responsibility for what happened to his wife.

While adrift in thought, Jillian wandered up the stone path walkway and stood staring at the front door, ornate with beveled glass and brass trim. The shrubs that were once on either side of the front steps were gone, replaced by an array of wildflowers and wispy grasses. Despite the hotter summers of late, the lawn was the greenest on the block, probably thanks to a sophisticated sprinkler system. She pivoted in place, devouring every detail. A birdbath made of stone and re-purposed wine bottles. A wind chime featuring blown glass. A lawn sculpture of a running woman was made entirely of entwined wire. Jillian was intrigued by the art, which was worth noting. It wasn't her taste, but something about it vexed her.

On the front porch, she reached out to the wind chime. The moving glass parts let out a jingling giggle and left Jillian's fingertips coated in dust—not unlike the ashes of all those years ago. She supposed the new owner of the house was either a collector or an artist, like Lyla Kyle perhaps.

Jillian traipsed around the side of the house, past more wildflowers, and toward the back porch. After climbing the back steps, she leered through a window. Beyond her faint reflection in the glass, the kitchen barely looked used. As a teenager, Jillian had sneaked in and out of her parents' house via the kitchen window. This house was no different from her childhood home, with the window above the sink, presumably so one could have a view of their children frolicking in the backyard while they washed dishes or prepared dinner. Here, though, there was no evidence of children or dishes or dinners, just takeout menus held in place on the refrigerator by vivid Andy Warhol magnets. Jillian observed the unlocked window and thought the unthinkable.

She whirled around and surveyed her surroundings, searching for faces in windows, people in cars. Nothing. Assuming the neighbors were probably at work—as she would be, if she hadn't had a cancellation—she applied the pressure of her palms to the glass, slid the window up, then hoisted herself onto the windowsill. Unfortunately, she was not as nimble as she was in her teens; when Jillian swung her legs inside, she accidentally knocked over a tiny can of red paint. It splattered everywhere, including Jillian's pants, unnerving her—it was the color of blood.

With frantic movements, she wiped furiously at the stains, only managing to smear it and coat her hands in the crimson substance. A distant voice inside her asked what she was even doing inside the house in the first place. In response, Jillian folded every corner of her consciousness upon the reflection, pushed it down into the recesses of her mind, and scrambled out of the kitchen and up the stairs. Just like ten years ago, but this time, without the knife.

Looking around, the layout was different than it had been before; Jillian could tell, even though she had been inside only once. She poked her head through each doorway, venetian blinds filtering the midday sun's rays into zebra stripes on the walls. First, a cheery, yellow bathroom. Next, a studio with easels, canvases, and countless more tins of acrylic paint. At this point, she ascertained that the homeowner was most likely the artist of the pieces on the lawn—which made her increasingly uneasy. Jillian continued to edge her way down the hallway, hoping her hunch was incorrect. She reached a sterile, plainly decorated bedroom, probably a guest room. At the end of the hall, the last remaining door opened into a master bedroom.

When Jillian entered it, she gasped and choked on the sudden influx of unexpected air. Her arms shot out from her sides to clutch at the doorframe. She scanned the space with darting eyes. The room was a nightmare: set up exactly as that where Calvin's wife, Susannah, had bled to death ten years ago.

Two cherry oak nightstands, topped with amber-hued oil lamps, flanked the queen-sized bed against the right wall. The matching bureau stood opposite the bed, with another taller dresser against the wall opposite the doorway. Two closets. Multiple piles of books on the floor like little literary islands amid the plush azure carpeting. Sketch pads and pencils scattered here and there were the only difference between past and present.

"Seemingly, the doorway to this bedroom serves as the entrance to ten years ago," Jillian quipped to herself, but the dry chuckle she intended as a distraction caught in her throat—she *knew* the owner of this house. The confirmation of her earlier inclination hit Jillian with a reeling effect. The location of the home. The artwork. The recreated bedroom where her mother was slain. *Lyla must have rebuilt the house with the insurance money.* At that moment, she happened to glance down at the blood on her pants. "It's not blood. It's just paint," she whispered over and over, the words running into each other like a Buddhist chant.

But it wasn't working.

Jillian slid down the crown molding of the doorway while hugging her knees, the not-quite-dry paint sticking to her fingers. She glared at her hands and clenched her eyes shut. *This isn't happening.* She shook her head violently back and forth, trying to shake free of the images she thought she'd managed to suppress years ago. She had worked through this. She had finished school. She was a recognized, prominent psychologist in the city of Philadelphia. Despite these accomplishments, nothing changed the fact that she was a killer, reduced to a blubbering mess of tears and flashbacks on the floor of a home she'd broken into. Not only a home with deadly ties to her past, but a home that housed an exact tableau of the setting where her traumatizing crime had taken place. The home of her client, Calvin's daughter. The home of Lyla Kyle.

Somewhere through the fog of her mind, Jillian heard a noise: a car door. She unfolded from her fetal position to rise to her feet and face reality. She needed to leave. *Now*. She eased down the stairs, not even sure if the noise was that of the homeowner's car in the driveway. It could be a neighbor. She strained to hear more, leading her descent with her right ear forward. She heard nothing, but still scrambled out the kitchen window the way she had come. The paint spill would give away the break-in, but there was nothing she could do about that now. She removed her cardigan and rubbed at the window in haste, attempting to remove any fingerprints, but leaving behind two greasy, telltale smudges. Sighing, Jillian tied the sweater around her waist, seeking to conceal the blood-red stains on her slacks.

Coming around to the front of the house, Jillian froze. A figure was climbing the front steps. A familiar figure. Jillian couldn't believe she'd ignored the obvious during her earlier exploration of the house. The insurance payouts would have amounted to a significant sum, considering the fire plus the death of both her mother and her father were separated only by a few days. Jillian swooned at the haze of her thoughts; they dizzied her along with the afternoon sun. She instinctively shielded her eyes, preparing to sneak back to her car, unseen by her patient. Before she could stagger forward, she lowered her hand—and found Lyla standing in front of her.

20
Lulls and Lurches.

BRIGHTHOUSE LEFT THE hospital with looser lungs, as though he were breathing easier. He felt accomplished. He may not have technically found his mark, but he saw Lyla and overheard her speak of visiting Derrick—moments before his death. Derrick was appearing more and more like a victim as the day wore on. Besides that, the deepest hollows of Brighthouse's gut spoke to him, cooing and insisting that Lyla was connected to the Alex Livanos case. He longed to speak to her for himself. *I need to speak to her for myself.*

Usually, Brighthouse would be confident that, whether or not she lied, he could analyze her expressions and behaviors to discern the truth. His father had showed him how. With Lyla, of course, it was different. His confidence wavered like the heat on the road in front of him. He hated to admit he drove with more than just the slightest thought of her. Her sweet aroma of fruit and flowers and that long, luscious hair mimicking her every movement. . . would he be able to see beyond her beauty, or would he get caught in the trap of his attraction to her? Would he be able to notice a shift in the bottomless wells of rich ink that were her eyes? Would he notice a scant hesitation before she spoke, or only that her smile resembled a string of diamonds dazzling in the midday summer sun? How about an uneasy change in her seating position? A squirm? Brighthouse could only hope he'd be able to concentrate on the cues his father had taught him.

After driving along silently, stuck between his own thoughts for a few minutes, Brighthouse decided he could indeed put aside his attraction to the enigmatic Lyla Kyle and perform his civic duty. He would make his dad proud. Part of the reason everyone mocked his own methods was because Brighthouse Sr., a well-respected homicide detective, had used his keen instincts to follow the lulls and lurches of his intuition—which were almost never wrong. Brighthouse preferred to rely more heavily on the evaluation of tangible evidence found at the scene, but since he wasn't a detective, he was taunted for even showing an interest in the forensic side of a case. Perhaps if he were more like his father . . .

Every now and then, Brighthouse was able to conjure up his late father's talents and feel his way through a detail—but never enough to be noticed—and he wanted so badly to feel his father now, beside him, inside him, even. As Brighthouse hoped his dad was beaming down on him from an otherworldly place, his phone rang, the CSI theme song. It seemed like weeks had passed since he'd last seen Blakely, though it had been less than twenty-four hours. Still, it was good to hear his voice.

"Hey kiddo, I thought I'd see you at the range this morning. You know how much I love showing you up in front of the guys."

Brighthouse could hear his friend grinning through the phone. "One time. One time that happened, Byron."

"And yet that's the time I seem to remember the clearest," He chortled. "Anyway, I was just checking in to make sure you were planning on showing up for shift tonight?"

"What are you talking about? I've never missed a day of work in my life. Not even when I bagged groceries in high school."

"Physically, no, but the last few shifts we've worked it's like your mind has been somewhere else entirely. Ever since we found that stiff on South Street it's like I've been working with a space cadet, man."

"I know. I just really have a good feeling about this case. And like I told you, I think it's tied to the other case. I could make detective if I get this right. Wouldn't that be something?" He brightened, thinking again of his old man. "By the way that guy, Derrick Warner, died today."

"Shocking. Not like he was in a coma or anything."

"Lyla Kyle was in the building when he died, Blakely."

"Coincidence, I'm sure, Lighthouse."

Man, he hated that nickname paired with that mocking tone. Yet he pressed on lightheartedly, "Oh, did I forget to mention that she knew Derrick?"

"You're kidding? You talked to her? And you didn't drown in your own personal puddle of drool?"

Brighthouse gave a hearty and sarcastic laugh, and then stopped for a deadpan "Go fuck yourself" before answering. "Not exactly, but I overheard her speaking to a friend, and I'm confident that said friend will contact me with additional information."

"Is that right?"

"Yes."

"Okay, so what you're saying is, I'll be working with a space cadet for yet another graveyard shift. Can't wait."

"All the more reason to embrace my ambition. Ride the wave with me, brother. We could make detective together. Aren't you sick of just being a beat cop? Think of your family."

"From what you've been telling me, you should be thinking of *your* family. I'm hanging up now."

That one stung. "Fine, but I'll leave you with this: I talked to our ME today, and she seems to think Alex Livanos might have been poisoned. I'm telling you, embrace my way of thinking. I'm going places. See ya tonight."

Brighthouse's phone rang again; this time it wasn't The Who. This time, it was Brian McKnight, which signaled a call from his wife. He groaned, but tried to sound chipper as he answered.

"Hey, honey, what's up?"

On the other end, his wife's voice was flat and without greeting. "Are you coming home before your shift tonight?"

"No, baby, I'm not. I have to interview another witness. I'm sorry—"

"I'm ovulating."

Brighthouse closed his eyes for as long as he could while driving, a small sigh escaping his lips. "I understand that, but I have to do this interview."

"No! No, you don't. You're not a detective, Jason. Your job is to ride around, fill out paperwork, and hand it off to the real detectives. You're not even on the clock, for Christ's sake! Who on Earth are you interviewing, anyway?"

"A woman, a possible suspect. She might be connected to the two different cases I was telling you about. This could make my career if I'm right about her."

"And if it breaks your career?"

"It won't. Don't be so negative. You want me to make detective, don't you? So I can better provide for our family?"

"What family? You're never home to make a family, Jason. Instead, you're off chasing down imaginary femme fatales."

"Okay, sweetie, now you're being a bit dramatic, don't you think?" Wincing, he regretted the words immediately after uttering them.

"I'm just not getting any younger, that's all."

"My God, Emma! If I had a dollar for every time I heard that line, I wouldn't even need to make detective." Brighthouse tried to bring levity to this exasperating conversation, but he knew that was a lofty goal. He switched tactics and made an attempt at rationalization. "You know, my mother had me when she was thirty-eight years old, remember?"

"Yeah, she was probably waiting for your dad to have a day off," his wife quipped sarcastically. "And aren't you an only child because of it? You know what? Whatever. At least he was a detective, and had a reason for never being home."

"Again, I'm *trying* to make detective. How do you think *he* made detective? It wasn't by just punching a clock, by coming home for dinner every night. He had to make sacrifices. And, for the record, I like to think I'm an only child because I was perfect and my parents knew lightning seldom strikes twice."

"Enough with the jokes. Are you coming home or not?"

"I'm not, Emma. I'm sorry."

The line went dead, and, as much as he wanted to believe otherwise, Brighthouse had a feeling his marriage wasn't far behind.

21
Cleaner of Body but Not of Mind.

LYLA MUST HAVE heard the rustling. Jillian imagined her client would have preferred to find a squirrel, or even a rabid raccoon. Judging from the slack-jawed expression on her face, Lyla definitely hadn't expected to see her psychologist meandering around her property.

"What are you doing here?" Lyla asked, with a slight shake of her head, eyebrows knitted.

"I was . . ." Jillian's mind surged to regain her composure and keep the conversational pauses to a minimum. ". . . concerned, due to the results of our last few sessions, so I wanted to check up on you." As the fabricated excuse escaped her lips, she felt her spine straighten with assurance, but she kept her hands out of sight and hoped her sweater was still covering the smears on her pants.

"And you knocked on the *back* door of my home?"

Jillian noted her client's incredulous tone. "Oh, no, of course not." Unfaltering, she added, "I heard a noise while I was on the front porch, and I thought it might be you, so I went back there, thinking you might not have heard the doorbell."

"What kind of noise?" Only one of Lyla's eyebrows was raised now. Jillian supposed it was progress, considering her previous expression.

"Well, it was more of a crash, really. I guess I went back to investigate."

Lyla snickered. "So you thought someone broke in? In the middle of the day?"

The irony did not breeze by Jillian lightly. "No, I mean, I'm not sure what it was. It could have been you; it could have been something else. Either way, I felt compelled to check it out, you know, since I was already here."

Jillian watched as Lyla's eyes narrowed into slits of suspicion. Why would a professional, paid by the hour, stop by for a house call? And put forth such an effort? She knew her story was just as transparent as the window she'd recently climbed through, which is why Jillian thought she heard wrong when Lyla shrugged and invited her inside with the offer of tea. The mere mention of tea brought with it flashes of the memories she'd endured inside just moments ago. The doctor's face drained, transforming her rich hue to the ashen color of sun-dried mud. Lyla, perhaps noticing the doctor's rapid color change, suggested another beverage option, but Jillian responded with a garbled mess of mumbled words as they rounded the corner of the house toward the front door. All the while, Jillian hid her hands, stained with blood-red paint, behind her back.

Playing the hostess—just like her mother had ten years ago—Lyla disappeared into the kitchen, leaving Jillian seated on a sofa set before a coffee table with a knotted driftwood base, and topped with a slab of tinted glass. Through the doorway, she watched her client, checking to see how concerned Lyla was with the blood-red paint splattered every which way on the floor. Apparently, she was only vaguely perplexed; after spotting it, Lyla scanned the kitchen, presumably searching for additional signs of a break-in. Satisfied her host wasn't going to accuse her of anything, Jillian called, "May I use your restroom?"

Lyla shouted the directions, but Jillian was well on her way, having already passed it when she'd explored earlier. She washed her hands thoroughly. It was funny; however hypnotizing it was watching the diluted red water circle and disappear down the drain, it wasn't enough to ease her mind. Not then, not years ago when she'd finally showered after three days of being encrusted with the blood of Lyla's mother. No, when she'd showered then, when the blood had swirled down and away from her guilty naked body, all Jillian had felt was disgust—even though she was finally clean.

Jillian returned to the sofa, cleaner of body but not of mind. She focused her attention on the unique coffee table where she noticed a burnt red stain on one of the wooden branches, barely visible. She shook her head. Again, Jillian couldn't believe the artful pieces throughout the home hadn't clued her in sooner. She had known her client was an artist. Was it so inconceivable for Lyla to reside at the same address her parents once had? Buried in thought, Jillian bolted upright when Lyla reentered the room, carrying a silver platter of teacups and other accouterments. If her sudden appearance didn't startle the doctor enough, the sight of the familiar tea set sure did.

"That's a gorgeous . . ." Not confident she could speak without stammering, she completed her thought by gesturing to the tray.

"Thank you, it was my mother's." Lyla spoke without regard to the unusually loud swallow that emanated from her guest's throat. "Fortunately, I was able to swipe it from the house right after my mom died, because the house burned down a few days later. It was missing a teacup, though. It must have broken at some point. But I always loved this set. It probably would have been the only thing I'd asked for in my divorce, had we actually gotten divorced," she said with a chuckle.

Jillian lifted the gold-trimmed, red bone china teacup to her lips, only to choke on her first sip. "I, uh, you never mentioned in any of our sessions that you were married." The revelation jarred her from the hellish déjà vu of the haunting tea set.

"Because I wasn't married long. He turned out to be just as unfaithful as my father was to my mother, but in the end we parted ways, in a sense." She took a long, seemingly soothing sip of tea, the corners of her mouth ever so slightly upturned in a smile.

Jillian opened her mouth to say something, but before words could escape, she was interrupted.

"I forgot I have to clean up a spill in the kitchen." Lyla shot up from her seat. "Excuse me." Lyla retreated to the kitchen and Jillian followed her, enveloping her in shadow. When Lyla turned on her heel, Jillian couldn't tell if she was uneasy or confused, possibly a combination of the two, as she seemed unsure of why she was being stalked by her unexpected guest.

"More tea?" she asked.

"Oh, no, I should get going. I just wanted to see how you were doing, and you seem fine, so I guess I'll see you at our next appointment, which is . . . ?"

Lyla knelt on the floor, scrubbing vigorously away at the paint stain that was already all but gone. She sprayed it with bleach, scrubbed, and repeated the process several times. Jillian cocked her head to one side. All Lyla said was, "Paint can be sticky," and resumed scrubbing.

"Right, of course. So, I guess I did hear a burglar or something?"

Lyla looked up from her crouching position on the floor. "What do you mean?"

"Oh, nothing," Jillian said, silently wishing she had a clone for the sole purpose of being able to physically kick herself.

"Yes!" Lyla punctuated the revelation by abruptly standing and punching the air with her scrub brush, spewing pungent droplets of bleach everywhere. "I guess *someone* had to knock over the paint." She eyed the tin cannister, still on its side on the floor. Picking it up, she looked at it for a moment, then tossed it in the trashcan. "I was just so intent on cleaning up the spill, I hadn't thought about it. I should probably call the police, right?"

"Yes, well, I'll just show myself out." Jillian's own words cut her deep. A decade ago, Lyla's mother had requested Jillian show herself out—right before Jillian killed her. They were the last comprehensible words the woman spoke; the rest had been a storm of shouts and screams.

Lyla stood, and Jillian thought she was actually going to escort her to the door, but instead she reached into the sizable purse she'd slung onto the kitchen counter earlier along with her leather jacket. She retrieved a cell phone after a moment of digging, and the next thing Jillian heard her say was that she was calling to report a burglary. Still intent on leaving, Jillian tiptoed toward the living room and the escape beyond the front door. Lyla called after her that she would see her at their upcoming appointment, then returned to her conversation with the 9-1-1 operator.

Lyla's front door closed behind Jillian without a sound but for the slight click of the catch. She retraced her steps with regret, hopped into her car, and sat with her hands on the steering wheel. She was finally free to tremble. Her body quivered and quaked as she pulled away from the curb and observed the glare of headlights behind her. The driver looked familiar, but in the diminishing daylight, having both traveled through time and lost track of it in Lyla's home, she couldn't be sure.

Jillian arrived at her own home almost an hour later and immediately headed straight to the back of her closet in the far corner of her bedroom. Throwing boxes of shoes and old yellowed photographs to the side and behind her, she pulled one particular shoe box out with care. She opened it gingerly and pulled out a plastic bag, removing the contents. Within minutes, Jillian found herself wearing the bloody clothes she'd worn ten years ago. Again she sat in a ball on the floor, picking at her nails, and sobbing silently among the pink sky of evening filtering in through the windows. Dusk was starting to creep in. *Dusk.* It dawned on Jillian then that she had been in that house for hours.

Déjà vu indeed. Jillian lifted an imaginary sip of tea to her lips from a gold-trimmed, red bone china teacup—the missing piece from Lyla's mother's set.

22
Subtle Seduction.

LYLA HAD BARELY hung up the phone when the doorbell rang. *There must've been a cop right around the corner.* Shuddering, she thought of the collateral damage of many years ago. Shaking that off, she put aside scrubbing the floor for a moment and answered the door. For the second time that day she was visited by an unexpected someone. The officer from the hospital stood on her front step.

"What a coincidence they sent you." Lyla beamed as she opened the door to the boyishly handsome man. She thought it strange they sent a plainclothes officer, but dismissed it, since jeans looked better than over-starched uniforms any day. "I've been seeing you everywhere, it seems. Anyway, please come in."

The officer walked slowly through the doorway with his head cocked, seemingly puzzled, but he entered the house anyway. Once inside, he pointed to his badge. "I'm sorry, I'm Officer Jason Brighthouse. And who supposedly sent me?"

Now Lyla was confused. She gave him an uneven look. "I called to report a burglary—well, a break-in. I haven't noticed anything that's been stolen as of yet. Are you not here in response to my call?"

"Um, no. I'm here to ask you a few questions. About Derrick Warner."

"Uh-huh." Lyla immediately thought of CJ. Instead of storming off, she should have taken the time to ease his mind. What if it was him who'd sent the police to her door? She would deal with CJ later. "Okay, well, please have a seat. Can I get you anything? Water? Lemonade? Hot tea?"

"A glass of iced water would be nice, thank you," he responded tersely.

This day's string of events had been both odd and exhausting. As he sat down, Lyla wondered if the couch was still warm from Dr. Atford's earlier visit.

She returned from the kitchen and handed him the water he'd requested, the ice tinkling against the glass. She chose to sit opposite him in a navy blue armchair, giving herself a clear path to both the front and back doors. Unsure where this questioning was going, she needed to be prepared to react if it headed south. She continued drinking the aromatic tea she'd brewed earlier, and sipped it slowly after pursing her mouth to blow over the top of the teacup. Even though it was no longer steaming, she wanted to subtly showcase her lips as she waited for him to begin.

The young cop squirmed, unsettled in his seat. Lyla just looked at him with an expression as sweet as the sugar in her tea. *Does he expect me to speak first?*

"Do you know why I wanted to speak with you, Ms. Kyle?" he asked.

"I'm sorry, I don't recall you ever asking my name, Officer," she said, crossing her lengthy legs for emphasis. She smiled, glad for the opportunity to showcase a different body part.

He swallowed hard, although he had yet to take a sip of his water.

"I know who you are."

"Is that right?"

"Do you know why I wanted to speak with you?" he repeated.

"Well you already said you were here to talk about Derrick."

"Yes. He passed away earlier today."

Lyla feigned a gasp of concern and placed her teacup gravely on the coffee table, uncrossed her legs, and leaned forward. "Oh my God. I didn't know." *So convincing.*

"You were at the hospital earlier today."

Maybe not so convincing? "As were you," she replied with a smile. "What are you implying?"

"How did you know Derrick Warner?"

"He goes to—went to—my gym." Lyla allowed the slip to escape on purpose. She didn't watch much television, but she once watched an episode of some crime procedural where an interrogator inferred guilt simply because the suspect used the correct tense when referring to the victim. *Though Derrick was hardly a victim . . .*

The reality of her being a suspect barely dawned on her when Lyla realized the officer had posed his next question.

"Yes, I've heard that you both attended the same gym. Was that your only connection?"

"I wouldn't call it a connection, really. But, yes. Why? Have you been speaking to Derrick's wife?" She refrained from saying "widow."

"No, I've been speaking to his friend, Jeremy. Do you know him?"

"If by 'know him' you mean did he confront me with his delusions, then the answer is yes."

"Uh-huh. Delusions." A few moments earlier, the officer had pulled a small notepad from the same shirt pocket his badge hung from. He scribbled in it now, appearing to underline certain points.

"Jeremy," she took another sip of her tea, "is under the mistaken impression that Derrick and I went out the night he ended up in the hospital."

"And you didn't?"

"No. Hence the phrase 'mistaken impression.'" She chuckled. "I like you, Officer . . . what did you say your name was?"

"Brighthouse." Lyla thought she spotted a shadow of a smile overcome the young cop's face, but he cleared his throat, and the smile right along with it. "Where were you that evening?"

"I painted. I'm an artist." Lyla gestured around the room to several of her works, thankful he didn't ask if they were *supposed* to go out that night. If he did ask, she knew to answer truthfully. She couldn't take the chance that Jeremy hadn't told him as much. "I could show you what I was working on upstairs in my studio, if you'd like?"

His eyes traced her movements toward the stairs then returned to meet her gaze, lingering. Another throat clearing quickly followed. "So you have no alibi for that night?"

"No, Officer Brighthouse, I do not. Do I need one?" she asked evenly.

He didn't answer the question. Instead, he fired off another of his own. "Ms. Kyle, do you know a man named Alex Livanos?"

"Who?" Lyla genuinely didn't recognize the name. "And please, call me Lyla."

"He was found dead in a parking lot off South Street last week."

Oh, that Alex. "And what does he have to do with Derrick?" she asked, careful not to betray her sudden recollection.

"So you didn't know him?"

"Are you distracted, Officer?" Her voice softened. His face reddened, but he gave no response. "I'm sorry. I assumed my initial response of "Who?" answered that already. But no, I didn't know him. I'm afraid my social life isn't what it used to be."

"And where were you the Friday evening before last, late into early Saturday morning?"

"*Again*, I was painting. The offer still stands to take a peek at my studio upstairs." She raised an enticing eyebrow.

"So *again*," Brighthouse good-naturedly mocked her, "you have no alibi."

Lyla perked up straight in the chair. Something had happened. His tone was lighter. It was almost playful.

She had him.

Lyla swallowed him with her eyes. "You know, if I knew I needed an alibi each night in case someone somewhere died, I'd make more friends," she said, grinning. "Speaking of which, what are you doing this weekend? I could use some company. You know, in case anyone else dies."

23
A Photograph Fades.

BRIGHTHOUSE HAD YET to sip his water. The glass started to sweat—and so did he. He tugged at the collar of his shirt with a clammy middle finger. The middle finger was fitting, considering how he felt about himself at that moment. Beads of sweat formed within the mess of his curls, like dewdrops in the brush. One such droplet made a run for it and streamed down the slope of his forehead. The officer caught it under the pretense of scratching his head in contemplation. Truth was, he no longer contemplated his interview, but rather his interviewee. The way she drank her tea, with her lips blowing innocuous air kisses with every sip. The way she changed positions, cascading one infinite leg over the other. The way she repeatedly invited him upstairs, even if just to show him her art studio. *She just wants to verify her alibi, right?*

He knew the answer.

Once he realized he'd failed to answer her most recent proposition, he opened his mouth to do so, but his response was unintelligible. Lyla giggled as she stood with an outstretched hand. At first, he thought she intended to lead him upstairs; instead, she reached for his glass. The ice had already melted, causing the level of the water to rise at the same rate as his body temperature. He handed her the glass, careful not to spill it, careful not to betray his nerves with a clash of his damp fingers.

"How about we get rid of this water that you're not even drinking, and this tea of mine that's gone cold, and break open a bottle of wine?" She beamed down at him; irresistible lips parted to reveal a dazzling smile.

"Oh no, I can't—"

"Sure you can. You don't look like you're on duty, so why should you act like you are?"

"I'm not technically on duty, but . . ." Brighthouse wondered why he'd broadcasted that information. *What am I doing?*

"Then I'll open the wine. I might have some cheese, also . . ." Lyla's voice trailed off as she disappeared into the kitchen. Brighthouse followed her.

"No really, I have a graveyard shift ahead of me," he pleaded.

"Fine. Then you only get one glass." She poked him playfully in the chest, then removed his badge and crammed it into his shirt pocket. "You might as well shove that notepad of yours in there, too."

He complied, but when he struggled to fit his pen in there also, she snatched it from him, bit on the end with a raised eyebrow, and then tucked it behind his ear. The tips of her fingers twirled his curly hair, and Brighthouse felt fireworks at the base of his neck, the sparks of which spilled down his back in a wave of shivers.

Lyla spun on her heel and reached for the wine, one of many dark bottles in a wrought iron rack against the wall. Then she changed her mind and instead grabbed a chilled bottle of white wine from among several nestled within the shelves of the refrigerator door. As she noisily searched a nearby drawer for a corkscrew, she began chatting about how wine was the preferred gift from most of her clients, and about how she really did need to make more friends to help her drink it all. Meanwhile, Brighthouse's fugue state faltered for just a moment—long enough to notice the faded crimson coloring in the grout between the floor tiles in front of the sink.

He waited for her to finish her train of thought, then stepped forward to ask about the staining, gesturing toward the spot. "What happened here? You must have cut yourself something good."

She repositioned herself, so she was standing directly over the area in question. "It's actually red paint." Her face darkened for only a second, then cleared, like the film of an approaching storm set to fast forward. "That's what clued me in to the break-in. It was knocked down from the counter while I was out. A, uh, friend, visited earlier, and said she heard a crashing noise come from the back of the house while she was up front ringing the doorbell." Lyla still hadn't shifted from the spot of the spill. "Speaking of which, I guess home invasions aren't really a priority, since the police haven't actually sent anyone yet."

"Yeah, I should probably call in to report that I'm here. I could claim that I heard it on the scanner or something." *I'm lying now?*

Brighthouse strode back into the living room to call the dispatcher, and while he explained the situation, he glanced into the kitchen. Lyla was on her hands and knees, scrubbing at the tile. She hadn't even finished pouring the second glass of wine. Once he finished his call, he returned to the kitchen. Lyla stood up abruptly, rushed a nervous smile, or perhaps a smile meant to mask embarrassment. She handed him the full glass of wine and topped off the other.

"Shall we?" she asked, waving him toward the living room.

Brighthouse sat on the sofa, but Lyla scampered back into the kitchen. "I almost forgot . . ." she called.

He watched her frown at the floor for a minute, then she shouted, "I don't have any salami or olives or anything, but I think fruit pairs better with white wine, anyway."

She pranced back in, carrying a tray of strawberries and assorted cheeses. When she plopped down next to him, his nostrils filled with her usual sweet scent of vanilla and pears. The fragrance mingled pleasantly with the citrus-laced aroma of the chilled Pinot Grigio.

She touched his knee. "So, you were born, brought home from the hospital, then what?"

Brighthouse guffawed. It was the first time in a long time a woman had made him laugh. "Is that from a movie? I could swear I've heard that line before."

"I'm sure I probably picked it up from somewhere."

They began talking about their experiences. The wine flowed through their bodies, as did the conversation from their lips, more readily from Brighthouse than from his hostess. He chatted about always wanting to become a cop. When Lyla confessed that she used to dream of being a physician, Brighthouse's reaction was typical:

his eyebrows shot up, and his mouth fell agape. The conversation then shifted to how Lyla had come to be an artist; it was like watching a time-lapsed video of a photograph fade before his eyes as the color and joy drained from her face. Both sipped their wine in silence. Several minutes passed before Lyla revealed that both of her parents were deceased, and eventually the stress of being alone drove her from her final year of residency.

"Lyla, I'm so sorry." He observed a glassiness in her eyes, most likely not from the wine. He grazed his hand across her leg. "My father died in a house fire when I was about that age, a couple years younger, actually. I couldn't even imagine losing my mother, too."

At that, Lyla sat up straight. In a small, solemn voice, she asked if his father had been a firefighter.

Brighthouse didn't understand why her eyes were closed, as if she feared his answer. "No, my dad was just in the wrong place at the wrong time: an off-duty detective trying to save another off-duty colleague's life in his burning home. In fact, I think it happened near here, somewhere in this neighborhood. I'm not sure though, my memory isn't . . ."

Lyla's eyes blinked open and stared at him, wide and somehow apologetic. Still, she sat there without a word.

Brighthouse continued, "Like I said, I don't know how you did it." He threw his head back and drained his glass. "You know, I almost couldn't go on myself, after . . . after my father died." He twiddled the stem of the wine glass between his fingers, fascinated by its pirouettes as he continued. "I attempted suicide with my father's old backup weapon. Luckily, his service weapon was in a commemorative lock box along with his badge. Without the larger revolver, I had to settle for his .22, the one he wore in his ankle holster. The bullet grazed around the circumference of my skull." Brighthouse turned his head and parted a few curls. "See the scar? My mother found me, told everyone it was an accident, and since I couldn't technically remember the incident—again, my memory from around that time isn't great—it never went on the record as an attempted suicide. It's how I was able to join the police academy.

Sort of a second chance all around, I guess."

"My mother committed suicide," Lyla blurted out, her voice cracking, like an old blues record.

"Oh, I'm so sorry. Wait, your father—"

She cut him off. "What hospital did you go to after your, er, accident?" Before he could answer, she interrupted. "You know what, never mind. I'm sorry. Do you mind if we change the subject?"

"Of course, you're right. Of course. Anything you wish to talk about. The floor is yours."

Brighthouse poured Lyla another glass of wine, and one for himself, too. They had almost finished the bottle, but he didn't care. He had a few more hours before his graveyard shift, and was sure no one would even notice. Besides, he was far from drunk. There were days Blakely came in with an intoxicating hangover cloud clinging to his skin, more drunk from the night before than Brighthouse was at that moment. Plus, Brighthouse was content. He felt comfortable talking to Lyla. She was so different from Emma, or rather, from whom Emma had become. His wife used to be flirty and conversational. Not anymore. Now she was selfish and acerbic. Did that justify what was happening right now? Did that justify the glass of wine before him, the hand on his knee, or the gorgeous woman leaning in inch-by-inch, dark hair trickling over her shoulders? Their lips were so close they shared the same air, warm and moist with lust, the space between them stripped, uncluttered of inhibitions.

But before their lips could touch, the officer's phone rang. All of a sudden, the lyrics to "Who Are You" had an altogether different meaning. "Who are you, indeed?" Brighthouse could hear his father asking, his words laced with contempt.

Brighthouse smiled and held up a finger to Lyla, seated so close to him he could taste the wine on her breath. She leaned in to kiss the finger just as he pressed a button to answer the call—without a thought as to who it might be.

"Brighthouse," he said through a flirty grin, winking at Lyla.

The person on the other end of the phone mumbled a greeting he didn't understand, but he recognized the voice, nonetheless. It was CJ.

The volume on Brighthouse's cell phone was loud enough for Lyla to overhear, plus her friend's voice was unmistakable. Just minutes ago, Lyla's heart had fluttered in a way alien to her for years. The feeling had overtaken her body, swept her up like a hungry tornado, and then, without warning, her heart had dropped with a thud at the sound of CJ's muffled voice.

For once, the impulse to kill philandering husbands had escaped Lyla's focus. She'd failed to ask Brighthouse about his wedding band or his wife. Normally she homed in to such things like an experienced carrier pigeon. With Jason she had flown, rather soared, past both. In fact, she'd basked in the warmth of his company, and wished she could preserve it in the empty wine bottle that had sat between them. She'd cork it, and enjoy it whenever she pleased. Then his phone had rang, cutting their evening short, and severing their intimate connection.

Lyla tried to suppress the nervous twitching of her foot, her anklet alive with jingling chatter. She bit her lip while she watched him across the room in the foyer. His attention shifted sheepishly from her questioning eyes down to a spot between his feet. When the call ended, the mood grew ominous, like the quiescent silence before all forms of wildlife flee an approaching tsunami. Lyla rose to her feet and crossed the room, reaching out to touch his arm.

He recoiled.

She wept.

He left.

The front door closed behind Brighthouse, but the sound was lost in the chaos of Lyla's thundering fury. She had overturned the glass panel of her coffee table. The momentous crash showered the room in shards and daggers. The wine bottle and glasses only added to the debris. Lyla cowered in a corner of her couch and stared at the twisted driftwood at her feet. Her sights turned to a small bloodstained area that she must have missed many years ago. It reminded her that this was the second time the glass tabletop had been broken in anger. The first time, a man had died.

24
Tumbling Down the Drain.

LYLA WAS GLAD for the distraction of the new meditation fountain, trickling and gurgling on the corner of Dr. Atford's desk. She admired its simple construction—stacks of river stones, with water bubbling out from the top—but was it supposed to be relaxing? Lyla didn't see the appeal, despite being grateful for something to focus on besides her own emotions. She asked Jillian about the new addition, and was briskly told it was a gift from a patient. Lyla supposed she wasn't the only person who received presents from clients, though in Dr. Atford's line of work, such behavior would probably be viewed as unethical. Lyla, lost in her thoughts, curious if her doctor was lying to her, jumped from her stance a little when Jillian cleared her throat, signaling the clock was ticking on their session. Lyla obediently scurried to her seat on the couch.

"I gather you know what I want to talk about today, don't you, Lyla?"

"Let's see . . . obviously not office décor. Would you like me to garner a guess? Because I prefer multiple choice." More than ever, Jillian didn't seem in a mood for games. In fact, she appeared as though she may have had a late night.

"Just because I've been to your home doesn't mean you can be brassy. Speaking of which, during my visit yesterday, you mentioned a husband and said you each 'went your separate ways.' Are the two of you divorced?"

"No." Lyla kicked the bottom of the couch with her heel, looking down at the floor, like a little kid. "Brassy," she scoffed under her breath.

"So you're only separated?"

Lyla hesitated before answering. "In a sense."

"Okay, forgive me. I must have missed him during my visit. All evidence of his existence, actually."

"Now who's brassy?" Lyla snickered under her breath.

"I'm sorry, I just—"

Lyla cut her off. "He's dead." The response was so starched and devoid of emotion that Jillian snapped backward in her seat, if only an inch or two. Lyla observed this, but made no effort to justify her tone. Rolling her eyes toward the window and the scattered people below, she continued, "Are you all right, Dr. Atford? You seem a bit . . . out of it . . . today."

Jillian swallowed the walnut that had manifested in her throat—a sound that could be heard throughout the office—before speaking. "Did you want to talk about it? How he died, or when? I mean, you don't seem all that upset—"

Lyla shrugged. "It was years ago."

"Well, your mother died years ago. And I don't have to remind you that you're still suffering the effects of *that* loss."

"My father died years ago, too. I'm not broken up about that either. No recurring nightmares there. No regrets. I guess I just feel the same way about my husband."

"I see." Jillian stared intently at Lyla, tapping her pen against her notepad.

"What's wrong? You're not shocked by the revelation of my father's passing?" Lyla taunted. "You're not going to press me to talk about that now?"

"I think we've touched upon that before, but if you'd like—"

"I've never told you that my father was dead."

Lyla watched as Jillian lightened a shade, as if all air had left the room, as if she had stopped breathing altogether. "Of course you have."

"No, I'm quite positive. Check your little notepad. Check my file." Jillian took the time to flip rapidly through a few pages. Lyla wasn't sure, but if she had to guess, her doctor seemed anxious. "Find anything?" Lyla asked casually, cheerfully.

"Perhaps you're right." Dr. Atford cleared her throat and crossed her legs in the opposite direction. "In any event, would you care to talk about your father's passing?"

"Not particularly."

"Well, we have to talk about something, Lyla."

"Let's talk about you."

"Nice try."

Lyla chuckled. "It was worth it. Anyway, my husband's name was Anthony. He fell."

"He . . . *fell*? What do you mean, like, down a flight of stairs, off a ladder, off a cliff?"

"No." Lyla straightened, and continued in a matter-of-fact tone, "One night we argued. I shoved him. Hard. He fell into our coffee table. Punctured both lungs. Died right there."

"And you harbor no ill feelings about that?"

"Should I?" Lyla shrugged again.

"Most people would feel guilt, remorse, shame. . ."

"I'm not guilty of anything."

"You pushed him."

"He cheated on me."

"Is that what the argument was about?"

"Well, it wasn't about a burnt pot roast. You know, I thought you were the psychologist," she sneered. "What else would get me that mad? He was no different than my father. But I wasn't my mother. I stood up for myself." Lyla shimmied in her seat with pride, head held high.

"By killing a man?"

Lyla glowered at her doctor. "I didn't kill him. I *pushed* him, and he was unsuccessful in steadying himself. Only a fool would fail to see the difference," she said keenly.

"And you think I'm a fool?" Jillian countered.

"You seem to think I killed a man."

"Or maybe I was trying to see how you viewed the situation by eliciting a reaction."

Lyla bristled at Jillian finally deciding to play shrink. Especially since, just a second ago, she'd mocked the doctor's intelligence.

Jillian eventually broke the silence with curiosity on her face and wonderment on her tongue. "Wait, did he fall onto the coffee table you have now?"

"Yes. It was the branches of the driftwood base and the broken glass that impaled him."

Incredulous, Jillian continued, "And you *kept* the coffee table?"

"Of course, it was a perfectly good coffee table. All I had to do was replace the glass panel and clean the—"

"You don't find that odd?"

"Again, should I?" Lyla refrained from shrugging this time, but she stared forward blankly, indifference evident on her face.

"I suppose not." Jillian pressed her lips together and resumed the staccato tapping of her pen against the notepad.

After several minutes, Jillian sighed. "Well, Lyla, I thought you were doing well the other day when I dropped in on you. Today, however, I'm concerned. You seem combative, but I'm trying to figure out if it's any more so than usual. You're a very hard woman to read, even for a professional."

"I don't know. Lately, I guess I just feel like my life is one big sink. I made a bad decision and now everything I thought I had control of is tumbling down the drain. But instead of trying to grab what I can before it's all out of reach, I just want to say 'Fuck it' and turn on the garbage disposal. Does that make sense?"

Jillian nodded. "I have, I mean, we all have our own skeletons coming to light. It's how we deal with them that matters."

Lyla let the words hang in the air, and then plucked at them one by one, tasting the wisdom. Finally, her psychologist had said something useful. How *would* she deal with this? Derrick was a problem, a mess she had managed to mop up. Now, CJ was littering up her life. *A mess is a mess*, she thought. CJ would have to be cleaned up, disposed of. The circumstances were unfortunate, but necessary. He had betrayed their relationship. He was no different than her father or her husband. He was no different than her other victims.

While Lyla thought about how to salvage her life from slipping down the proverbial sink, Jillian was muttering. Lyla had tuned her out, as she often did, until now. The more she listened, the more it seemed the psychologist was speaking from personal experience. Jillian's attention was on the passing cars below, and, while she was sputtering, she kept shaking her head. It was as if she were no longer speaking to Lyla, but talking to herself, like a hobo on the corner. Lyla couldn't take her eyes off her. She began noticing the details, observations she had attributed earlier to a late night of partying and drinking. Jillian's hair, usually in tidy twists, was ratty and uncombed. She wasn't wearing any makeup. Her legs were crossed, and Lyla saw Jillian's socks did not match, and the small patches of visible shin appeared unshaven. Also, there only seemed to be one word written over and over on her notepad, but Lyla couldn't decipher it from her angle of view. *Maybe something with a C?*

Lyla continued to observe the outward details of her doctor's anxiety, wondering if the meditation fountain had been purchased as a means of remedy, when she caught something that seemed unexpected even to Jillian. Somewhere in her ramblings, Dr. Atford said, "Calvin wouldn't want that." *Did she just say my father's name?* Lyla abandoned her studious interpretations for just a moment. The age matched. So did the skin complexion. Could she have been her father's lover all those years ago? Lyla wasn't sure; she had only seen him with her once. Lyla stared at her psychologist. It was possible, but it was also improbable.

Their session ended, but not after more rambling on Jillian's part, and intensive listening on Lyla's. She scoured every word for another clue. Nothing. Then Lyla remembered that Dr. Atford had also known her father was dead, even though they had never discussed it. It made her wonder. *What was she really doing at my house?*

Lyla decided to deal with Jillian Atford later. Her traitorous friend CJ proved a more pressing matter.

25
To Friendship.

LYLA THREADED HER SUV through mid-morning traffic, blew through a red light, and spoke through clenched teeth into the air, her cell phone connected to the SUV via blue-tooth.

"Hi Cheryl, it's Lyla Kyle . . . Yes, I know, I'm sorry I missed you yesterday, too. Listen, is CJ working today . . . No? Okay, great thanks. See you soon, take care."

Her quick call to West Philly Gen confirmed CJ had the night off. If she knew him as well as she thought she did, he would be home. The poor thing enjoyed even less of a social life than she did. Lyla may have said the same about herself to Brighthouse, but at least her life was bereft of social events on purpose. Lyla decided to pay him a not-so-friendly little visit. *He could use the company, right?*

After picking up a few things, Lyla eased into a space in front of CJ's West Philadelphia apartment building, broken glass crackling beneath her rolling tires. At the door, she pressed repeatedly on the plastic strip of a doorbell marked with CJ's last name, but apparently the intercom system was as busted as the rest of the building. Patiently, Lyla hung around and waited, unwilling to risk a call to CJ from her cell phone. When another resident exited the building a few minutes later, she sneaked in behind her before the door slammed shut.

Inside, Lyla removed the baseball cap she'd been wearing and pulled her hair out of the collar of her shirt and jacket, shaking it out a little, hoping she hadn't been noticed or recognized. In the lobby, she trailed a finger across the cluster of steel mailboxes until she found the dented one belonging to CJ; he lived in apartment 4A. As Lyla climbed the stairs to the fourth floor, her stomach stirred. The fetor of urine overpowered her nostrils. Every landing revealed a cache of cigarette butts, while cigar guts sat on random steps like incinerated caterpillar carcasses, their husks used for marijuana. Occasionally, Lyla caught a few stale whiffs of marijuana smoke, thankful that it managed to cut through the stench of urine. She crumpled her nose as she scrambled through the detritus, finally reaching the door to CJ's apartment. In a cheery fashion, she knocked on the flimsy wood once, thrice, then twice more, whistling when CJ opened the door.

"Hey there, Calvin-Klein-Christoph." He'd barely opened the door more than a few inches. Tension hardened his features, so she held up the six-pack of Leinenkugel's Summer Shandy beer—CJ's favorite—and the greasy brown paper bag full of Chinese food containers. "Glad I caught you. Peace offering?"

He shrugged and stepped aside, fully opening the door. "Come on in."

"I got you shrimp pad Thai, no peanuts. Still your favorite, I hope?" Lyla placed the food on his coffee table with a thud and threw her light leather jacket on the couch. "Listen, I'm sorry about yesterday. I got a little defensive and, well, a little rude."

"It's all good. But I should probably tell you—"

"I don't want to hear it," she shushed him. "I was in the wrong, and I'm sorry."

In the kitchenette they gathered plates and utensils and chatted about their respective days. CJ shared stories of his morning errands and the mean lady in line at the post office. Lyla managed to fabricate a few anecdotal tales from her non-existent veterinary office, all the while she made it a point to ease his mind. Frequent laughter and friendly touches peppered their conversation. More than once she maintained eye contact for just a moment longer than necessary. She even rested her hand on the small of his back when reaching past him for a bottle opener. By the time they headed for the living room, CJ had returned to his usual, affable self.

Lyla sat on the couch perpendicular to CJ, who slouched back into a matching leather recliner. The set was secondhand, and she wondered if the worn, cracked leather scratched his skin the way it clawed at her forearms. They popped open their beers and raised them in salute.

"To friendship," they said in unison.

"I'm sorry I jeopardized it," Lyla added. They each enjoyed a few swigs before hurrying to prepare their plates.

Using his fork, CJ twirled a fistful of lo mein from Lyla's untouched plate. "No peanuts?" Lyla shook her head, smiling, and he shoveled the ball of noodles into his mouth, following it up with a forkful of his own pad Thai

"You're a lifesaver, Lye-dye," CJ garbled between swallows. "I was all set to have cereal and bologna for dinner. I really need to make grocery shopping more of a priority." He chuckled. "Aren't you going to eat?" His laughter morphed into a cough.

It was a silent cough. Void of air. Dry.

Lyla sat motionless, a slippery smile rising on her lips. She had never intended to eat. Instead, she watched her friend of over a dozen years. She watched his eyes abound, his pupils growing to drown out the blue. She watched his eyebrows shoot up above his darting gaze. Anguish took over his look of surprise as he realized Lyla hadn't so much as stirred from her seat to help him—she was sitting back, enjoying the show.

CJ clutched his throat and clawed at the air to stand up. Lyla deduced that he was heading somewhere with purpose, probably towards an EpiPen, so she rose from her seat and stood defiantly in his way. He tried to squirm past her and was met with a swift punch to his chest, ridding his body of its last remaining stores of precious air. CJ fell to his knees. Lyla, her head askance and rotating like a praying mantis, inspected her friend's every twitch and grimace.

She crouched down next to him, met his eye, then leaned in beside his ear and whispered, "Oh, did I say that dish had no peanuts? I misspoke." She retrieved a small bottle of peanut oil from her nearby jacket pocket and held it up for him to see. He tried one last time to push through, to push past. Lyla shoved him to the floor.

Confident her quarry was no longer ambulatory, Lyla strutted around the coffee table, hands on her hips. When she spoke, her voice was airy and casual. “So, again, I just wanted to apologize. And in the interest of full disclosure,” she whipped around, her hair flowing over her shoulders, “I think I should come clean. Although it *is* true that I didn’t sleep with Derrick, we *did* go on one measly little date, after which he wasn’t supposed to live to see the next day.”

CJ’s eyes were losing the fight to stay open. His ragged breathing grew fainter, drowned out by Lyla’s frighteningly calm diatribe.

“But he did live.” Lyla sighed and plopped down into the recliner, crossing her legs. “And that was kind of annoying. So I smothered him.” She stared down at CJ, who was positioned at her feet, gasping, silently dying. “You know, I had that detective eating out of my cleavage last night until you called?”

She reached over to the table and pulled an egg roll from its crinkled wax paper wrapping. She bit into it, leaning over to face CJ. The crumbs sprinkled down onto his face and Lyla brushed them off roughly with a paper towel before going on.

“I think I even liked him. Maybe that’s how you came to call. Is that it? Did you feel something in your gut?” She squinted mockingly. “I know you’ve always been in love with me,” she said between exaggerated bites of the egg roll, ever the seductress. “Be that as it may, I might have to dispose of the young officer now. By the way, if it comes to that,” she pointed at him with the stump of egg roll, “his blood is on your hands.” More flakes speckled his face. She didn’t bother to wipe them off that time.

Lyla rose to her feet, bent to retrieve her beer, and stepped over CJ’s body just as she had stepped over the trash that littered the destitute stairwell. She rummaged around the apartment and tied up a few loose ends, ridding the place of all traces of her visit. She had been cautious not to touch much, but what she did touch she wiped down quickly. Before she walked out the door, she glanced back, regretting the gross waste of Chinese food.

She never gave Christoph a second look.

26
A Goaded Gargoyle.

BLAKELY TURNED TO Brighthouse sporting a broad grin, momentarily ignoring the road. "So you got yourself a little strange, huh?"

"I told you a million times," Brighthouse said rubbing his face with both hands, "nothing happened."

"Yeah, well, you used the words 'hot' and 'heavy.' You can't fault me for prying. Just a few more details, come on?"

"Fine, but there was no 'strange,' as you so eloquently put it. Therefore, no details. My witness ended up calling and, uh, *interrupted* before anything actually happened. And am I ever glad he did. That woman," Brighthouse shook his head, still looking out the window, "had me hypnotized, or entranced, or something, man. I can't explain it."

Byron Blakely nodded in understanding, but Brighthouse had trouble believing his partner could relate. *How could he?* Only someone who knew Lyla, and knew what it was like to be within her clutches could possibly fathom what she was capable of. He let himself loose in the world of his own thoughts, and Blakely was silent as well, until the squad car came to a stop at the next red light.

"I hear you, man. So, you still like her for your so-called serial murders?"

"I did. I do . . . like her . . . for the killings, I mean."

"Right," Blakely said with a schoolboy smile.

"Shut up."

"I'm just saying—"

"No, I mean it, shut up a sec." Brighthouse waved off his partner's words in a frenzy and focused on the hurried but monotonous voice coming through from dispatch. "What was that address?"

"What? What are you talking about?" his partner asked, flashing his eyes between Brighthouse and the road ahead of him.

Brighthouse shook his partner's arm wildly. "I think I recognize that address." He turned up the radio's volume. Static and a stern voice flooded the car. "Oh, no. Turn the car around. Turn it around!"

"All right, all right, but why? That's not our beat, and another unit already responded."

Brighthouse exhaled heavily and sunk his chin into his chest, smothering his solemn reply as he shook his head limply. "I recognize that address."

"Yes, I gathered that. Whose is it?" The strain in Blakely's voice indicated he was wrestling with impatience.

"I think it's my witness's, Lyla's friend. I ran a routine background check on him when he called, you know, to be thorough, seeing as how he works around some serious drugs all day and he's kind of squirrelly, and if he's gonna testify I need him to be credible and—"

"Get to the point, bro."

"Yeah, well, whoever just called to report a dead body, reported it at his current address."

"Is it a house or an apartment?"

"It's an apartment building. I think. Why does that matter?"

"Well, there you have it. West Philly? It could be any one of the residents in that building."

Brighthouse conceded his partner's point and silently prayed he was right, prayed the young guy with the acne-spotted face was home watching whatever awkward pharmacists watched on TV after work. He also found himself praying that if CJ had met with foul play that Lyla was in no way involved. He immediately scolded himself.

The streets were ablaze with whirling red and blue lights, silently serenading Blakely and Brighthouse as they drew near. They parked the squad car as best they could, with multiple spaces blocked by the responding patrol unit and the obligatory ambulance. Brighthouse jogged over to the detective who appeared to be first on the scene.

He was clean-shaven, except for a thick broom of a mustache that seemed to have crawled right out of the seventies. He, of course, met Brighthouse with sarcasm.

"Officer Lighthouse, we didn't call for your, um, *expertise*," the man said with a snicker. Brighthouse stiffened at hearing his much maligned nickname had spread to outside precincts.

"Yeah, yeah, you got an ID yet?"

"What's it to you?"

"One of my informants lives here."

"Beat cops have informants now? Must've missed that one."

Mustache turned his back to face another detective. The taller, dark-skinned man had yet to utter a single word in the exchange, but didn't seem averse to joining in his partner's fun. They both shared a hearty chuckle, and Brighthouse felt the heat in his face contrast with the cool summer breeze.

"He called me about a person of interest for a case. An angle, I'm working—"

"Whoo-hoo-hoo, you have informants *and* angles now, huh?"

"Look, I just want to make sure he's all right, and I thought I would do you the courtesy of not stomping up to your crime scene to check for myself, but obviously you're not the type to appreciate such civility, so—"

Blakely interrupted. "Can you give up the damn ID and stop giving my partner a hard time?" He'd probably spotted his partner's fist clenching. Luckily, he jumped in right as Brighthouse was about to wind up.

"We haven't gotten one yet."

"And why not?" Blakely asked as Brighthouse stormed off, kicking a piece of trash in the gutter.

"We just got here, haven't gone up yet. What's the rush? Look where we are." He held his arms out like a pompous ruler, perched on the balcony of his castle, overlooking the peasantry. "It's probably a junkie up there. Another OD."

"Who called it in then?" Brighthouse chimed, back from his momentary loss of cool.

"His boss over at the hospital." Brighthouse shook his head; he couldn't believe their ignorance. "Said he hadn't shown up for his last three shifts and couldn't get a hold of him. Sent a coworker to check in. Poor girl cut outta here as soon we showed up." The detective and his partner enjoyed another sturdy laugh. Brighthouse inched toward them, glowering, but Byron placed a hand on his comrade's shoulder and stopped him where he stood.

"And you know a lot of junkies with jobs?" Brighthouse grumbled, as Blakely inquired as to why the coworker was not questioned. Detective Mustache ignored Byron and chose to address the other question instead, shrugging his round shoulders.

"He works in a pharmacy. He could be a white-collar junkie. What difference does it make? A junkie's a junkie."

"Well, here's your fucking ID: the kid's name is Christoph Lahm. If you don't want the case, if you feel like it's a waste of your precious time, we'll gladly take it off your hands. Save you the paperwork. You can head over to the bar early, get drunk off your ass, and crawl on top of whoever you cheat on your wife with—"

A calming hand on the shoulder was no longer sufficient to quell his rising fury. Blakely had to step in front of him, steeping Brighthouse in shadow. The darkness highlighted his anger, twisting his face into that of a goaded gargoyle.

The detective scoffed; his mustache twitched, and he rubbed his hands together with exaggerated flare to signal that he was washing his hands of the entire situation. He and his partner walked off, but that wouldn't be the end of it. This wasn't Brighthouse and Blakely's district, and they weren't detectives. Nevertheless, Blakely, as per usual, offered to scrounge up some witnesses while Brighthouse hurriedly signed the Crime Scene Entry Log and went up to have a look around CJ's apartment. They would sort out the repercussions later.

During the walk up, Brighthouse hated to admit it, but he could see how the detective might assume the death he was climbing toward was another typical junkie OD. He was correct about the neighborhood, and, from the look and smell of the stairwell, he was also right about the building. Briefly he wondered why a young pharmacist would live in such an area, but then Brighthouse remembered that he lived in a similar apartment in North Philly until the day he was married. The thought of Emma caused his chest to tighten. He had come so close to cheating on her he couldn't stand it—and with a suspect. *What was I thinking?*

He shook off his momentary lapse in judgment, willpower, and overall morality to focus on the possibility of his dead witness. *What are the odds that two hospital pharmacists live in this building?* But he knew better. As soon as Brighthouse reached the threshold of the apartment, the odor of the decomposing body within knocked him backward, almost back into the hallway. He stole a glimpse through the open door: the bloated, discolored body slumped on the floor was indeed CJ.

Without a handkerchief handy Brighthouse lifted an arm across his face to guard against the smell. He started to duck under the crime scene tape blocking off the entryway, but, seeing no one inside, thought better of it, not wanting to disturb any evidence inside the apartment. While he waited for other personnel to arrive, he stared at CJ—or rather, what CJ had become—from where he stood in the hallway. Brighthouse's reluctance to investigate the body of a man he once knew, even if briefly, was palpable. Once again, he found himself reciting a silent prayer that Lyla Kyle did not have a hand in the scene beyond him. And, once again, he chided himself.

27
Carefully Feigned Emotion.

THE SKY ABOVE Lyla was an inky azure, almost black with night. The horizon was visible between breaks in the rows of the self-storage units, and appeared almost foamy, infused with the eerie amethyst of the approaching storm. She stared at it, mesmerized by its misty allure. Exhaling with content, she was pleased that the debacles caused by Derrick and CJ were behind her. Lyla had even gotten past her brief attraction to Officer Brighthouse, and he hadn't called upon her since he dropped by her house a couple of days ago. With another gratified sigh, she looked down to where Dr. Theodore Stone lay sprawled face-down on the cement floor at the entrance of her unit, his silver-speckled hair reflecting the light that spilled out into the alley.

Of her many kills over the years, this one proved bittersweet. It was supposed to be celebratory, what with so many wrongs being righted, but she and the handsome doctor had actually enjoyed their evening of potent cocktails and gleaming conversation. With every flash of his smile, with every playful joke about his hairy arms, Lyla had imagined she was on an actual date with a real man, one whom she had met in a hospital elevator only a few days prior. Yet when he excused himself to make a call, she knew she needed to choose between her want of normalcy and her desire for justice. In the end, she settled their tab and bowed to her desires. Still, Lyla had fought herself when they stood in front of the corrugated metal door of her storage unit. It hadn't helped when, during the awkward silence, he'd kissed her. Knowing what she had to do, she stabbed him in the chest with a syringe, counting on his hirsute body to the conceal injection site. Now, Lyla paused, taking a few minutes to appreciate the beauty of the sky, building up the energy needed to drag his dead weight inside the storage unit.

Before she could properly dispose of her kill, she noticed movement out of the corner of her eye as she bent over her prey; a figure dressed in head-to-toe steel gray, strolling in her direction. His familiar features gradually came into focus, the mess of curly, reddish hair and the pale, freckled skin. *The new guy*. Lyla let out an exasperated sigh. The security guard whose name she'd never bothered to learn was watching her intently as he advanced. She shuffled through the various ideas racing through her head and chose one. Lyla chose to run out to greet him.

"Help! My friend . . . he passed out! Please hurry." Lyla's voice cracked with carefully feigned emotion as she frenetically waved her arms about.

The gray-clad man quickened his pace to a moderate jog. When he arrived, out of breath, the usual responses sputtered from his mouth like water from an old spigot. "Oh, my go—! Miss. Wh . . . What happened? Who . . ."

Ignoring every word he spoke, Lyla grabbed his arm. Pleading with her eyes, she ushered him to the doctor's side. He knelt down, reaching out with two fingers to take the prone man's pulse. Lyla swiftly jabbed him with her last syringe, plunging the chemical into his bloodstream and his body into paralysis. In a few moments, she would have two dead men at her feet.

Lyla hauled both men inside her storage unit, her muscles screeching at the added effort of moving two bodies instead of one. The glaring lights of her workspace glinted off the new guy's security badge, as well as the sterling silver ballpoint pen protruding from Dr. Stone's breast pocket—presenting an idea. She hastily searched both men, emptying their pockets down to the lint and spare change. Within minutes, she found a tiny Ziploc bag in the new guy's pants pocket. The white, powdery substance had a slight yellow tinge to it, and when she poked her finger inside, rubbing the drug between her thumb and forefinger, its coarseness confirmed its identity: heroin. She recognized it from her days volunteering at a halfway house, many years ago as an undergraduate. Back then she'd confiscated all kinds of drugs from the residents and heroin abuse explained the constricted pupils and shortness of breath she'd noticed when she first met the new guard.

Other than a platinum wedding band in the folds of his wallet, Lyla found nothing of interest on the doctor, but, given her familiarity with the stress of working in a hospital—and inspired by what she'd discovered on the security guy—she removed his shoes and socks on a hunch. Doctors and hospital staff sometimes took the edge off with prescription meds, and when they built up a tolerance to oral ingestion, they often turned to intravenous use. Lyla pried apart Dr. Stone's toes and was thrilled to discover puncture marks between several of them. It seemed Dr. Stone needed to take the edge off every now and again. There weren't any actual track marks yet, and she didn't know what his drug of choice was, but she had to admit the situation was fortunate and would help sell the stage she was preparing to set. Lyla shook her head at him disapprovingly, but, armed with a fully formed plan, she went to work.

Disposing of the security guard was easy. After Lyla wrapped him in burlap, she wheeled him out to the main security post on her dolly. Wary of the operational cameras around the perimeter of the facility, she kept her head down and rolled him around the side of the scant building to an area outside the view of video surveillance. As she had done countless times before, Lyla unwrapped the guard and dumped him on the ground, letting his limbs and his stringy red curls lay as they fell, splayed in multiple directions. She pulled a utility knife from her purse and stabbed him several times in the chest with all the force she could muster.

The guard's heart was paralyzed from the injection, so blood had stopped pumping through his body, but it still seeped from his torso and spread a bouquet of crimson blooms throughout the front of his shirt. She kept stabbing. Because of the blunt angle of the blade, the tip eventually snapped off inside his ribcage. *Oh well.* She lint-rolled the body, wiped the knife handle clean of her prints, and took it with her, gripping it with a tissue. Following a final inspection to ensure she hadn't missed anything, and grabbing a few items from inside the security post, Lyla left the new guy—now the dead guy—to be discovered in the morning.

Dealing with the doctor proved more difficult, so it was a good thing Dr. Stone insisted on driving so he could show off his sleek new Porsche. Lyla placed him in the driver's seat of his own car and made herself comfortable in the passenger seat beside him. Summoning her little knowledge of heroin use from her days at the halfway house, Lyla had brought a few items with her: a metal spoon and a bottle of water she'd found inside the security post near the microwave, the cotton pad of a Band-Aid from her purse, a lighter from the new guy's pocket, and one of her empty syringes.

Using her phone to consult the Internet, Lyla confirmed her memory of the procedure, drew up the prepared heroin—filtered through the cotton—and injected the dead doctor with the drug between his big and second toes. Lyla left the needle sticking out from his foot to stage the scene as much as possible, making sure to place his fingerprints on the plunger. She also wrapped his fingers firmly around the bloody utility knife before tossing it under the driver's seat. Then, just as Lyla had done at the scene of the guard's body, she wiped everything down and gave the Porsche a final parting glance.

Lyla expected both bodies to be found long after she'd left, probably in the morning. At first glimpse, the guard would appear as just another victim of senseless Philadelphia violence. Once they located the second body however, the authorities would conclude that the security guard was killed by the junkie doctor. Lyla didn't care what motive they attributed to the scenario. Most likely they would assume the guard was the doctor's dealer, and they'd fought over quantity, quality, or price. In his near-withdrawal state, the doctor had killed the guard before staggering off to his car, and then accidentally overdosed in his hurry to get high.

Lyla beamed with pride and confidence, her head held high as she strolled back to her unit, checking the cash in her wallet. Satisfied she had enough for a cab ride back to the lounge where her car was parked, she pulled out her cell phone. Before she could dial a single digit, she spotted Willis. The fatherly security guard she had known for years was dressed in plain clothes and plodding around the grounds with a cheery gait. It was too late for her to duck out of sight; he'd recognized her instantly.

"Well, hello, Miss Lyla. Burning the late night oil again, I see," he said with a friendly chuckle.

Lyla returned the laughter. "You know me, Willis. Time is money, and I don't waste a single cent."

Once Willis caught up to her, Lyla made up a lie about her SUV being detailed after having spilled paint on the rear seats. When he insisted on walking with her to the main street where she planned to catch a cab, Lyla's heart began a drumbeat of anxiety as the meager security post came into view, a single leg peeking out from its shadow. They reached the spot where she had staged the new guy's demise. One look at the messy, red head of hair and Willis gasped. He ran to kneel beside his coworker and Lyla knew what she had to do.

She had to play along.

28
Elements of the Milieu.

THE PUTRID STENCH was almost unbearable.

"Thank goodness it wasn't too hot this week," Brighthouse mumbled to himself, swatting at the flies buzzing around CJ's bloated corpse and the rancid spread of Chinese food. Maggots wriggled and writhed intermittently throughout the room, but were most concentrated nearest the food and CJ's open orifices. The officer entertained the briefest comparison between the swarms pudgy white larvae and rice pudding and suppressed a gag. He was determined to contain his last meal. He also made a mental note to avoid rice pudding for the rest of his life.

Brighthouse didn't see anything out of the ordinary as he surveyed the scene. His gaze wandered around the various elements of the milieu, resting on each momentarily before moving on to the next. He was engrossed in thought when he heard creaking floorboards behind him. He spun around, thinking it was another CSU tech, but a pair of latex gloves soared across the room, hitting him squarely in the chest.

"I know you know better, so I assume you didn't touch anything," Dr. DiCicco said dryly from the doorway.

"Of course not," he said through the crumpled napkin he'd found in his pocket and had been using to protect against the offensive odor.

"What good is that doing you?" she asked, meaning it as more of an observation than an inquiry. She hurried up to him and smeared a generous amount of Vick's Vapor Rub under his nose. The powerful mix of menthol and camphor was a welcome relief. "There," she said satisfactorily. "But you'll have to get a tech to document that." She pointed at the glob of petroleum that had fallen to the polished wood floor with a splat.

Dr. DiCicco turned from Brighthouse to inspect CJ's body, careful not to disturb anything in her path. She massaged CJ's mouth open, scooping maggots out of the way with two fingers, and her face brightened with discovery. Watching her cast aside those maggots was almost too much for Brighthouse, and he ran off to the kitchen. She found him a minute later bent over the sink; he'd found something curious.

"What are you doing? I expected to hear retching, but heard none. Thank God. Go outside if you're going to be sick."

Brighthouse sniffed loudly. "No, I'm fine now. I'm smelling the drain. What are you doing?"

"Oh, nothing. Just this little thing I do called finding tentative COD." As always, her tone was dry as a desert.

"Well, you'd better note suspicious circumstances."

"And why would that be?" When he didn't respond she called, "Cause of death is asphyxiation from anaphylactic shock, in case you're interested."

"There are only five bottles," Brighthouse said, his face still out of sight within the sink, muffling his shouts.

"What?"

"Only five beer bottles." He emerged from the depths of the sink and shrugged. "I'm willing to bet this was a fresh six-pack, probably purchased at the same time as the food. Five bottles. Where is the sixth bottle?"

"You're kidding."

"It would be here somewhere. In the trash. On the counter. On the table. But it's nowhere to be found. I don't see any broken glass . . ."

"And you think it disappeared down the drain?"

"No, I think someone poured it down the drain and took the bottle with them. Even over the Vick's, I can smell stale beer in the drain. And Chinese food. Someone must have dumped some of the food down there, washed it down with the beer, and then turned on the garbage disposal."

"Why would someone do that?" Even though her voice was still flat, her words bore a distinct hint of mocking.

"Exactly," Brighthouse shrieked. "Why wouldn't they leave it? Unless they didn't want to leave a trace of themselves. Maybe they already sipped from it. Maybe they wanted to make it look like he was eating alone. That would explain the food down the drain."

"I guess that makes sense, albeit still a little far-fetched."

"Everyone's a cynic," Brighthouse said through a sigh, shaking his head.

"I believe you're looking for the phrase 'everyone's a critic,'" the medical examiner corrected.

"Yeah, that too. So, you said he choked or something?"

"He suffocated due to an allergic reaction. From the scene here, I'm guessing it was something in the food."

"If he were that allergic to something, wouldn't he have one of those pen things?"

"Epinephrine, an EpiPen. I'm sure he would have. Why don't you use your astute powers of observation and look around for one?"

He chuckled. "You kill me, Doc."

Brighthouse stood in the middle of the living room and closed his eyes, trying to put himself in CJ's position. Assuming he was alone, his take-out food arrives, he digs in. Either he didn't know he was allergic to something, or he did and specifically requested that the food be prepared without it, but they neglected his instructions. If the latter was the case, why didn't he use his EpiPen? He wasn't some uninsured slum-dweller. He was a hospital pharmacist. Good job, good benefits. He would most definitely have one. Brighthouse combed the bathroom, figuring CJ would keep it with his other remedies, in the medicine cabinet, perhaps. Nothing. He checked the kitchen. Nothing. He searched the bedroom. Again, nothing.

"Hey, Dr. DiCicco," he called out from the bedroom, "any chance you could tell me what the victim was allergic to? Like, maybe he didn't know he had allergy? I haven't found a single EpiPen in this place."

"No. I can't tell just from looking at him what he's allergic to. Sorry."

"What's the matter, you missed that class in med school?" he shouted, laughing to himself as he imagined the look of irritation on her face.

"When I check his medical records and compare it to his stomach contents, I'll let you know," she said, disregarding his joke.

"It looks pretty disheveled in here. Maybe someone already took them?"

"Yes, the same someone that dumped the Chinese food and the mysterious sixth beer down the drain," she replied incredulously. "*Or* maybe he was looking for them himself. If the victim was aware of the allergy, which he probably was, he might not have needed to use his EpiPen in a long time. Years, even. Also, let me ask you this: How clean was *your* apartment when you were a young bachelor, hmm? Perhaps his apartment always looks like this."

Fair point . . . But still. "My money's on someone already took them," Brighthouse mumbled.

"You're just trying to turn this into a suspicious circs case," she said, exasperation tainting her voice. "Everybody's right about you—"

"Hey!"

"I'm sorry. I suppose you were onto something with those other cases. I'm still waiting to hear back from the lab about the samples I sent out, by the way."

"Okay, Doc. But you know what bothers me about this case?"

"Do tell."

"That kid in there was a friend of the woman I like for those other cases. And he called me. Wanted to tell me about Lyla. I met with him, and he told me she hadn't been the same since she quit her medical residency after her parents died. I mean, she'd told me about all that, but . . . Anyway, he said she was supposedly working in some veterinary clinic here in West Philly. I went to every one of them in the area. No one has ever heard of her. No one recognized her license photo. So the drugs she's been having CJ smuggle out of the hospital for her? What is she using them for? I'll tell you what. They're probably the drug you're testing for. They're probably the drugs she's been using to kill these men right under our noses without anyone suspecting anything. Well *I* suspect something. *I* know she's involved. And *I* intend to put her pretty ass away for it."

Brighthouse concluded his rant and looked up at the medical examiner, who was staring at him with an intense expression of bewilderment. Her face suddenly looked like a delicate sheet of pale, crinkled rice paper, drained of all color. Before he could think to ask her anything, he looked down at the pen he'd been using to jot down notes. He inspected it, as though it were now foreign to him.

"Doc! Do you have access to that hair I collected from the Alex Livanos scene? I'd handed it off to a crime scene tech that night." His hands were on her shoulders now, shaking her.

"I . . . I . . . I think so," she sputtered. Brighthouse retreated slowly, concerned; he'd expected a terse reaction to his physical outburst.

He tentatively handed her his pen. "Can you run this pen cap for DNA and then compare it to the follicular tag on that hair?"

Momentarily ignoring whatever had ailed her, she raised an eyebrow. "Do I even want to know what she did to the end of your pen cap, Brighthouse?"

"She put it in her mouth, in a, uh, playful manner," he said, blushing, suddenly very interested in his shoes.

"Do you know this woman?"

"No, I was at her house—"

The doctor's jaw fell from its hinge. "Her house?"

"Long story. Can you run the stuff or not?" He'd endured enough accusations from his partner, and was in no mood to defend himself to yet another person. Besides, he'd berated himself enough already.

"Not personally, but I can make the request," she said calmly, before pausing. When she continued she was notably closer to the officer, approaching him with the apprehensiveness of a stray cat. "Can I ask you something?"

"I didn't have sex with her. Blakely swears I—"

"No, no, not that." She swallowed what looked to be a sizable ball of nerves. "You said her name was. . . Lyla?"

"Yeah, Lyla Kyle. Why?"
"You may not know her, but I do. She's my niece."

29
Uncovered Skeletons.

THE SOFT SOIL beneath her was cool and damp. The bitter moisture seeped into the seat of her pants, chilling her spine, just as it had the last time she was there. Jillian sat, cross-legged, and wondered if soil always felt that way, or just at cemeteries. She wondered many things as she stared at the granite slab in front of her, its color like that of a low-hanging storm cloud. Calvin Kyle's name was etched broadly across the surface, staring back at her. So did the phrases 'Loving Husband' and 'Beloved father.' She chose to ignore those.

She didn't need to see the dates on the stone to know it was Calvin's birthday; she had remembered after all of those years. Jillian thought it was a sign. Concerned with her actions of late, and knowing it had all started with him, she had returned for answers and inspiration once again. After Calvin died, Jillian had experienced her own poignant version of a living death. Overwrought with grief, she had stayed in her house for months, sleeping more than she had to, eating only because she needed to.

Six months after the funeral, on a particularly radiant winter afternoon, Jillian had left her apartment for the first time, determined to grease the wheels of her life, intent on moving forward. Her first stop had been the cemetery. She remembered a crisp, cool day, and the many willow trees throughout the grounds had been bare, like so many branches of bony fingers swaying in the wind, clawing at the ground. That day she had said goodbye to Calvin, and goodbye to her past. Now Jillian had returned, hoping to rebury the recently uncovered skeletons of her youth.

"I'm a psychologist now, Cal." With her lips parted, words trickled forth like a stream, awkwardly at first, as if obstructed, but before she knew it, she was speaking casually to the gravestone before her, seeing only Calvin's rugged face. "Yeah, I finally started my own practice. After I got over you, of course. Though I guess the fact that I'm here proves that I've never actually done that." She gulped, unsure of what to say next, so she stuck to the current topic. "My office is in the heart of Center City, just like we used to talk about. Great view. Sometimes the PPD sends me guys to clear for duty. They always remind me of you," she said with crackling words and welling eyes.

Jillian imagined Calvin—Cal, as she liked to call him—sitting across from her. She pictured the fine lines engraved in his face and around his dark eyes, coupled with a few gray hairs and silver stubble.

"When I see them, and I think of you, I transcend to a world where we were able to have a life together. A world where you left your wife, your daughter wasn't an issue, and we were free to marry. Our child would play 'cops and robbers' in the yard with the other neighborhood kids, always insisting on being one of the cops because he idolizes you so much." Jillian sighed as these images danced around in her head. "Cal, it's a world where you would come home to me, and I'd greet you with a cold beer. I'd fuss in the kitchen over a hot meal, and then we'd all sit around the table and chat about our days." Her lips curled into a desolate, half-hearted smile.

"Usually these thoughts comfort me," she continued. Her voice kept morphing between honey and gravel, between smooth and strained. At the moment, it was once again taut. "That's what daydreams are for, right? To comfort us with what could be, or, in this case, what could've been," she said with a dry chuckle. Even now, the playful projections of suburban bliss scattered in her mind, making way for the darkness. "Lately, however, I've been having a little trouble, unable to indulge in such escapes." Tears were flowing now, as freely as her words. "No mental relief for me," she cried, blending sobs with near-maniacal laughter.

"Do you wanna know *why* I'm without respite, Cal? It's simple."

Jillian's tone had become even again. "You see, your daughter is one of my patients now." She paused, as if giving her deceased lover time to let this information sink in. "She's beautiful, creative, and strong-willed. Just like you. The strong-willed part, I mean. I'm sure she got the creativity from her mother. If I remember correctly, you could barely draw a stick-figure." She sniffled through a giggle. "Lyla looks just like you, but I'm sure you already knew that.

"Anyway, ever since I figured out who she was, which didn't take long, I've been preoccupied with all these ghastly thoughts and loathsome emotions. Things I've suppressed since the last time I was out here ten years ago."

"When I see your daughter, I'm reminded of you. Not in the way the officers remind me of you. I'm reminded of your death. I'm reminded that we don't have a sunny life in the 'burbs. I'm reminded that I never got to say goodbye." Though her voice was clear right now, Jillian wiped at her sniveling nose with a rumpled tissue, staring off into the distance, as if unable to make eye contact. "I couldn't even catch a parting glimpse of you because there was hardly anything to bury. Jesus Christ, Cal, it was a closed casket funeral! What the hell happened that night?" The tears flowed once more.

Several minutes wasted away in silence. Each blade of grass shivered in the breeze. The large willow tree whispered incoherently as its longest branches tickled the ground at its roots. Jillian's upper body nodded back and forth, as though invisible arms were rocking away her despair. After a while in this state, she glanced around, surveying the seemingly endless rows of tombstones. Confident there was no one within earshot, she composed herself once more before she continued.

"Cal, there's something else that comes to mind when I see Lyla. Not only am I taunted by the life we never had and the child we never raised—the child you hadn't even known I was carrying—but I'm also reminded of Lyla's mother. I suppose it's a good thing your daughter resembles you. If she'd been blessed with her mother's blonde hair and blue eyes, things would probably be so much harder on me. Despite the contrast, Susannah is brought to the forefront of my mind all the same. Yes, I eventually learned her name. And her blood-streaked hair and dead eyes the color of faded hyacinth are haunting me again," Jillian said through choked back tears.

"I never told you this, Cal, but I was there when Susannah died. It wasn't a suicide. I'm so sorry."

30
Something More Sinister.

"SHE'S YOUR NIECE!" Brighthouse exclaimed, extra octaves in his voice.

"Yes," Dr. DiCicco said sorrowfully. "Her late father was my brother. It always bothered me how both of her parents died so close in succession."

"Wait. What do you mean?" he asked with a raised eyebrow. "I know she told me they had both passed away, but she never mentioned a time frame or anything."

"They died less than a week apart."

"I thought her mother committed suicide?"

LeeAnn DiCicco seemed exhausted, like she wanted to plop down in the cracked leather chair, despite the decomposing balloon of a corpse rotting at the base of it. Instead she was forced to stand while she spoke. "It began with the death of my sister-in-law. I wasn't the chief medical examiner back then and was doubly distanced from the case because of my familial relationship. When my boss ruled Susannah's death a suicide, I stayed up nights, studying reports and photos of the scene, concerned by the blood smears on the walls. To me, they indicated a struggle, but without any evidence of another person, an actual attacker, my concerns were deemed unfounded. I ceded the point at the time and gave up my useless protestations. Then my little brother, Calvin, died in a house fire days later. The night of Susannah's funeral, in fact."

Brighthouse stiffened at the mention of a house fire, but allowed LeeAnn to continue.

"Lyla never showed up at the repast following her mother's funeral. She also seemed oddly emotionless at her father's services, which were held exactly a week later. Everyone viewed her stoic demeanor as simply the shock of losing both of her parents so unexpectedly, but I was never convinced. I investigated Susannah's and my brother's deaths in my spare time, but was unable to find anything probative. There was a storm the night of Calvin's death. The lights went out. Melted wax at the scene indicated Calvin must have lit a candle, and then passed out drunk. According to the autopsy report, his blood alcohol level was more than twice the legal limit. Even the Fire Commissioner himself assured me nothing was amiss. Still, I obsessed over the reports and photos. In particular, I noted a mound of colorful melted glass in the living room, near the body, in the vicinity of the coffee table—"

"Colored glass?"

"I had given Susannah two matching, blown-glass oil lamps one Christmas. She kept them on their nightstands. The melted glass was consistent with the lamps, given the heat of the fire and the hydrocarbon accelerant held within. But I always wondered why only *one* of them was in the living room if he had a candle? I suppose he could have used the candle to light the lamp—it wasn't implausible—but it just never felt right to me. He was obviously drunk. What did he need so much light for? And would a drunk *man* really think to go get the decorative oil lamps from the bedroom in a blackout? I highly doubt it. I know my brother. He was a real man's man. He probably didn't even know those lamps existed. And where was the second lamp? There was no corresponding mass of melted glass in the bedroom. I checked the photos." LeeAnn shook her head, obviously still befuddled after all those years. "Anyway, I haven't even spoken to Lyla since her father's funeral."

"So that solidified it for you then, I'm sure," Brighthouse mused.

"Yes. Especially since I called her several times. She never returned any of my calls. After the house was rebuilt, I stopped by. She wouldn't even answer the door."

"And how was Lyla toward her parents before they died?"

"That perplexed me also. She was Daddy's little girl, as they say, and she adored her mother very much. Neither had an ill word to say about her . . ."

"But?" Brighthouse pressured.

"She always had to be in control. I watched her make an omelet once, and when she turned it over, it broke. She threw the biggest tantrum I've ever seen. Threw the pan—omelet still inside—across the room, breaking a window. It was surreal."

"Anything else?"

"Yes. Calvin and my husband at the time bought her a Dalmatian puppy when she was nine years old. She brought it to mine and Calvin's parents' house so they could see it. She was absolutely giddy, until it nipped our mother's hand. She strangled it the next day and cut it open. Kind of an amateur necropsy.

"But it wasn't just *that* dog. Lyla could never keep a pet without . . . killing it. She enjoyed dissecting things. Her parents applauded it, said it was scientific curiosity, which is why I encouraged her to become a physician, but deep down I'd always hoped it wasn't something more sinister than that."

"Curious," Brighthouse mumbled the understatement with raised eyebrows, taking furious notes with a pen he'd borrowed from LeeAnn.

"Exceedingly," she agreed.

"Run the samples?"

"Absolutely. But you know the pen won't be admissible. No chain of custody."

"I get that. I just need to know."

"Me too."

They exited the meager apartment just as the ME's assistants prepared to remove CJ's body. On their way down the stairs, Brighthouse and Dr. DiCicco passed several more members of the CSU team. The two groups, threading through one another in opposite directions, maneuvered down the narrow staircase awkwardly, concerned with both avoiding the trash and each other. Suddenly the building felt crowded, and Brighthouse was relieved to be heading out into the evening air.

Outside, Brighthouse spotted Blakely speaking with a squirrelly, shaggy-haired man, scratching at his hands and arms but ignoring his nose, which ran like a faucet. His eyes were sunken, yellowed, and bloodshot. Brighthouse was impressed he'd notice the man's eyes since they darted about, like they were following a rapidly paced tennis match. As he neared the conversation, he overheard the junkie trying to trade information for money. Blakely didn't oblige, and the gaunt man reduced his demands to a single cigarette. This request went denied as well, since neither officer smoked. They were just about to leave when a woman walked up hugging a brown paper bag full of groceries.

"Is everything all right? What do you want with my cousin?" she asked, adjusting the bag so she could peer over it to make eye contact with them.

"Nothing ma'am. We were just asking him a few questions. Do you live here?"

"Yes. My cousin's just staying with me. I'm tryna dry him out, ya know?"

"Good luck with that," Blakely grumbled under his breath.

Brighthouse shot a brief glare at his partner before continuing, "Listen, have you seen anyone unfamiliar around the building, a few days ago maybe?"

"Nah, not that I can remember."

Brighthouse held up a finger while he accessed a photo on his phone. "This woman, perhaps? Seen her in or around the building?"

"Um, I'm not sure. I did see someone. Maybe this past Wednesday? Not sure if it was her, though. I think she was wearing a hat. I don't remember all that hair."

Blakely rejoined the conversation. "What else do you remember?"

"Her jacket. Definitely her jacket."

"Her jacket?"

"Yeah, it was gorgeous. Very expensive." She pursed her lips. "Chocolate brown, buttery leather. Belted. Flared out a bit at the waist. If I owned something that posh, I wouldn't ruin the look with a raggedy old Phillies cap, ya know what I mean?"

Blakely rolled his eyes, but then he must have seen his partner's slack-jawed expression. He elbowed him. "Everything all right, man?"

"I know that coat. Lyla was wearing it the day I saw her at the hospital. And I think I saw it folded on the counter near her purse when I was in her house."

"You may seriously be onto something with her."

"Bro, you don't know the half of it."

While Brighthouse had his attention, he told Blakely that Lyla Kyle was Dr. DiCicco's niece. He also told him about the doctor's suspicions regarding the deaths of her brother and sister-in-law. Given those stunning revelations, he'd almost forgotten his disappearing bottle theory. Blakely opened his mouth, probably to ridicule him, but abruptly stopped himself. Brighthouse grinned. He had led with the info about Lyla's past because of its shock value, and because he wanted to circumvent the mockery that would surely ensue when he mentioned the missing beer bottle. Instead, Blakely asked what their next plan of action was.

A few yards away, CSU collected some of the trash from around the front steps to the building, as Brighthouse had suggested, on account of his missing bottle hypothesis. He was about to answer Blakely regarding their next move when one of the techs approached with a glass bottle in a plastic evidence bag, the yellow Summer Shandy label dingy from the gutter, but still readable.

With wide eyes, Brighthouse pointed to the curb and requested they note the bottle's original location—where the responding detective's taunts had prompted him to kick it in anger about an hour or so prior.

31
Collateral Damage.

FOR THE SECOND time that evening, Lyla faked an emotional response to a dead body, one whose death she hadn't intended to be directly responsible for. When Willis ran to his coworker, Lyla saw no other choice than to flank the opposite side of the corpse. She briefly considered killing Willis also, but that was not possible. The eyeglass case she carried only fit four syringes comfortably. Two held the paralyzing agent, both of which she had already used, and the remaining two were empty, used for gathering her trophy blood samples. She had used both of those on Dr. Stone: one to extract his blood moments before the security guard had spotted her, and the other to stage his heroin overdose.

Lyla hadn't followed her usual ritual with the new guy; she viewed him as collateral damage, just as she had CJ. The thought of viewing Willis in the same way upset her. She was too fond of him, which she hated to admit. It was bad enough she'd had to kill CJ, but he had betrayed her. Willis had done nothing.

Kneeling on the ground alongside the new guy, the pock-marked surface of the concrete dug into her knees. No amount of shifting her weight alleviated the discomfort. Regardless, Lyla was forced to push it from her mind so she could focus on her dramatic performance. She fumbled with her phone, dropped it once, and misdialed it twice. When she finally reached the 9-1-1 operator, she stumbled through the details of the situation: dead guy, stab wounds, no pulse, please hurry. She provided the address to the storage facility, making sure to quiver her voice all the while. The operator asked for her name. She froze and handed the phone off to Willis. Lyla wasn't pretending; she was hesitant to have her identity connected with the scene. He grabbed the phone from her, and only then did she realize the futility of the gesture: her name would appear on the 9-1-1 transcript anyway. *Oh well.* At least the moment of indecision helped seal her act of forced distress.

Willis spoke to the operator in an even tone, but with downcast eyes and an air of solemn regret evident on his face. He hadn't stopped shaking his head. Lyla paused to appreciate just how young the new guy had been. With his fresh face and thick, shiny red hair, he barely looked old enough to drink, let alone have a wife at home who was interested in Lyla's artwork. In an instant, she felt a pang of something she had only experienced once before: the night an unsuspecting off-duty cop had run into a burning home in an attempt to save her father. Yes, for the first time in a long time, Lyla felt regret.

Fortunately, the emotion was fleeting. Willis's voice interrupted her thoughts. "The lady on the phone said the police folk will be here shortly." Lyla couldn't help but stifle a smile. Part of Willis's charm was when he spoke she pictured a Southern grandfather, in a rocking chair on his front porch, chewing on a toothpick.

"Okay, good," she replied through tight lips with a curt nod.

They sat, bathed in an uncomfortable silence for more than twenty minutes. Willis kept fussing over the new guy's body: straightening his collar, flattening the wrinkles in his shirt, checking to make sure his pants were completely zipped. All the while he cooed over him as though over a baby, telling him that he needed to look respectable, even in death. Lyla started to tell him he shouldn't disturb the scene, but thought better of it. In fact, she would let Willis contaminate his heart out. Lyla, however, steered clear of the new guy altogether; she hadn't touched him once since her and Willis happened upon him. The last thing she needed was evidence connecting *her* body to *this* body.

Just then, all other thoughts screeched to a halt, then faded into the background. *What if Brighthouse was dispatched to this call?* He worked nights. *Is this his jurisdiction?* Lyla didn't know, but she needed to leave. *Now.*

"Willis, are you okay waiting for the police alone? I really have to get going," she said with a sweet softness to her tone, blanketing her anxiety.

"If you have to go baby-girl, I understand, but I could sure use some company. I ain't never been 'round no dead body before." He paused, then hung his head somberly. "Christ, I just referred to ol' Kevin here as a dead body. Poor kid."

Lyla cringed at the sound of the new guy's first name. She had never heard it spoken before. Willis shook off a sniffle. As touched as Lyla was by his despondence, she couldn't afford to linger. She stretched her legs to stand up, and Willis followed her movement with sad eyes. "Now, I don't know much about such things, but wouldn't it be best if you were here when the police got here? Like a witness, or something?"

Willis was right. He didn't know better than not to touch the body, but even he knew it would seem more suspicious if she left. Lyla had been forced to use her cell phone to call 9-1-1 since Willis didn't carry one, so her name was already on the record. The police would certainly track her down for questioning. There was no avoiding it; she had to play witness.

Lyla's ears prickled to the sound of cars as her eyes focused on the swirling red and blue lights that rapidly wove through the storage facility. The staccato of multiple sets of footprints grew louder. Lyla held her breath, steeling herself to face the ambitious Officer Brighthouse. Three cops rounded the corner, and she exhaled in relief; he wasn't among them. Instead, a squat man of about forty hitched his dress pants up while he walked, barking orders to a wiry man in uniform who peeled off from the group to secure the perimeter. A diminutive, but no-nonsense looking woman, also in uniform, followed the detective, her eyes drawn to the corpse on the ground.

"I take it you two are the ones who called this in," the detective asked, gesturing toward Kevin's body with the butt of his chin. The female officer wandered off, presumably to help check the premises.

"Yes, sir," Willis replied. Lyla just nodded, thinking it a dumb question to lead with.

Her statement was taken first while the detective continued to adjust his pants, shuffling his digital recorder between hands to do so. Lyla was surprised the process proved particularly painless. She explained that she was there to store several of her paintings and sculptures, which she often did at night right after she completed them. Willis, who of course was privy to her habits, vouched for her. In the middle of her statement, the female officer gave a shout from the direction of the parking lot. She must not have been sure she was heard, because she followed up with a radio call, or perhaps that was protocol, Lyla wasn't sure. After assuring the detective that they'd never strayed from the spot of Kevin's body, Willis was told to stay put while the hefty man jogged off in the direction of the female cop's shout. Lyla was allowed to leave after he hastily handed her a business card. She reached for it like one would a relay baton. Over his shoulder, the detective shouted for her to contact PPD in case she remembered anything of value.

Lyla finally resumed her walk to the main street, and observed a white SUV turn the corner and head in the direction of the storage facility from which she'd just left. The lettering on the side panels identified it as belonging to the office of the medical examiner. Lyla smirked. She hoped they had an extra body bag in the back since the urgency in the female officer's voice indicated Dr. Stone's body had been located. A geeky young man sat in the passenger's seat, fiddling with the dashboard-mounted GPS system, the screen bathing his face in a bright green glow. Her aunt was driving. Lyla chided herself for not leaving sooner and hoped LeeAnn hadn't seen her.

32
Puzzles.

BRIGHTHOUSE WAS GLAD to finally have a day off—mainly so he could focus on work. He needed time to piece together all the intricacies of the various cases he suspected Lyla Kyle had a hand in. He was confident the DNA samples Dr. DiCicco was having compared were an essential piece to the riddle. Unfortunately, he knew it would be an eternity before the results were available, and even then, he'd be lucky if they got him a warrant. But they'd be a start, just like when he and his father would put together jigsaw puzzles when he was a boy: they would start at the outer edges while the middle pieces sorted themselves out. He frowned at the fond memory; it stung with the reality that he'd be solving this puzzle on his own.

Brighthouse sat down at his makeshift desk in the dining room. Every seat but that at the head of the cheap birch wood table bore a kitschy vinyl placemat, depicting images of 1940s housewives doing tasks like pulling a roast out of the oven, or frosting a cake. Emma always nagged him about doing his paperwork at the table, even though he and his wife were seldom home together to share a meal. *Maybe if she got rid of these damn placemats,* he often mused. With his morning coffee in hand—it was too early for Red Bull—he settled into the creaky wooden chair, and shuffled through a heap of loose papers. Just as he began to skim his notes and reports, he heard his wife in the kitchen slamming cabinet doors and going out of her way to sigh audibly. After the fourth such exhalation, he let out one of his own, snatched up his mug, and set out to see what had incensed his wife this time.

When he entered the kitchen, she was pouring his pot of coffee down the drain.

"Hey," he said with pleading outstretched arms and a forced smile spreading across his face. He didn't want to be confrontational. Not on his day off.

"What?" she asked without even turning to face him.

"What do you think you're doing with my coffee, little lady?"

"It's old."

"I just brewed it." He held up his still steaming cup, and playfully wafted it in her direction in a vain attempt to lighten her mood. She rolled her eyes and began rinsing out the coffeepot. "What's wrong? I thought you'd be happy I'm home."

"I am. Or *I was*, until you sat down at that damn table with your notes."

"I was just looking over a few things while I drank my coffee. What's the big deal? You were messing around on your tablet while you had breakfast, reading yesterday's 'digital' Sunday paper." He rolled his eyes. "It's the same thing."

"Is this what you're going to be like when we have kids? Home, but really gone?"

"Only if the kids want to play Hide-n-Go-Seek." Brighthouse wore another foolish smile, though somewhat forced. Emma turned from the sink and leaned against the counter. Her face twitched with anger, and her eyes filled with water. He stepped toward her and rested his hand on her arm—she began to weep freely as though he had flipped a switch. "Whoa, whoa, whoa. Okay, sweetheart. What's this really about?" he cooed.

"You know what this is about," she whimpered.

Brighthouse dropped his head in exasperation. He did know what this was about, but chose not to utter a word. Instead, he just held her, hoping the silence itself would soothe her.

"I stopped taking my birth control," Emma sobbed into the crook of his shoulder.

He slowly disengaged her from his grasp and held her at arm's length. "Well, I don't know why you would do that." He enunciated his words to steady his voice, to keep from shouting. "I thought we weren't ready to start a family yet."

"No. *You're* not ready, Jason. But I figure if I become pregnant, maybe that'll finally put things in perspective for you." She had stopped crying and now glared at him with reddened eyes.

Brighthouse exploded. "You're impossible. Unbelievable! You know that? Here, you can pour this down the drain, too, because I'm leaving." When she reached for the extended mug, he purposely let it slip and crash to the floor. Emma hopped backward to avoid the scalding coffee and the sharp ceramic fragments.

"What are you afraid of? The coffee's old, remember," he said reproachfully before storming from the kitchen in disgust.

Despite the bitter autumn morning air, Brighthouse grabbed his keys and left wearing nothing but the T-shirt and shorts he'd slept in. He drove around for most of the morning and into the afternoon without a definite destination. His thoughts wandered between Lyla and Emma, back and forth. Finally, tired of driving but unwilling to return home, he headed to Mickey's pub. To his surprise Blakely was already there, honoring the common 'it's five o'clock somewhere' mantra. Brighthouse pulled up a high-backed barstool to where his friend was chatting with a veteran detective. The man possessed an imposingly broad build and his thick mustache seemed to move of its own accord as he spoke.

The detective must have known Brighthouse Sr., because he smiled at Jason warmly. Blakely nodded in his partner's direction. "Speak of the devil. Here's the man working on something that might get us both promoted. And I fully intend to ride his bullet-proof vest tails the whole way," he exclaimed, already slurring and raising his frosty mug of Yuengling at the two of them.

The detective, clearly impressed by whatever Blakely had already told him, raised an eyebrow at Brighthouse before he introduced himself as Swartz. "Your father was a good man, and a damn fine cop," he said.

Brighthouse had a firm grip, but Swartz nearly broke his hand. Still, he nodded in appreciation of the acknowledgment. He tried not to cringe when he wrapped his sore fingers around the highball glass that had been set in front of him the moment he'd sat down. *Mickey's as reliable as Old Faithful.* He sipped on the J&B on the rocks and savored the liquid heat trickling down his throat, and the calm that coated his chest.

"So, you're gonna follow in your old man's footsteps, huh?" Swartz slapped Brighthouse on his back, exhibiting the same strength as his handshake. "What's this monster case your partner says you're putting together?"

Brighthouse told Swartz everything, excited to have someone that wasn't going to mock him, and even more excited that his cynical friend had sparked the conversation in the first place. He explained the time of death discrepancy with the Alex Livanos case, and the suspicious circumstances surrounding Derrick Warner's coma and eventual death. He told him about the previous cases he'd found, and how even the medical examiner believed the victims were linked—and poisoned. Blakely jumped in to disclose CJ's recent demise and Lyla's connection to both him and Derrick. Brighthouse reluctantly admitted he couldn't prove Lyla knew Livanos until the ME ran the hair from the scene against the other samples, the pen and the beer bottle. He almost forgot to tell him about the witness in front of CJ's building who described the jacket, but was able to blurt it out in the end, when Swartz was about to offer a comment. Of course, Brighthouse managed to sidestep his time spent at Lyla's house—much to the amusement of Blakely—but the seasoned detective didn't seem to notice anything was being withheld.

The three continued to discuss the assorted connections, laughing all the while and patting one another on the back, but Brighthouse felt he was being watched. On the other side of the bar, seated in the corner, was a female cop with a youthful, yet ascetic face. Her brow was knitted, and her dark, glossy hair pulled back into a tight bun. Brighthouse recognized her from around their precinct and thought her last name was Montoya; it was a sign of respect that no one ever called her by her first name, as they did most of the other female officers. He had noticed her staring in their group's direction for some time. After receiving a fresh beer, she stood up to her full height of five feet and ambled across the length of the pub. She approached the guys, and asked about the woman they were talking about named Lyla. Normally the guys would have dismissed a female cop trying to join in on their chat, but her reputation of capability preceded her by a mile. She was tiny, but stout, and could cuff her own perps, no matter their size, and drank many of her fellow officers under the table. Brighthouse, basking in the attention his off-duty investigation was garnering, retouched upon some of the higher points of the discussion for the newly arrived member of their group.

"Huh," she said. "I met a Lyla the night before last, at a scene. She was one sweet looking witness. . ." Blakely practically fell off his stool. Swartz clumsily cleared his throat and took another swig of his whiskey. Brighthouse, already aware the rookie was gay, didn't bat an eye. Instead, while the other two men composed themselves, he asked her to describe the witness.

"She was tall, slender, but still curvy." She gestured an hourglass shape with her hands. "Long, dark hair. Very dark eyes. Olive-ish skin. Just an absolutely gorgeous woman. Told us, she was an artist, kept her work at the self-storage facility."

"And what kind of scene did you say it was?" Brighthouse asked through an embittered breath.

"Two DBs, although the original call was only for one. An off-duty guard was walking Lyla to the street to hail a cab, and they found another guard stabbed to death outside his post. Then I encountered a second body in a car while walking the premises. ODed. Seems to me like she's in the clear. Doesn't sound like any of the cases you described."

"Poisoning someone with their own food allergy doesn't fit her MO either, but I'm way past giving her the benefit of the doubt."

33
Awash in Bewilderment.

LYLA HAD SPENT most of the remaining weekend painting Dr. Theodore Stone. She loved the way his neatly-trimmed hairline shimmered gray around his ear, so that's what she focused on. For the ear itself, she used red paint, tainted, of course, with his blood. Every now and then she'd held out her right hand in front of her to admire the metallic, matte sheen of his platinum wedding band. She didn't know why she'd kept it, but there was no engraving, and she didn't think it could be traced back to its owner. She held it out again and twisted it. Despite the good doctor's nimble, surgical fingers, the ring was still a bit loose, so Lyla wore it on her thumb—fitting, since that was the finger she had used to inject death into Dr. Stone's neck.

"New ring?" Jillian asked from the doorway of her office.

"Yes," Lyla replied, flustered. She'd almost forgotten where she was, seated in the waiting room outside Dr. Atford's office.

Jillian ushered her inside with bright eyes and a warm expression on her face. Lyla thought maybe her doctor was just pleased that she hadn't burst in on her previous patient's session like last time. They entered the office and sat in their usual respective seats, with Lyla in the center of the couch and the doctor in the matching armchair perpendicular to it.

"How have you been since we last spoke, Ms. Kyle?"

Ms. Kyle? "Well, I tidied up a few loose ends in my life," Lyla said with an accomplished sigh. "I'm feeling better."

"Any nightmares?"

"No. Well, a brief one a few nights ago, but not as intense. And you, Dr. Atford?"

"Are you asking if *I've* had any nightmares?" Jillian asked, with a forced chuckle.

"No, I'm asking how you've been." She paused and then altered her tone. "But feel free to tell me if you've also experienced nightmares regarding your past." The last words dripped from Lyla's tongue like venom from a viper's fangs.

"Oh, thank you for asking," Dr. Atford cleared her throat. "I've been fine."

"Good to hear. You know, because you seemed distracted during our last session," Lyla said. Jillian nodded. She opened her mouth to speak, but Lyla cut her off. "And you also appeared—what's the word?—disheveled."

Lyla narrowed her gaze at the doctor, scrutinizing every inch of her. Jillian's eyes looked strained, and her clothes wrinkled and rumpled, even though her socks matched today. Her reckless demeanor had, in fact, calmed down from the previous week, but Lyla had clearly just rattled her nerves. The psychologist still hadn't spoken, so Lyla continued, sitting relaxed with her legs crossed and her arms spread out over the back of the couch.

"I was thinking about something. Last week you mentioned the name 'Calvin.' That was my father's name. Did you know him?"

"Did I know your father's name was Calvin? No."

"You misunderstand," Lyla sniggered. "I'm asking if you personally knew my father, Calvin."

Jillian looked her in the eyes, unwavering, and said, "No, I don't believe so."

"How can you be sure? It's entirely possible that you did know him."

"I'm sure it's possible."

"What did your Calvin look like?" Lyla intertwined her fingers over her knee with exaggerated interest.

"I hardly think that's appropriate—"

"Well, people say I look like my dad. Dark hair and eyes, golden complexion. Tall. Does that sound familiar?"

"That sounds like a lot of men I know," Jillian said, clearly no longer in charge of the therapy session—as Lyla had planned it.

"I see. Are, or were, any of them named Calvin?" Lyla asked

nonchalantly.

Lyla leaned forward in her seat, demolishing the doctor with an icy stare, wrenching her with each vice-like word. Jillian squirmed in her chair, then hurriedly excused herself to run off to the restroom. Lyla wasn't even sure if that was allowed. "You're deducting this little break from your hourly rate, right?" she called after her, amused. Driving the psychologist from the office hadn't been her intent, but Lyla had to admit it presented a unique opportunity.

When the door closed behind Dr. Atford, Lyla bounded across the office in a flash, sidestepping the coffee table and plopping into the chair behind the desk. She opened every drawer until she found the psychologist's purse. She rummaged through it, found a wallet, and removed her driver's license. She entertained the thought of stealing it, but decided against it and instead committed the address to memory. While repeating the house number and street name to herself, Lyla hastily replaced the license in the wallet and planted the purse back in the drawer, exactly the way she'd found it. When Jillian returned, Lyla was still standing behind the cherry wood desk. She pretended to be fascinated by the babbling water fountain.

"I was thinking of getting one of these for my art studio," she said, gesturing to the trickling water and river rocks. A few drops of water splashed on her hand, and she playfully flicked her fingers in the air before wiping them on her trousers.

Jillian disregarded the statement. "So, you keep insisting I know your father. Is that your way of wanting to speak about him?" she asked, returning to her seat in the armchair.

"Perhaps," Lyla said with a mischievous grin, winding out from around the desk. She watched Jillian's chest heave, and when she exhaled, relief washed over her face.

"Good. What would you like to talk about?"

"I'd like to talk about how my father ruined our family by constantly sleeping around on my mother. I'd like to talk about how my mother committed suicide as a result of his despicable actions. And I'd like to talk about how the night of his death he was too drunk, after one of his dates, might I add, to drag himself from our burning home."

"Uh-huh." Jillian pressed her lips together thoughtfully. "That's a lot to have to deal with as a young woman. I can see why you'd harbor such angry feelings towards your father."

"I'm actually pretty angry with a lot of people," Lyla stated coolly.

"Okay, this is good." The psychologist settled deeper into her seat. "Who else are you angry with? I know you once said you were angry with your mother for allowing the infidelity to take place. Is there anyone else you'd like to discuss?"

Lyla held her gaze. "I'm not angry with my mother," she said flatly.

"Great. That's progress. You've forgiven her, then?"

"More like . . . focused my anger elsewhere."

Lyla observed Jillian, watched as the doctor realized that she had never really regained control of the session. She wriggled in her seat, trying to writhe free of Lyla's influence. "I see," she said finally.

"My mother was a fool. Naive. But you know who I'm really angry with?" she asked, the question obviously rhetoric. "The women who knowingly carried on affairs with my married father. I mean, who does that?"

Jillian didn't answer, so Lyla repeated the question with added fervor. "No, seriously? Who does that?"

Lyla never received an actual answer from the psychologist, but the intended damage had been done. The appointment ended awkwardly. Lyla exited the office with her doctor awash in bewilderment. Lyla herself was all but certain that Jillian knew her father—so she passed the time in the elevator repeating Dr. Atford's address softly under her breath.

34
Obstinate Actions.

BRIGHTHOUSE DOWNED HIS remaining scotch and slammed the glass on the bar, agitating the ice cubes into a second of frenzy. The discovery that Lyla was connected to yet another crime scene left him hunched in a heap of frustration atop his barstool. Despite his anticipation of the results, he knew that even if the DNA connected her to the other scenes, the evidence was circumstantial at best. He realized there was nothing he could do at the moment except order another round. By then, Swartz and Montoya had gone their separate ways, and it was just him and Blakely.

Brighthouse stared into the fresh drink Mickey had placed before him. He watched the melting ice create translucent trails and swirls in the amber-hued spirit until he felt the bar owner nudge him.

"Don't worry. You'll get her, Junior."

"I know."

"So what else is eating at you?"

Brighthouse lifted his head to face the bartender with pensive eyes. "Emma, my wife."

"Oh here we go . . ." Blakely leaned over and began gesturing slowly with his arms, stroking an imaginary violin. When Brighthouse failed to react, he put his hands in his lap sheepishly.

"She's just really pushing this 'hurry up and start a family' agenda of hers. Told me today she'd stopped taking her birth control." Brighthouse shook his head, still beyond belief at his wife's obstinate actions.

"Really?" Mickey and Blakely asked in unison. "What did you do?" Blakely added.

"I left." Brighthouse motioned to his shorts and threadbare T-shirt.

"Wow, I must've really been knocking 'em back. I didn't even notice you were dressed for a pick-up game of basketball at the park," he joked. "So what are you gonna do? You have to go home sometime. Are you gonna give in? Because if you do, I have some great tips for you. Like, with boys, make sure you stand back a bit when you change their diapers, because they'll just pee right up—"

"No. I don't think so," Brighthouse defiantly cut off his partner's colorful anecdote, no doubt pleasing the nearby patrons Mickey had now returned to.

"What?"

"I need to make detective before I can even think about supporting a family."

"Hey! I support my family just fine with the salary we make."

"Oh, don't even! Listen, you inherited that house, and *your* wife works."

Blakely shrugged and then raised his pint of beer. "These are the facts."

"And we would eventually have to get a bigger house. And a second car."

"All valid points." He saluted Brighthouse a second time.

"We just can't do it right now. It's not practical."

"Buddy, you know I'm here for you, for you to vent and all that, but, um, did you tell Emma what you just explained to me?"

"I'll tell you what, if you tell her and she listens to reason, I'll give you a million dollars." Now it was Brighthouse's turn to raise his glass. "You know Emma," he continued, "when she has her mind set on something, there's no stopping her. She's like a charging rhino."

"Can I tell her you called her a rhino?"

"New plan: I'll pay you a million dollars not to," he said with a flicker of playfulness.

Brighthouse ordered a fifth drink in a feeble attempt to steel his nerves to face Emma. Mickey set the drink down on the bar and the officer smiled; he'd made the drink heavier on the ice, just like the one before, to keep him safe on the road. *Good ol' Mickey*, Brighthouse thought as he chugged the weakened scotch.

Brighthouse arrived home thirty minutes later to a still, chilly house. With his scant attire, it was like walking through a furnished tundra. The eerie silence unnerved him; he didn't hear the usual murmur of music, or the television. As he searched the first floor for his wife, he perceived the constant whoosh of running water originating from the upstairs bathroom. Brighthouse took the stairs two at a time, but his steps lacked their usual bounce. The hiss of the water grew louder. He approached the master bathroom cautiously; the door was barely ajar, so he used his elbow to nudge it open the rest of the way. Emma sat on the floor across from the toilet, clutching her knees to her chest. The faucet was turned on full force and sputtered water into the air like a hard rain on a stone step. He reached to turn it off, all the while inspecting Emma to ensure she was unhurt. She met her husband's glance with her blue doe eyes. He parted his lips to speak, then looked past her. A pregnancy test rested precariously on the ledge of the bathtub. Even if he could read it from where he stood, he didn't know how to decipher such things—but he didn't need to. Emma's demeanor said it all. She was pregnant.

Emma spoke before Brighthouse had a chance to. "I wanted to tell you this morning," she said between sniffles. "I wasn't sure, but you were so upset about the birth control thing that I took the test, hoping it wasn't true."

Brighthouse felt torn. He wasn't ready for this, but the woman he had loved secretly in high school but hadn't had the guts to approach until after his accident, was balled up at his feet, sobbing because she was carrying their child. His child. When he thought of it that way, the shame enveloped him like a cloak. He fell to the floor and embraced his wife even more tenderly than he had that morning.

Slowly, Emma's heaving sobs subsided, and she melted into his arms. He nestled his face into the crook of her neck, kissing it more out of habit than desire, but before he knew what was happening, her lips found his. They kissed in a way they hadn't since they were teenagers. Hungrily. Feverishly. As if nothing else mattered. Not even stopping to breathe.

Entangled on the floor, together they inched over to the wall of the bathtub. Brighthouse sat with his back leaned against it while Emma removed his shorts. He pulled his shirt up over his head and tossed it aside. The cool ceramic surfaces contrasted with the heat he and his wife exuded. He reached for her, pulled her clothes this way and that. She straddled him and they became one rhythmic movement. They severed from each other's lips just long enough to allow the occasional moan or grunt. At the height of their passion, Brighthouse hoisted Emma up into the air and laid her on her back. The fleecy bath mat beneath her tickled them both, and Emma giggled. Brighthouse lowered himself on top of her and firm legs wrapped tightly around his waist. A cacophony of groans bounced off the walls and surrounded them like an orchestra of passion. Again, it was as if nothing else mattered.

Exhausted and salty with sweat, Jason and Emma relished the chilly tiled floor of the bathroom, reaching out for it as they had reached out for each other just a while prior. They had fallen asleep there, entwined on the floor. The positive pregnancy test had long ago fallen into the bathtub, out of sight and equally out of mind.

Brighthouse awoke several hours later, his muscles stiffened from the cold. He was surprised to find he had room to stretch. He was alone. Assuming Emma had awakened sooner and unable to rouse him from his deep sleep, had headed to their bedroom, Brighthouse retreated down the hall after her. What he saw in the bedroom caused his body to tremble.

The bed was still neatly made with the hospital corners Emma's grandmother had taught her as a girl. In the center of the flowered bedspread sat a large, empty suitcase, the largest of their matching set. Inside was a handwritten note that read, "Jason, we want different things. I'm staying with my sister for a few days, and I think it's best you move out. Emma."

Below the note was one of their wedding photos. Emma had torn it in half, right down the middle, separating the bride from the groom. *She sure has a knack for symbolism.* Sitting on the edge of their bed,

Brighthouse's bitter chuckles were soon dampened by silent rivulets of tears.

35
A Sliver of Light.

WHEN DARKNESS FELL that night Lyla wore it like a costume. She embraced the evening by squeezing into tight, black pants and stretching a long-sleeved, black shirt over her head. After using a black marker to color in the white and worn areas, she stepped into a pair of old cross-trainers. With leather gloves and baseball cap in hand, Lyla drove to the address she had memorized. During the drive, she continued to repeat the number and street. She'd already absorbed it but sustained the chant out of anticipation.

Lyla passed the two-story brick colonial once, twice, several times, until one by one all of the lights were extinguished, and the house was claimed by darkness. She parked around the corner in the shadow of a towering maple tree, where the fallen leaves gathered in the gutter softened the sound of the tires. After lingering a half an hour longer, just to err on the side of prudence, Lyla left her car and cut across Jillian's neighbor's lawn, sprinting from tree to tree, shrub to shrub. When she arrived at the back of the house, she pressed her body to it, hugging the cool bricks and hoping her heartbeat did not jostle the foundation.

Lyla circled the perimeter, but after finding nothing but locked doors and storm windows, she was about to give up. Then she noticed the small rectangular windows along the bottom of the house, close to the ground, that undoubtedly opened into the basement. Crouched down low—careful not to disrupt the freshly planted mums—she inspected the windows. She struck out several times before she found one that gave way after the screen was removed. Dr. Atford had probably opened it to let out some of the moisture and mildew of a recent heavy rainfall. The undersized window opened inward, and Lyla was able to slither through it feet first, though the space became tight around her hips, and she had to shimmy. She landed lightly on a rickety folding table full of unpaired socks and assorted laundry detergents. A bottle of fabric softener danced dangerously close to the edge. She caught it.

After her eyes adjusted to the unlit basement, she retrieved a small pen-light she'd tucked into her sock. She surveyed the room with the handheld sliver of light to gain the layout of the basement. Within the silence of the space, a squat, boxy silhouette in the corner begged for her attention. Illuminated, corner by corner in the beam of her flashlight, appeared an old-fashioned crate.

A fine layer of dust and cobwebs covered everything in the basement—except the crate, which must have just been placed there from somewhere else in the house, or recently acquired altogether. It reminded Lyla of her own trunk, the one that housed her private collection, but the key to her trunk hung inconspicuously from the charm bracelet on her ankle, while Jillian's key was still protruding from the lock. Lyla shook her head in mock disappointment, whispered a, "Tsk, tsk, tsk," and lifted the lid with gloved hands. The hinges were stiff, unlike those of her own chest, which were loose and well-worn from years of frequent deposits.

Lyla thumbed through the contents and quickly found the proof she sought. Slack-jawed, she leafed through several envelopes addressed to her father in what she assumed to be Jillian's hand. The letters had "Return to Sender" written in what she knew to be her mother's handwriting. Lyla's eyes moistened at the thought of her mother having to handle such mail. *Why didn't she just throw them out?*

Beneath the collection of returned envelopes, there was a single photograph of her father in uniform. It seemed to have been taken without his knowledge; he wasn't centered in the frame or looking at the camera, and the corner of a car's side-view mirror was visible in the foreground, as if the shot had been taken from the inside of a vehicle.

Lyla shuffled through a few more letters and random keepsakes and found a shoebox. She opened it and a gasp tumbled from her lips, and the cardboard lid slipped from her fingers. Inside was the missing red bone china teacup from her mother's set, placed daintily atop a stack of folded clothes, stiff with dried blood. Concealed within their folds lay a red-handled kitchen knife, which also matched her mother's set from all those years ago. And Lyla was willing to bet the blood on the clothes could also be matched to her mother. *Not only was Jillian Atford sleeping with my father, but she was involved in my mother's death, too?* It didn't make sense, didn't add up. Yet the evidence was staring Lyla in the face.

From above, the basement grew slightly brighter. A soft fluorescent glow escaped from under the door to what Lyla assumed to be the kitchen at the top of the stairs. Lyla froze behind a bag of topsoil and snuffed the beam of her small flashlight. She listened and heard a refrigerator door open, then close a minute later. Footsteps traveled across the ceiling above her, painfully close to the basement door, then they receded. Lyla took several moments to restore the chest's items back to their original arrangement, then closed the lid and replaced the key. She hoisted herself up to the window and pulled herself free from the home with her forearms, inch by inch, trying not to claw at the earth outside.

Lyla had barely pulled the window back into place behind her when the basement she had just left lit up fully. She rolled over onto her stomach, clenching every muscle, afraid to even breathe, as she saw slippered feet creep down the steps into view.

She watched as Jillian clutched a single photo of a cinnamon-colored infant in both hands, sniffling, before placing it gingerly in the trunk. Then she lowered the lid, turned the key, and removed it from the lock, taking it with her upstairs.

36
A Dangling Key.

LYLA HARDLY SLEPT the night, anxious to return to Jillian's house to carry out her plan. All these years spent luring married men, murdering them in the name of what her father drove her mother to, and it wasn't even entirely his fault. Lyla even shed a few tears of guilt over killing her father, but quickly talked sense into herself. He may not have driven her mother to suicide, but if it weren't for the affair he'd carried on, Jillian wouldn't have killed Lyla's mother. *Did Jillian kill my mother?* Lyla still wasn't sure. But why else would she hoard the bloody clothes and knife? If only Lyla was still in good graces with her aunt in the ME's office. She would know who to contact, who could analyze the clothing. Then again, Lyla didn't want to involve the authorities—her own methods of punishing Dr. Atford would be much more enjoyable.

Day finally broke, and Lyla entered her studio, gently touching the surface of her most recent painting. Dr. Stone's ear seemed dry enough for transport, so she wrapped it in wax paper and set it by the top of the stairs. She took a few minutes to get dressed, grabbed the parcel, and placed it in the back of her SUV, heading for the storage facility.

Arriving about a half hour later, and feeling lazy with exhaustion, she pulled up in front of her unit instead of in the parking lot. Lyla gathered the painting in her arms, and the wax paper crinkled in protest against her grasp. She disregarded the patrol car parked a few spaces from her, assuming the police had come with follow-up questions to Saturday's incident. But she doubted her assumption just as quickly as she had formed it when she recognized Officer Brighthouse. Even from behind, his mess of frat boy hair and defiant stance were unmistakable. He hadn't seen her yet, so she backed up slowly and put the canvas back in her trunk. When she closed the hatch, another officer was standing there. She smiled warmly. His nametag read BLAKELY.

"Beautiful, young, dark-haired." The cop peered into the back window at the wrapped canvas. "Artist. Ms. Kyle, I presume?"

"Do I know you?"

"No, you haven't had the pleasure," he said with a wink, probably to let her know her beauty didn't faze him. "But you know my partner, I believe. Jason Brighthouse?"

"We're acquainted."

"Excellent. We're, uh, actually here to . . . well, let's just say you have excellent timing. Walk with me."

Lyla obliged, once again thinking their presence was connected to Saturday night. As she expected, Brighthouse probably learned through the thin blue grapevine that she was a witness at the scene, smelled blood, and therefore felt the need to pounce.

She walked up to Brighthouse wearing an expansive grin. "You don't call, you don't write, you don't stop by uninvited . . ."

She saw his partner stifle a laugh, but Brighthouse's expression was like chiseled marble and just as cold.

"Ms. Kyle, we would like to take a look around your unit, with your permission, of course."

"Is that how you address me now? 'Ms. Kyle?' How formal. I'm afraid I'll have to follow suit and formally deny your request."

"I thought you'd say that."

"Then I'm sorry you wasted a trip."

"Not all is lost." He pointed behind her, and Lyla turned to scan the alley.

Willis appeared from inside the security post and purposely avoided the dark brown stains in the concrete upon his approach.

"Darlin', it seems I have to let these here officers in. My hands are tied. Sorry, love."

"They can't possibly have a warrant—"

Brighthouse broke in. "No, but I had your friend Willis here call the property manager, and it turns out there's a clause in your rental agreement that states the facility maintains the right to enter the unit if they believe illegal activity is occurring."

"Yup, and we were very convincing," Blakely added.

"Fine," Lyla said curtly. "I don't know what you hope to find in there, but fine."

She stepped aside with a broad sweeping motion of her arms, signaling them to proceed. "Forgive me, I left my red carpet in the truck."

"I like this one," said Blakely, chuckling.

Brighthouse stoically stood aside while Willis fiddled with an overwhelming ring of keys, searching for the right one to her unit's disc lock. He glanced over his shoulder and shrugged at Lyla. She nodded understandingly.

The two officers tackled opposite sides of the space, poking at things from time to time. Lyla followed close at their heels. She was certain that if they didn't have a warrant she didn't need to wait outside. Their lack of objection confirmed her assumption.

Brighthouse moved a sculpture out of the way that was sitting on a wheeled, wooden platform. "Careful with that," Lyla called. "It just sold for more than your entire department makes in a month."

Lyla watched Brighthouse approach her trunk with interest and bit her lip for the slightest second.

"Open it," he said.

"No."

"Open. It."

"For that, I do believe you need a warrant." She had no idea, but hoped she was right. Brighthouse's sigh told her she was.

"Fine, we'll be back with that warrant."

"Good luck with that," she quipped. Again she was bluffing, hoping she didn't sound like a television police procedural. She didn't know what Brighthouse and his partner were looking for, but she figured if they had enough for a warrant, they would have had one now. Which made her think of something else: if they were as determined as they seemed to be, they might actually come back with a warrant. And they would be able to take a closer look.

Possibly run tests. She didn't know if her special blend of paint would withstand such analysis. "On second thought, why not? I have nothing to hide." She removed the charm bracelet from her ankle and used a dangling key to open the lock. "Voila," she said, stepping aside.

Blakely stood over his partner with a flashlight while Brighthouse thumbed through the canvases. He extracted several of them halfway, noted their peculiar subject matter with squinted eyes, and then slid them back into place. Satisfied, though visibly perplexed, he closed the lid and nodded to his partner. They emerged from the storage unit and thanked Willis for his cooperation. Instinctively polite, Willis nodded. "Any time."

Lyla reminded him that she understood he couldn't do anything, handed him one of her smaller sculptures as a gift, and hopped briskly into her car.

Before she had a chance to drive away, Brighthouse pulled the patrol car alongside her and rolled the window down. "By the way, I'm sorry about your friend, CJ," he said.

"Yes. A true tragedy."

"I missed you at the funeral."

"I didn't think you were so close."

"And I don't think you were ever as close as you led on, Ms. Kyle." The cruiser sped off. Without anything else to do that day, Lyla followed them.

37
Call It a Quirk.

BRIGHTHOUSE'S SCAR FELT inflamed, his ears hot and most likely red with anger. As a distraction from his marital woes, he'd requested the photos from the storage facility crime scenes. He immediately recognized the body in the Porsche as the doctor he'd met in the elevator at West Philly General Hospital. He recalled entering the elevator and interrupting a conversation between Dr. Stone and Lyla, which, at the time, had hardly impressed him as platonic. Brighthouse knew in his very core that Lyla's presence at the scene of the doctor's supposed overdose was about as close to a coincidence as he and Emma were to reconciliation. *Damn.* He promised himself he wouldn't think about that right now. His fingers gripped the steering wheel with brute strength, knuckles whitening with each passing city block. Blakely cut through the silence first.

"You wanna tell me why you dragged me outta my house early for shift just for me to be right?" he asked.

Brighthouse rolled his eyes. "Can't you just say, 'I told you so' and be done with it, like a normal person?"

"I told you so."

"Yes, thank you."

"And what did I tell you?" Blakely asked, in a playful version of the tone he usually reserved for his children.

"That the storage facility would be a waste of time," Brighthouse paused, "but there's just one problem: I don't think it was a waste of time."

"Of course you don't." Blakely breathed out, and made a move like he was trying to open the car door and jump into the surrounding traffic. Brighthouse guffawed at his partner's antics. When the laughter subsided, his stomach was tight, but he straightened in his seat and continued.

"I'm serious. Okay, so there wasn't a stack of dead bodies or a step-by-step bulleted outline of how she manages to kill these men and make it look natural . . . but what about that trunk?"

"What about it? It was chock full of paintings of nostrils and other creepy body parts." Blakely shuddered.

"Yeah, but you don't think that's odd enough in itself? None of it resembles the rest of her work—"

"Oh, so you're what? A curator, now?"

As usual, Brighthouse ignored him. "No, just the way she refused access so adamantly, then simply stepped aside . . ."

"Because it was just a bunch of paintings, Brighthouse."

"Exactly, but if it were 'just a bunch of paintings,' why did she refuse us access in the first place?"

"I don't know. Preservation of her civil liberties or something, maybe?"

"Then why the sudden change of heart?"

"Who knows why anyone does anything? Like, who knows why she locks up those creepy paintings in the first place?"

"Byron Blakely, you're a goddamn genius!" If he weren't driving, he would have kissed his partner on both cheeks.

"This I know," his partner said confidently, before pausing with confusion. "But why this time?"

"Why would she keep the paintings under lock and key? Why?" He hit the steering wheel with both palms in frustration. Neither of them spoke for several blocks. Finally, he said, "We have to get that warrant."

"With what? We have nothing substantial, Jason. If we did, we'd already be sitting pretty, tearing through all her creepy stuff."

"Will you stop using the word 'creepy?' Anyway, I think we should go see Dr. DiCicco. Maybe she has something."

"Don't you think she would have called you by now if she had something? She might be busy. It is Philadelphia. Plenty of bodies to grace her table."

"All the more reason to stop by her office and be sure the results haven't slipped her mind," Brighthouse said.

"Listen, man, are you sure you're not grasping at straws here? You know, trying to keep occupied because of you and Emma? The whole separation thing?"

Brighthouse didn't answer as he neared the University of Pennsylvania, where the ME's office was located—he was too busy eyeing the black SUV a couple of car-lengths back.

Lyla's black SUV.

Brighthouse made a sharp U-turn, and Blakely clung to the passenger-side door. The silence became peppered with Blakely's protests and inquiries. "Are we . . . going *back* to the storage facility?" he asked. When no answer came, his voice rose an octave. "Have you completely lost it, man?"

Brighthouse drove past the storage facility, the rows of corrugated metal structures streaking past them. He was glad to see Lyla was no longer behind them. Blakely's face contorted in confusion but remained quiet.

"Ms. Kyle was following us. I spotted her. Didn't want to tip our hand. Definitely don't want her to know her aunt is helping us out directly."

"That doesn't exactly tell me where we're going . . ."

"I'm separated," Brighthouse said finally, turning his head to face his partner. "I need a place to stay."

Blakely remained puzzled until they pulled up to a motel, not a block from the storage units.

"What better place to stay than somewhere I can keep an eye on my favorite suspect? Maybe I'll even get a glimpse of her comings and goings from the storage unit. See what's so damn special about that damn trunk."

He parked the patrol car in front of the motel office. They hopped out, and Brighthouse chimed, "By the way, did you notice she keeps the key to that trunk hidden on a charm bracelet on her *ankle*?"

Blakely just smirked as they entered the office. A short woman with stringy, over-bleached, bottle-blonde hair read a magazine behind the counter. The exaggerated movements of her jaw as she chewed her gum could be heard throughout the dingy lobby. Brighthouse approached while Blakely hung back and toyed with his phone.

"I need a room. Non-smoking, if you don't mind," he said with his best boy-next-door charm.

"All the rooms are non-smoking. People smoke on the balconies." She stopped to cough, hardened mucous rattling around in her chest. "Even I have to smoke outside," she said, despite the overflowing ashtray on the floor beneath her stool. The woman's voice was raspy, dulled by years of cigarettes—and hard liquor, if Brighthouse's nose detected correctly.

"Okay, then. I need a room. Do you have anything facing east?"

"Which way is that?" she spat out through another wave of coughs.

"Umm, that way." Brighthouse pointed. Blakely also gestured, never looking up from his phone. "Toward the storage facility?" Brighthouse added.

"17A work?"

Does she think I've been here before? "Uh, sure. As long as it faces toward the storage facility, it'll work just fine," Brighthouse said lightly. The woman grunted while she reached behind her for one of the keys with the plastic, oval-shaped tags hanging from them.

As he and Blakely started to walk away, apparently left to find the room themselves since the woman offered no directions, she called after them. "You ain't doin' no stakeouts are youse? City don't pay right away!"

"No ma'am," Brighthouse called back. "I just like to face east. Call it a quirk."

38
Shockingly Chilly.

LYLA HAD WATCHED in vain as the police cruiser, a few cars in front of her at the stoplight, flashed its emergency lights. A short siren sounded, followed by a few honks that sounded like an angry, oversized goose. The patrol car peeled out, made a squealing U-turn, and, as it passed her in the opposite direction, Brighthouse had glanced her way. She shrugged with both palms up and out. *Can't blame me for trying.*

When the light had turned green, she'd surged forward with the flow of traffic, the lanes of cars moving like herded sheep. She'd searched the surrounding buildings as they streaked past and fell behind her in blurs, trying to ascertain her location. Finally, when Lyla came upon a few familiar street signs, she figured out the boys had probably been headed to UPENN. Autopilot kicked in, and she'd arrived on the stately campus twenty minutes later.

But *why* had they been heading there? Were they actually heading to West Philly General to question the doctors again? That couldn't be it. The Derrick Warner case was closed, wasn't it? Well it was on her end, but Lyla had no idea if the police were still investigating it. Still, perhaps there was another reason.

Lyla reached a suitable place to park and sat staring, pondering. She spotted a petite, black-haired woman rushing by—Aunt LeeAnn. Lyla had seen her arriving at the storage facility crime scene Friday night. Maybe she and Brighthouse were working together. He probably interacted with her on a regular basis, surely at other crime scenes. It was plausible that they had discussed the possibility of Lyla as a suspect. *LeeAnn never liked me.*

***

Lyla walked with brisk steps to the entrance of the building that housed her aunt's office. A towering cop with a shiny head, presumably just passing through, looked at her quizzically as they crossed each other on the stairs. He called back to her from the lower landing.

"Hey, miss? No civilians up there. Hey!"

Lyla descended, retracing her steps to meet him. "Oh, it's okay. I'm meeting my aunt for lunch. LeeAnn DiCicco? Chief ME?" Her voice was sweet as syrup as she looked up at the officer with innocent saucer-wide eyes.

"Dr. DiCicco's your aunt?"

"Yes. My late father's sister. You may have known him also. Calvin Kyle? He was a detective for—"

The officer, seemingly unimpressed with her name-dropping, cut her off. "Do you have ID, miss?"

"I do, but it's in my car. I just wanted to let her know where I was parked in case she wasn't ready. I'll be quick, I promise."

The officer considered her pleading and sighed. "Okay," he finally said.

Lyla clapped her hands together in gratitude and re-climbed the flight of stairs. She pressed her ear to the door and didn't hear anything. She checked the time on her phone and surmised that LeeAnn was already out to lunch. She chuckled. After all these years, her aunt still stopped everything at exactly two o'clock to have lunch. She tried the knob, surprised—no, shocked—to discover the door wasn't locked. That was new. Probably on account of one of the interns or assistants who didn't know any better. They would certainly get an earful later.

Taking advantage of their oversight, Lyla let herself into the office. It was cold and dreary gray, just like her aunt. Every cement or metal surface was shockingly chilly to the touch. The whole room was filled with stainless steel scales, shelves, tools, tables, and gurneys. She tiptoed past it all to her aunt's desk and rifled through the various papers in the tiered organizers, but found nothing—until she opened the top drawer. Among the pens, white-out, and shiny digital voice recorder was a lone set of stapled papers: a DNA report comparing 'Suspect 1' with two exemplars. The suspect's name wasn't listed, nor was the nature of the samples, but Lyla knew it was her own DNA. Why else would her aunt keep the report? And in her desk drawer, at that? The papers fluttered in Lyla's hand, her fingers trembling with fear.

Lyla didn't know what to do. Destroying the report wouldn't do any good; surely there was a digital copy in some computerized filing system. Not to mention if the report disappeared, there was a skeptical bald-headed cop who could attest to her presence in the building. She hoped Brighthouse hadn't seen it yet, but if he hadn't, he soon would. Then he might get his precious warrant.

Lyla put the papers back in the drawer and rose from her aunt's desk on shaky legs. Checking the time on her phone, only six minutes had passed. She hadn't lied to the cop in the stairwell; she had been quick, as promised. Lyla exited the office, locking the door behind her. The least she could do was save the absentminded intern from a stern talking-to. Despite her current situation, a smile crawled across her face; she wasn't completely without good deeds.

Not to be discouraged by losing her tail on Brighthouse and his partner earlier, but presently motivated by what she'd found in LeeAnn's office, Lyla decided to wait for the officers. She still felt they were heading there, so what did she have to lose by sticking around? Only her time, she decided, which would be well spent if they did turn up. She sat at the base of a nearby tree with a clear view of the entrance to the building.

Memories of her life there flooded her thoughts while she waited. Touring the campus with her parents. Meeting her would-be husband at the computer lab. Countless lunches with CJ sprawled on the grass beyond the line of food trucks parked end to end like a choo-choo train. Dropping off the lifeless body of an unsuspecting grad student in a shady corner of the quad after nightfall.

Over an hour later, Lyla spotted Brighthouse and Blakely across the street, saving her from herself—though not entirely. The truth was the subjects of her memories were all dead. Mostly by her own hand.

39
Some Semblance of Levity.

BRIGHTHOUSE AND BLAKELY knocked on the ME's door. No answer. The door was locked. He called her cell phone, and ringing echoed in the stairwell below. He hung up just as she answered it, and he heard her huff at the dropped call. Rather than shout down to her, Brighthouse sat at the top of the stairs, legs wide, arms hanging between them, waiting.

"Hey, Doc. Remember us? Two cops, patiently waiting for important scientific charts and graphs and stuff to prove our main suspect is a cold-blooded serial murderer?"

"Apparently, not all that patiently," she muttered.

"What was that, Doc?"

"Nothing." Dr. DiCicco unlocked the office door and let them in ahead of her. The heavy door drew shut on its own, slamming behind them with authority. Inside, the doctor had little time to settle herself before Brighthouse closed in with the purpose of their visit.

"So, the report? Have you—"

"Yes, yes. I was going to call you after lunch. I just got the report this morning. It's promising, but . . ."

"Let me guess, won't hold up in court?" Blakely asserted from across the room. Though he always stayed behind when Brighthouse went off on his forensic conferences and seminars, he was still a cop.

LeeAnn nodded. "Exactly."

"I knew it," Blakely continued. "When we talked to the captain about getting a warrant, it didn't happen. You told him what evidence you had pending. If he thought it was something substantial, don't ya think he would have said to wait until the reports came in?"

Brighthouse couldn't deny his partner's logic. He opened his mouth to speak, but LeeAnn's voice filled the room instead. "Well, I'm afraid I spoke to someone I know in the DA's office, and even though all three DNA samples match, there's nothing you can do except keep an eye on her and wait for her to commit an error."

"Which means waiting for her to commit more murders," Brighthouse said, throwing his hands up in exasperation.

Blakely was across the room, touching various jars and reference materials around the office, just as Brighthouse had when he'd first visited.

"You know, people say you guys are polar opposites, but I don't see it," LeeAnn said sarcastically. Brighthouse laughed. His partner just shrugged, returning a jar containing an enlarged human heart to its rightful place on the shelf. He set it down just a bit too harshly, and the major veins and arteries jiggled in the aqueous fluid like tentacles.

"May I see the reports, Dr. DiCicco?" Brighthouse asked, with an outstretched hand.

LeeAnn plopped down in her chair, still managing to do so with an air of prim and properness, opened her top drawer, found the papers, and handed them to Brighthouse. He looked them over; not yet a detective, he'd only seen DNA reports at his forensic seminars, but he got the gist of it. All three samples matched each other, one of which was the known exemplar, the pen cap with Lyla's DNA definitely on it, but Blakely and LeeAnn were right. The hair was only evidence Lyla had been on South Street. It could have drifted to Alex Livanos's car on a breeze from a block away. Also, the beer bottle had been found outside. She and CJ could have shared a beer on the steps before he went up alone and met an accidental death by pad Thai and of the three samples, only the hair and the bottle were collected properly by CSU and adhered to chain of custody procedures. They had nothing. Nothing warrant worthy, anyway. No way to more closely examine the contents in that trunk. No way to stop Lyla Kyle.

Brighthouse hadn't realized he'd said the last part out loud, not until LeeAnn spoke. "I didn't say all was lost. You can't arrest her, can't convict her on this," she snatched the report from the desk where Brighthouse had tossed it, "but perhaps you *can* get a warrant on it. Talk to your captain again. He might have thought you were reaching when you presented your theories the first time."

"You're right. Too bad we didn't come by here this morning . . ."

LeeAnn glanced back and forth between the two officers, confused. Blakely explained how his over-ambitious partner had dragged him to Lyla's storage unit. He told her they had been granted access to everything, her unit and the items in her locked trunk, but good ol' "Lighthouse" still wasn't satisfied. Blakely's animated portrayal of the morning's events caused the usually solemn doctor to laugh heartily, rattling her tiny frame.

Brighthouse ignored his partner. It was the story of his life, especially as of late. Instead, he felt newly invigorated by the possibility of obtaining a warrant. Despite the fact that Blakely was bringing out some semblance of levity in the medical examiner, a side of her he was unfamiliar with, Brighthouse had to interrupt their reverie.

"We have to go," he said.

"Okay, where to, bro?"

"*I'm* going back to the motel. I'll drop you off at the station, and you can talk to the captain about the warrant. He likes you better, anyway," Brighthouse said, sounding like a spoiled young boy.

Brighthouse didn't give his friend time to answer. He was already out the door, waving goodbye to LeeAnn over his shoulder. Blakely followed close behind. Unbeknownst to both of them, so did Lyla. This time, in a yellow cab.

40
Estranged but Ever Present.

BRIGHTHOUSE COULD ONLY hold his breath for so long against the musty smell of the motel. *People smoke on the balconies. Yeah, sure they do*, he scoffed to himself. With strained lungs, he committed himself to purchasing an air freshener later on to bring back with him when he returned that night. He wished he could remember the brand of air freshener Emma always bought for the bathroom. The memory of that scent—tropical, like pineapples—brought Brighthouse back to the previous night, when they'd made love on the cool tile floor. The previous night, when she'd asked him to leave while he slept. He sighed longingly, and like voodoo, his cell phone rang. Their wedding song bounced off the flimsy walls of the motel room. Brian McKnight's voice used to soothe him like a lullaby, but now it assaulted him like gunfire. He stepped outside to the balcony and answered the phone as quickly as he could, fumbling to remove it from its belt clip. Shot through the soul by the pain of their song, he answered the call with as light an air as he could muster.

"Jason." Emma's voice was dry, formal; she was all business with him lately.

"Emma, estranged but ever present love of my life?" The words were meant in jest, but he found them weighed down with sorrow.

"Cut it out, Jason. This is hard for me, too."

Brighthouse detected a sliver of warmth in her voice but shooed it away. This was, after all, her doing. "Fine. Whatever. What can I do for you?"

"It's what you can do for yourself, actually. I wanted to let you know that I'll be going to a spa resort with my girlfriend. I'll be back on Friday, so in the meantime, if you wanted to go through the house and gather some of your things . . ."

"You'll be back on Friday. I have until then. Okay." Awkward silence overwhelmed the line, broadening to fill the miles between them. "Where, what resort?" he finally mustered.

"I don't see how that's any of your business."

"Oh, congrats on the new job, then."

Emma paused, then asked, "Job?" Her voice was high-pitched with frustrated confusion.

"Yeah, because the only way it's not my business is if you aren't using money from our *joint* bank account or one of our *joint* credit cards to finance your little excursion. Since I provide the funds for both . . ." His voice trailed off, letting her complete his point for herself.

"Just come get your things before I hold an impromptu yard sale in order to 'finance my little excursion.'" As soon as the rapidly spat words escaped her lips, she hung up.

"If she had a dollar for every time she hung up on me, she could finance her trip just fine," Brighthouse grumbled to himself, stepping back into the room. When his cell phone registered that both parties had hung up, he stared at the screen. A wedding picture of him and his wife stared back at him. The two of them, kissing, embracing one another on the church steps. Confetti was raining upon them. Bright rays of sun glittered off the sequins of her dress, and their brand new wedding bands. The shot had been taken a few frames before the picture Emma had torn in half and set in his suitcase. The joy of that day seemed like centuries ago. Brighthouse's cellphone screen timed out and went black. How fitting.

He stifled a cough. The smell of cigarette smoke proved more unbearable by the lungful. He could hear the Blonde Bombshell—that was the sarcastic nickname he and Blakely had given to the front desk harridan—hacking a near-death rattle in the lobby. Thin walls. He should pick up some earplugs, too.

Then he heard another sound—a rustling, like leaves crunching underfoot—and the rhythmic creak of a glass bottle rolling across concrete. When Brighthouse left the room and searched the area from the balcony, he didn't see anything probative, and figured it was probably just another tenant.

Brighthouse made a quick call to Blakely. Still no warrant granted, his partner told him, but they were given tentative permission to all but formally tail Lyla Kyle. He'd take what he could get, he decided. He told his partner he had to stop by his house—his actual house—before he met up with him on shift. Blakely promised to cover for him if he was late. Brighthouse left the room, and as he passed through the lobby, Blonde Bombshell dropped her magazine in an effort to hide her cigarette. She coughed and smoke escaped her thin mouth as though from an exhaust pipe. She managed to call out something about stakeouts again, but Brighthouse dismissed her smoky protests with a wave of his hand.

41
Pack Up and Leave.

LYLA'S PORES HAD tingled with the new knowledge about her unlikely nemesis. She'd known that if she followed Brighthouse long enough she would be presented with a solution. That is precisely why she'd hopped in a cab after she'd spotted them leaving her aunt's office. When Lyla had seen him enter a lowly motel in close proximity to the self-storage facility—*her* self-storage facility—she'd figured it was for surveillance purposes. She'd circled the property until she spotted him through the parted drapes of a window. Brighthouse stepped outside to take a call and she'd cowered around the corner from the balcony where he stood. She'd overheard everything. A conversation between the officer and someone Lyla assumed to be his wife. *His estranged wife.*

A plan began to take its devilish shape. All at once, she'd realized how to exact her revenge on Jillian Atford and Jason Brighthouse in one final, despicable act—and she'd hoped it would be her last. Afterward she would pack up and leave. She had sold enough of her largest sculptures as of late to disappear to a sunny place without an extradition treaty. She would leave all of her guilt, all of her past discretions, all of her victims behind.

At the mere thought of it, Lyla had stomped her feet in delight. The autumn leaves beneath her had crinkled and crunched, and an empty Snapple bottle she hadn't seen tipped over and rolled down the sloped sidewalk and into the gutter of the parking lot. The cyclical rattling seemed like the only sound for blocks. Lyla had held her breath, waiting for Brighthouse to do what he did best: investigate. She'd heard something—footfalls—but they hadn't drawn near enough for him to spot her. Silently crab-walking backward behind the building, Lyla had felt ridiculous. She'd crept forward, not wanting to miss Brighthouse as he left, needing to follow him, curious to see where he ended up next.

Before she'd drifted too far, she'd heard the young cop's voice once more, seemingly on the phone again. Lyla had opened her eyes wider, as though it would have a similar effect on her ear canals. She'd been certain he was talking to Blakely. Though she couldn't make everything out, it had sounded like he was headed home to pick up some things while his wife was out of town for the next few days. *Perfect*, Lyla had thought. She'd waited until she saw the patrol car reverse from its parking spot before jogging to the awaiting cab around the corner.

The cab sat idly in the lot of a nearby warehouse, credit card tab running a marathon. Lyla had given the driver a couple of twenties at the start of the trip and promised a couple more at its conclusion. Honestly, the heavily-accented man appeared delighted just to have a beautiful woman in the car with him. Always able to feign the damsel, Lyla had fed the cab driver a tale: the officer was her boyfriend, and she suspected him of cheating. At that, the cabbie was only too happy to follow the patrol car across the border to Mexico if she so desired.

As they entered the suburbs and the dense Philadelphia traffic thinned, the yellow cab became much more obvious, like a banana tree in the desert. Lyla, anxious that Brighthouse would catch on, instructed the driver to hang back, almost to the point of losing the cop car altogether. She was certain they were close, as a neighborhood enclave now surrounded them. Lyla told the driver to search the area in a methodical, grid-like fashion—block by block, street by street—until they found the police cruiser parked in front of a house or in a driveway. The driver did as she asked, but to no avail. Just as Lyla was about to hand him a couple more twenties to bring her back to UPENN's campus, where her SUV was parked, they saw the patrol car sitting in front of a house dwarfed by its more stately neighbors. The house was dilapidated; roof shingles were missing, crab grass infected the lawn, the driveway was a slab of crumbling asphalt, and the house itself was riddled with swaths of peeling paint. Slipping a pair of twenties through the plastic partition, she asked the driver to let her out around the corner and wait for her.

Then a knock came at the window opposite Lyla's.

She turned to find Brighthouse standing outside the cab, waving merrily at her. She stared at him in disbelief before exiting the car and telling the driver to wait around the corner as planned.

Brighthouse chuckled. "I would say 'I didn't know you lived around here,' but since I know exactly where you live, well, ya know . . ."

"And *I* would say 'I was just in the neighborhood,' but something tells me you'd be skeptical of that explanation."

"Why are you following me, Ms. Kyle?" The friendliness had been a front, and Lyla watched as it drained from his face.

"I don't know what you're talking about."

He stepped closer, mere inches from her. She had only been this close to him once before, under much more affectionate and intimate circumstances.

"Why are you following me, Lyla?" He stretched out the syllables of each word in a singsong manner, as if he were scolding a small child.

"I thought maybe I could find a cause, a reason for your obsession with pinning murders on me. My storage unit? Really? You know I'm an artist. What did you find? Art. I bet you feel like an ass now, don't you?"

"Why do you keep that trunk of yours locked?"

"The trunk I unlocked for you? The trunk I allowed you to look in? That trunk?"

"Why is it locked in the first place?"

"Those paintings are special to me. They're not for sale. They're . . . cathartic."

"Bullshit. I'll get my warrant. I'll find out the truth. But for right now, I'll settle for you telling me one thing."

Lyla looked at him impatiently.

"Do you stalk your victims like this before you kill them, before you dump their dead but otherwise healthy bodies? Is that why you're following me?"

"Officer Brighthouse, that's not one thing, that's two things. Besides, you're not my type."

"Could've fooled me."

"Think about it. Say hello to the wife for me."

With that, Lyla spun off and returned to her cab. The tab had grown close to her car payment, but she wasn't worried about that number. Instead she occupied herself with a different number: Brighthouse's address. She added it to Jillian's. She would need them both in the coming days.

42
A Tongue Slicked With Oil.

HE KEPT WATCHING HER. He and his partner trailed her. Other patrol units, at Blakely's pleading, kept an eye out for her. Brighthouse himself stared at the storage unit across from his motel room until his eyes demanded to close, like angry bouncers at a nightclub, turning the lights off on their patrons. So far, nothing had happened. Lyla Kyla had done little besides drive from her home to various spots around the city, like any other citizen. She hadn't been to see Jillian Atford once, but she'd bought art supplies several times, and met with a buyer, who purchased a giant sculpture of a fly made out of metal leaves. Her visit to West Philly General Hospital seemed promising, but when the personnel was questioned, everyone sang the same song: Lyla had stopped by to say hello to the staff, and she did that quite often.

Brighthouse stood on the cement slab of balcony outside his motel room. He still hadn't mastered breathing without coughing. His cell phone rang, interrupting his constant praying for a break in his case. It was Blakely.

"Good news, bro. The little lesbian rookie spotted Lyla in a Home Depot buying rope and duct tape. What are the odds? A lesbian in a giant hardware store, right—"

He loved Byron, but before he could continue his wholly inappropriate quip about the young officer they'd chatted with at Mickey's, Brighthouse promptly cut him off. "Did she approach Lyla? By the way her name is 'Montoya.' Please stop referring to her as 'the little lesbian rookie.'"

"She did." Blakely cleared his throat. "Excuse me, Officer *Montoya* did, in fact, approach the suspect. At first she said Lyla avoided eye contact and when that didn't work, she'd tried to scurry away unnoticed. When Officer *Montoya* caught up with her, Ms. Kyle explained that she was working on a new sculpture. Montoya also muttered something in Spanish. I don't remember much from high school, but I think it translated to something like Lyla's 'tongue was slicked with oil.' I guess that means she thought she was lying."

"Nothing gets past you, Byron. So, uh, this is all great, but why the phone call? Couldn't this have waited until—?"

"Not at all."

"Why not?"

"Because I need you to meet me somewhere. Right now."

"Fine. Where?"

"Lyla Kyle's house. We got the warrant."

"What?"

"After Montoya told me about her encounter with Lyla, we went together to approach the captain for a third time about a warrant. The circumstantial DNA evidence, coupled with our uneasiness about Lyla's intentions for the items she'd purchased, plus DiCicco's two cents . . . let's just say the captain became a bit wary of having Lyla Kyle's latest victim on his conscience."

Brighthouse didn't care what had finally persuaded him; as far as he was concerned, the third time was the charm. As he hung up the phone, he returned his focus to the storage unit for just a second before grabbing his keys and readying to leave. Of course, *now* there was finally something interesting happening: all of Lyla's things were being moved from her storage unit by two burly men in matching shirts. He couldn't read the logo, but he figured they were professional movers. They seemed to be rolling everything via a pair of dollies into a mobile self-storage pod. Everything was being transported: sculptures of all sizes, art supplies, easels, floodlights—and Lyla's precious trunk.

43
A Spirit Newly Released.

LAST WEEK'S VISIT to Calvin's grave proved just as therapeutic as it had been years ago. Jillian should know; she was in the business of therapeutic practices. Now, after a long day of dishing out therapy to others, the last such day for a while, she just wanted to relax. She could do that now. *Relax.* The word no longer flowed foreign within her mind. The concept was no longer chased from her thoughts by the nightmares of her past. She could relax.

Her keys dangled and jostled from her hand as she unlocked her front door. Jillian entered her home, closed the door behind her, and leaned against it, an exaggerated sigh of relief escaping her like a spirit newly released. She set her purse down on the coffee table and shuffled through the small stack of mail in her hands, not necessarily interested in it, but reveling in the normalcy of the act itself. She shifted her gaze to the now empty dining room table where she'd recently gathered all the items that she had amassed in her youth, those that reminded her of Calvin. She'd since moved them, permanently, to a trunk in the basement—letters, pictures, elements from the night of Susannah's death, an old birth certificate—all stowed safely below.

That day, the doctor had instructed her receptionist to contact all of her patients to let them know she'd be going on an indefinite sabbatical. Lyla Kyle hadn't answered the call, but she'd also missed their last session earlier in the week. With crossed fingers, she hoped Lyla had found a replacement psychologist. Then Jillian could return from her time off to her practice, to her life. No remnants of Calvin throughout her home. No Lyla in her office. She thought it an excellent plan to reclaim the new life she had built for herself a decade ago. With her future in sight, she poured herself a glass of wine before even bothering to remove her jacket. She took a swig of the wine. It tasted a little strange. Jillian shrugged, chalked it up to the bottle having been opened two days prior, and emptied the rest of the wine into her glass. Finally, she removed her jacket, slung it over the back of a chair, and headed upstairs to draw herself a bath.

God, I don't even remember the last time I took a bath. She climbed the steps, and her legs felt heavy. An avalanche of exhaustion fell upon Jillian like boulders down a mountainside. She trusted a long, luxurious bath would do her good.

After preparing the tub, she paced from the bathroom to the adjoining bedroom. The water rose; the salt and bubbles crackled behind her. She sipped her wine, resigning to ignore the odd taste. Instead, she focused on the fragrances of lavender and chamomile filling the bathroom. The aromas overflowed into her bedroom, where she undressed and slipped into a plush terrycloth robe. She turned on her laptop and chose an Etta James playlist on Pandora. The iconic lyrics of "At Last" emanated from the tiny speakers, and she enjoyed both the acoustics and the aromas. Jillian hummed along sleepily and stumbled back into the bathroom. She lifted one leg to test the temperature of the water, wine glass still in hand, but found she needed to steady herself. Jillian grabbed the towel rack weakly. Her sight blurred, and spots pranced across her vision. The wine glass fell into the tub, cushioned by the clouds of suds, the light golden elixir blending with the salty, scented bath water.

Jillian fell next, but she didn't make it into the tub.

44
Past All of It.

LYLA WHISTLED A cheery tune as she drove. There were only a few more ducklings to round up and set straight. She had managed to operate normally over the past few days, despite the constant tailing by Philadelphia's finest. She'd even waved a couple of times to Brighthouse and Blakely. There was one unfortunate run-in with that feisty Latina cop from the night of the storage facility incident, but she didn't think anything had come from it. Therefore, she'd set her plan in motion, like a car with a brick on the accelerator. She had gathered materials, gotten rid of the tainted red paint in her studio room, conducted another thorough scrubbing of the kitchen floor tiles, and picked up some goodies from West Philly Gen—which proved decidedly more difficult without CJ. Maybe she missed the little guy after all.

Meanwhile, movers were currently packing up everything from her storage unit into a portable storage pod. Including her private collection. She wished she could be there to see the look on Brighthouse's face when—*if*—he arrived with his warrant to search an empty storage unit.

With the first stage of her plan behind her, barely visible in the rear-view mirror, she slowed the rental SUV to a crawl. Rather than switch the license plate with her own—which would have been counterproductive—Lyla had altered a few of the characters with masking tape, for depth, and paint, for overall appearance. If anyone spotted her in either neighborhood, the plate number wouldn't come back to the rental agency—which was in Delaware.

Lyla glanced once more in the rear-view mirror, and focused on the items on the backseat. The trunk had been locked this time, unlike her first encounter with it, and she'd had to search for the key, which set her back a few minutes more than Lyla would have liked. She didn't blame her unwilling hostess; it wasn't like Dr. Atford knew Lyla had a schedule to keep.

She took another peek into the back, past the objects she'd stolen. Past the backseat, the right side of which she'd folded down to afford her a clear line of sight. She looked past all of it—to the unconscious Dr. Atford, lying in a heap in the trunk, covered in a picnic blanket. The soft rise and fall of her breathing was eerily slow and rhythmic.

45
The Clarity of Near-Death.

JILLIAN CAME TO, and her surroundings were unfamiliar. As was the smell. Each home had its own unique scent, and she was sure she'd never been here before. She tried to move, only to find her upper arms bound to her torso by rope, and her wrists and lower legs fastened to the chair with duct tape. She was alone at the head of a cozy dining room table. Jillian tried to listen, straining for a clue as to where she was or why, but heard nothing

The last thing Jillian remembered were two lengthy legs stepping over her. She had been immobilized, but had willed her limbs to move, begged them. Then, there was silence. The music she had put on had ended. The water that had been streaming into the bathtub, filling her ears with the echo of a waterfall, had stopped abruptly. The sounds of relaxation had been replaced by the harshness of suction and gurgling. The tub had been drained. So had her awareness. Then she'd drifted off into the blackness.

Now Jillian heard nothing, could do nothing, and she knew nothing of who had done this to her. She closed her still unfocused eyes in despair, her head thudding heavily into her bosom.

She sat like that for hours. Though her eyes were closed, she kept track of the time. Seconds. Minutes. Hours. She counted, perhaps for the last time in her life.

Finally, a sound. Jingling. Keys. A lock's tumbler turned. Door hinges creaked. Past the arcing entryway to the dining room, a pretty young woman entered, lugging a small suitcase behind her and a tote bag on her shoulder. Her blonde hair rippled with her struggle. She brushed it aside.

Her face now visible, Jillian realized she didn't recognize the woman any more than she recognized the rest of the setting.

She watched her waltz right up the hall, past where Jillian was being imprisoned, without looking into the dining room. Either the woman was oblivious to Jillian's predicament, or she was privy to it—and didn't care.

The following minutes—and the terrifying sounds trapped within them—told Jillian it was the former.

A squeal of surprise was followed by the thud of someone hitting the floor. Then came screams of blood-curdling anguish. Then gurgling—just like her bathtub—but it was the gurgling of a woman losing the battle with her attacker. She was choking on her own blood.

Jillian squeezed her eyes shut tightly, awaiting the same fate. It never came.

She opened one cautious eye minutes later. *What is happening?* Jillian opened her other eye. A tall, lithe figure approached, winding deftly around the dining room chairs. The person was clad in black, except for the shirt. The shirt used to be white. It used to belong to Jillian. She recognized the dried blood stains immortalized into the fabric, visible only where fresh blood hadn't splattered and obscured them. Jillian's vision was still blurry—and her newfound terror had brought on a curtain of tears—but she could tell the figure's arm was raised, and wielding a kitchen knife. The sight of the red handle widened her eyes even more than she thought possible. It was the same knife that had killed Susannah Kyle ten years ago. The same knife that was supposed to be locked away in Jillian's trunk, along with the attacker's old bloody shirt. *What is happening? Who is doing this to me?*

Frightened that reality had long ago slipped from her grasp, she wanted to scream herself out of this nightmare. The hazy figure drew nearer, its arm still raised. Just as Jillian winced, bracing for death, the attacker's other hand rose. Jillian never saw the syringe, but she felt its needle enter the side of her neck near her hairline right before she began drifting off for the second time that day. Again she asked herself: *Who is doing this to me?*

But with the clarity of near-death, she knew. Deep down, Jillian thought she knew.

46
A Cyclone of Violence.

LYLA EXTRACTED THE needle from Dr. Atford's neck. The woman's head rolled to the side, then bowed forward and came to rest. It was much different from the usual scenario: no paralyzed limbs or wild eyes. No watching her terrified prey perish before her. No, her psychologist was simply unconscious. Temporarily so, at that. Still, plunging a needle in her neck had been much more satisfying than spiking every beverage in her refrigerator.

Lyla took the knife that was in her hand, her mother's knife, and wiped the familiar red handle clean, careful not to disturb the blood on the blade. Of course she was wearing gloves, but she wanted a pristine surface to work with. She paced behind the chair where Jillian was tied and placed the handle of the knife in the doctor's right hand. She closed her lean, limp fingers firmly around it. With the fingerprints in place, Lyla leaned out into the foyer and tossed the knife near the body she had slain.

Lyla untied the ropes that held Jillian's torso to the wooden spokes of the dining room chair and cut the duct tape from her arms and legs. In one quick movement she ripped the duct tape from Jillian's mouth, her head bopping violently with the action. With an alcohol-soaked pad, Lyla wiped away any adhesive residue she could find on her face and limbs and also checked Dr. Atford's clothes for any signs of the duct tape. She shoved the used alcohol pads, the rope, and the discarded tape into a paper bag, to be disposed of later. Lyla grabbed the bottom of her shirt—technically Jillian's decade-old shirt—and pulled it up gently over her head. She untied the belt at Jillian's waist and removed the robe from her slumped over body. Once she got it off, she rolled it into a compact ball and stuffed it into the paper shopping bag with the other discarded items. She wrestled with Jillian's torso until the psychologist was once again wearing the bloody shirt she'd worn the day she'd killed Lyla's mother.

Lyla heard sirens far off. The woman in the foyer had screamed loudly a neighbor must have called 9-1-1. Lyla hoisted Jillian off of the chair, hooked her arms under her armpits, and dragged her into the foyer. She unceremoniously dropped Dr. Atford on the floor next to the lifeless figure sprawled before her—that part was no different from her other staged scenes. To add to the tableau, Lyla crashed a nearby vase over her psychologist's head. Finally, Lyla toured the downstairs level of the house like a cyclone of violence, carefully avoiding the pool of blood so as to not to track her footprints throughout the rooms. She knocked over pictures and potted plants. She yanked drawers from bureaus and purged them of their contents. She upturned the dining room chairs and brushed the papers and horrid vinyl place mats from the table, littering the floor with tacky housewives. All the while, the sirens grew louder.

47
Unknown.

OFFICERS BRIGHTHOUSE AND Blakely wore latex gloves—two pairs each—but touched very little. They wanted the search of Lyla's home to be exquisite, a work of art, forensically speaking. Jason instructed the techs to pay special attention to Lyla's upstairs studio, and a particular spot on the kitchen floor where he remembered her scrubbing with unusual vigor. He also rummaged through her closet until he found a supple, leather jacket, earthy brown, with a belt. He removed it from the closet by the hanger, and inspected it. His cell phone rang, and, with his free hand, he checked the display. He didn't recall the number, and there was no name accompanying it, just the word 'unknown.' Brighthouse deferred the call to voicemail and whistled for one of the technicians.

"Hey, Byron, you have the contact info of that woman outside of CJ's place, right?" He raised an eyebrow at his partner and held up the jacket before handing it off to one of the crime scene guys to photograph. Blakely nodded and gave an enthusiastic thumbs up.

Brighthouse scurried behind various people in paper shower caps and matching booties, both to keep abreast of what they were doing, and because their field fascinated him. He remembered his dad always telling him about new breakthroughs in technology and techniques. Maybe if he had gone to college like his father had wanted he could have become one of them. But that was an obsession for another day. One obsession at a time, as Blakely would say. So he focused on the one that brought him to Lyla Kyle's home. He made sure the techs were on the lookout for drugs that could incapacitate a grown man without a trace. LeeAnn had specifically mentioned something called succinylcholine. He also wanted them to look for peanut oil, since Dr. DiCicco had contacted him with the results of CJ's autopsy and medical records, which confirmed his peanut allergy. His stomach contents contained traces of peanut oil specifically, though pad Thai, the suspected dish, traditionally called for a peanut garnish only, not oil. Brighthouse thought that was odd. He also thought Lyla had something to do with it.

Brighthouse's phone rang again. Same unknown number. He was about to answer it when he heard a bit of commotion outside. He opened the drapes of Lyla's bedroom window and saw the storage pod he'd witnessed being packed earlier pulling up to the front of the house. With the department vehicles in the driveway and the immediate space in front of the house, the pod was forced to park one house over. The heavy-duty pickup truck spit out its occupants, and they dismantled the hitch from the pod in minutes. As they drove off, Detective Swartz, who'd volunteered to oversee the serving of the warrant, called three techs over and sent them down to the pod.

The officer beamed proudly. He had her. He had his warrant. He had the walls closing in around her. He continued to smile to himself, walking through her home, waiting for an *Aha* or a *Gotcha* moment. Instead his phone rang. Again. Same number. This time he answered it.

From down the upstairs hallway Blakely called to him. Brighthouse held up a finger, but as he listened to the words flowing from the other end of his cell phone, his hand dropped limply to his side. He watched as concern knitted his friend's face, and he felt the color completely drain from his own. The phone crashed to the floor and Brighthouse sunk into a wall; he barely missed scraping his head against a sharp sconce.

Blakely rushed to retrieve the phone. "Hello? Hello?"

"Yeah, Officer Danillo here. We got a 9-1-1 call. Brighthouse's house. It's his wife. We've been trying to call . . . it's bad."

48
A Flower Among Chaos.

JILLIAN WAS TIRING of fading in and out of consciousness. She awoke again on a hardwood floor, a blood-streaked wall before her. She unfolded her body and scrambled to a seated position. Bracing her arms behind her, her hands landed in a pool of blood, and her right arm bumped into something. Something *soft*. She turned to peer over her shoulder. Confusion cleared like fog from the morning, and memories flooded her mind. Her bathroom, then being tied to a chair, then a woman. So many screams. *Oh, God.* That screaming woman was now the body stretched out behind her. Jillian stood up slowly, feet slipping and sliding in the sticky, syrupy blood. She steadied herself on the wall, adding a crimson handprint to the fury of splotches and spatter, a flower among chaos.

She was still groggy—had been all day—but when the haze lifted, and her swimming vision caught up to the fact that Jillian was standing completely still, she crept closer to the body. She nudged the woman's leg with her foot. Nothing. She bent over and groped the woman's neck and wrist for a pulse. Nothing. Jillian turned the woman over and jumped back. Her blonde hair was full of blood. Her blue eyes were vacant of life. She looked so much like Susannah Kyle. Younger sure, but given the circumstances, the resemblance was unnerving. Jillian's gaze fell to her own shirt. The shirt she herself was wearing. Years before it had been stained with Susannah's blood. Now it was stained with the blood of this unknown woman.

Jillian's eyelashes tried to trap her tears, but they escaped. They ran down her cheeks and plopped down to her chest, which heaved with sobs. Jillian needed to escape, too. She shuffled forward, continuously planting her hands on the wall for balance, and leaving a trail of blood-red blossoms in her wake. She stepped over a wedding picture pinned under broken glass and a cracked frame, marred by blood droplets. The woman smiled happily, the man appeared young, but familiar. Jillian contemplated bending to retrieve the picture, to get a closer look and maybe find a clue as to her whereabouts, but she never finished her thought.

The front door crashed open on its hinges. Wood splintered into the entryway and angry voices invaded the silence. Officers barreled through the foyer, shouting, guns drawn—aimed at Jillian.

49
The Man You Made a Widower.

JILLIAN STUDIED HER fingers, splayed in front of her on the cold metal table. Keeping them on the table eased their trembling, and she was grateful for that. There was blood caked in the crevices of her knuckles and under what was left of her fingernails; they were clipped as part of her processing. Still, she stared at them, wondering if they were capable of such heinous acts twice in one lifetime.

A loud thwack filled the room. The table vibrated violently. The detective in front of her had slammed down on the table with both palms, lifting her own hands from the cool surface, snatching her away from her musings.

"Why did you kill that woman?" he asked with calculated enunciation. "I'm sorry, she had a name. Her name was Emma." Now he was shouting. "Why did you kill Emma?" He whacked the table again.

Jillian cowered in her chair, shrunk into herself. "I . . . I . . . don't think I did."

"*You don't think you did*? Take notice, Ms. Atford. We took your clothes and you're *still* covered in blood. So what did she do? Sleep with your boyfriend? Because I can understand that."

"I don't have a boyfriend," Jillian said meekly.

"Were you having an affair with her husband? Because I can work with that, too."

"I don't even know her husband."

"Sure you do. One of our own. One of *your* own—"

"I don't know what you're talking about. I—"

"I'm talking about Officer Jason Brighthouse. You saw him several times. Mandatory sessions, to clear him for duty after his shooting. Ringing any bells? Now do you know what I'm talking about,'Dr. Atford? I'm talking about his wife. Recently deceased. Recently *murdered*, in cold blood. Emma Brighthouse."

"I still don't think . . ." Jillian's whole body shook. There wasn't a table in the world big enough to steady herself on anymore.

The detective continued berating her. "So, tell us. Tell me. And everyone watching, including Officer Brighthouse, the man you made a widower. Tell us all why you don't think you killed Emma."

"I may have been drugged . . . I think. Yes. I came home from work, was going to take a bath, then I woke up in a strange house. Tied up. Then the screams, the awful screams." Jillian's tears fell again and she shook her head, trying to loosen the shrieks from her memory. "I thought I was next. Then I woke up. Next to that poor woman. And there was so much blood, and then I thought the police were gonna shoot me, and—"

"So you're claiming you were drugged at your house, relocated, and when you came to, you were tied up. Then you woke up again next to Emma, who was already dead. And you were . . . untied?"

"Well, I know it sounds—"

"So, why did you have your secretary cancel all your appointments? Indefinitely? Did you foresee this drugging? Are you one of those psychic therapists?"

"No, I was going on sabbatical."

"Such short notice?"

"I needed the time off . . ."

"To kill Emma and flee the country?"

"No!"

"Ms. Atford, if you don't tell me what your plans were, your every intention, I can't help you. If you do tell me, I can and will help you. We can have the DA make you a deal, maybe reduced sentence? You won't have to wear an unflattering color for the rest of your life until your appeals run out."

Jillian's sobs overwhelmed her. The thought of killing Susannah Kyle had haunted her for years. Now there was a second death, so eerily similar. And a client's wife. A cop's wife. They were both cops' wives. And with their appearances so strikingly similar, a pattern would be established. Jillian sobbed louder as she realized she would probably get the death penalty. Her only hope was not to tell them about Susannah Kyle.

But that meant she couldn't tell them her suspicions about Lyla.

50
The Animation of Life.

THE DETECTIVE HAD been bluffing; Brighthouse wasn't observing Jillian Atford's interrogation. He didn't even know she was in custody. Brighthouse was racing through Philadelphia in his own car, the portable siren and lights kit wailing and whirling on his roof. He hadn't even waited for Blakely, who was following close behind him in a cruiser.

They arrived at Brighthouse's home with a brief symphony of screeching tires. Brighthouse hopped from his car, keys still dangling from the ignition. The engine grumbled behind him. He ran through the personnel flitting about on his dead rust-colored lawn and through the open front door. When a fellow officer realized who he was, he grabbed him by the shoulders. Brighthouse resisted, and the man slid his grip down to a less aggressive location, sympathy filling his eyes and voice.

"I don't think you should go in there."

Blakely jogged up behind them. "I don't think you can stop him. What if it was your wife?" he said, nodding to the man's wedding ring. A frown of acknowledgment shrouded the man's face, and he let his arms fall to his sides. Brighthouse stormed past the officer, glad he didn't have to shoot him to get to Emma. He pushed through more personnel, past the chaos of his overturned possessions, oblivious to the disarray and the din.

Emma's body was lying awkwardly on the foyer floor, the pool surrounding her a ruddy brown. Her once luminescent skin was now simply pale and marred by drying smears of blood. Her clothes were torn in the obvious struggle and peppered with puncture wounds. So many puncture wounds.

Brighthouse barely realized Dr. DiCicco was in the room until she reached up to put a hand on his shoulder, cautioning him not to kneel beside his fallen wife; doing so would disturb the evidence. He nodded absentmindedly, heeding her warning, but still didn't entirely acknowledge her presence. He gawked at his wife, his precious Emma, lifeless as she was, sprawled on the floor. It was amazing how different a person looked without the animation of life. If you took away the streaks of blood, removed the awkward angle of her limbs, she still appeared foreign to his eyes. Without the flush in her snowy cheeks, and the sparkle of the sun in her sky-blue eyes she was almost like a stranger. Jason Brighthouse wept as LeeAnn and Byron flanked his sides and gently led him away, their jaws tightened and their eyes glassy.

The trio stood outside and was soon joined by a detective from homicide. Brighthouse sat on the front steps to his home, knees bent and far apart, elbows resting on them, fingers intertwined between them. Before the detective could begin the hard, but necessary, inquiries, Jason spoke first.

"Lyla Kyle did this."

Unfamiliar with Brighthouse's current obsession, the detective glanced at Blakely for clarification.

"Lyla Kyle is a suspect he, I mean, *we* have been pursuing for a number of suspicious deaths," Blakely said. LeeAnn nodded her agreement, aware of Brighthouse's less than respected reputation throughout the force.

"Anything like this?" the detective asked, gesturing in the direction of the crime scene. Brighthouse had to admit his question was a fair one, which was probably why no one spoke. "Okay, we'll explore the Lyla Kyle angle, but you should know, Jason, there's already someone in custody."

Brighthouse's hanging head rose slowly from where his sights had fallen to his interlaced fingers. His eyes were wide, imploring the detective to continue.

"The department's outsourced psychologist, Jillian Atford. She was on the premises, covered in blood, when the police responded to the call."

"Jillian Atford? *Doctor* Jillian Atford?" Brighthouse shook his head in disbelief.

"Yes, I've been told you saw her after your shooting?"

"Has she confessed?" Brighthouse asked, ignoring the question.

"Well, no. Not yet. The responding officers said she was pretty out of it. But she was here, in the house, when they arrived. And, like I said, she was covered in blood. Murder weapon was on the floor. Visible prints on it, as well as the walls. If they match, we might not need her to confess."

Brighthouse stood, and everyone's feet shuffled uncomfortably around him. "I need to talk to her," he said.

"I don't think that's wise, Jason," Blakely said. His partner's voice was soft and gentle, his arms crossed tightly against his chest. Again, LeeAnn nodded her concession, her eyes wide and still gleaming.

"Fine, I'll observe," Brighthouse said with a curt nod, his jaw set as firmly as his resolve.

"No problem. You can ride back with me," the detective said, placing a hand on Brighthouse's back, ushering him gently.

Dr. DiCicco had already headed back inside. Blakely squeezed his shoulder. "Jason, I'm gonna hang around here, keep an eye on things for you, okay?"

"No. Head back to Lyla's. I trust LeeAnn's eyes here. I want someone I trust's eyes there."

Blakely nodded, and Brighthouse acknowledged his friend with a second of eye contact before he ducked into the detective's unmarked sedan. A few minutes had passed after they'd pulled away from Brighthouse's home when he realized he hadn't caught the detective's name. Almost as if the man was reading his mind he said, "Name's McHenry, by the way. Lawrence, if you prefer." Instinctively, Brighthouse foolishly opened his mouth to offer his name as well, but stopped himself.

He was thankful Detective McHenry allowed them to ride in silence for a while, but he was the first to break it. "I know Lyla Kyle did this, Lawrence. I don't know how, or why she dragged Dr. Atford into it, but I know it was her."

51
A Cycle of Fire and Ice.

JILLIAN WAS DRAINED, her mind and body alike ravaged by unknown drugs and never-ending emotional trauma; but the most tiring aspect was trying to convince the detective across from her that she was a victim, not a murderer.

Her interrogator glowered at her, bored into her with a permanent scowl of massive disbelief. Jillian didn't care. She was tired, and not a word she could utter would make him believe her. So she returned his unyielding glare.

The door to the small room flung open, interrupting their unblinking connection. A second detective spoke briefly with Detective Scowl and they performed a relay of sorts, a brown folder acting as the baton. The new detective was still firm, but softer. If Jillian had to guess, he was the 'good cop' in the age-old dichotomy. He introduced himself as McHenry, and despite her situation, Jillian's mind automatically wandered to the candy bar. *Oh Henry!*

He was sweet, she thought, since he bothered to introduce himself at all. She couldn't recall her previous inquisitor having done so. As her newest captor dove into his line of questioning, Jillian realized the oddity of her trivial stream of thought. She was fighting for her life in there. She needed to act like it. She needed to focus.

"They tell me, Dr. Atford, that you think you were drugged."

"That's correct; I do," she said softly.

"And what makes you think that?"

"I already told the other detective—"

"I know, I know. I want you to tell me now. Every detail. From the moment you got home from work. You unlocked the door, right? It wasn't forced open, nothing amiss that you remember?"

Jillian shook her head meekly, and then repeated her story for the detective. Each infinitesimal movement, everything she could recall. When she concluded her tale, McHenry let out an exaggerated sigh. He rubbed his belly, leaning back in his chair.

"I'm starved. You hungry? You must be hungry."

Jillian said nothing. She couldn't even think of food. Not after that scene. Not with blood literally on her hands. She looked down at them again. The detective continued, abandoning the lunch break idea. "Your story sounds . . . far-fetched . . . but, plausible." Jillian looked up at him with hopeful eyes. "Can you think of anyone who would want to do this to you? Someone with a connection to you, Officer Brighthouse, and his wife, maybe?"

Jillian began to weep again, her shoulders shuddering with snivels. Her story was ridiculous. The detective's assertion that it was only 'far-fetched' was nothing short of kind. But she couldn't answer his questions—not without incriminating herself further.

The door squealed opened again. Since she hadn't provided any new details, Jillian assumed it was the 'bad cop's' turn, a never-ending cycle of fire and ice. Instead, a uniformed officer entered and handed McHenry a second folder. He glanced at its contents, snapped it shut, and glanced up at Jillian. She met his gaze, and he cleared his throat.

"Dr. Atford, we already know that Officer Brighthouse was one of your patients, but we subpoenaed your patient list. What can you tell me about Lyla Kyle?"

52
Traces of Blood.

WITH THE DOOR to the interrogation room open, Brighthouse shifted his focus; the sudden open portal called to him through the closed-circuit monitor. He left the observation room and scurried down the hall to steal a glance at Jillian Atford, who was looking at McHenry as though something had just dawned on her, as though she knew something. It was all he could do not to tear the door off its hinges and beat his former doctor with it. Despite his feelings about Lyla's involvement, seeing Jillian sitting there—her skin dotted with traces of blood that used to course through Emma's veins—he wanted her dead.

But Brighthouse steeled himself. McHenry had promised to check out Lyla Kyle, and he didn't disappoint. After Brighthouse had told him he'd seen Lyla in Jillian's office, the detective asked the DA to obtain a subpoena. With Lyla confirmed as a patient, McHenry might see the connection that was so obvious to Brighthouse. Perhaps Dr. Atford's knowing expression had been in response to the detective's mention of Lyla's name. At the thought, he folded his arms across his wounded heart, took one last glance into the interrogation room before the door closed, and hurried back to the observation room.

"Ms. Kyle is a patient," she said, dragging out her words. Brighthouse had the feeling she was holding something back. He squinted his eyes in concentration as he continued to listen.

"We know that. So, Officer Brighthouse was a patient. Lyla Kyle was a patient. Is there a connection you want to help us see?"

"A coincidence, I'm sure. Well, I assume."

"Were you . . ." McHenry paused, as if uncertain of what he was about to say next. "Were you aware Lyla was being investigated by

Brighthouse?"

Jillian's muscles went rigid and her eyes bulged. The slightest of gasps escaped her lips. She stumbled over her answer. "No . . . No . . . She barely discussed her personal life. She had . . . difficulty opening up, as do most of my patients."

"Didn't discuss her personal life? Doesn't that defeat the purpose of going to a psychologist?" Jillian only shrugged, so he continued. "Why did Lyla seek your professional services, then, if she wasn't there to discuss her personal life?"

"I cannot discuss that." Jillian straightened in her seat, suddenly formal and officious. "You subpoenaed my client list. You can just as easily subpoena her patient file."

"Fair enough, but did you have any mishaps during the course of her treatment? Or did you notice anything out of the ordinary about her general behavior?"

Brighthouse watched on the monitor as Jillian thought about her answer. Regardless of her predicament, she seemed to be an upstanding doctor, hesitant to violate her profession's code of ethics. When she eventually spoke, she weighed her words. "Lyla was becoming increasingly agitated, but it had nothing to do with her treatment."

"What did it have to do with then?"

"Lyla was under the impression that I knew her father," Jillian said with an anxious sigh.

"Knew? As in, past tense?" Brighthouse was impressed with how astute McHenry was. It reminded him of his father.

"He's deceased," she said quietly. Almost a whisper, in fact.

"*Did* you know him, Dr. Atford?"

Brighthouse leaned closer to the screen, observing Jillian as she winced at the question.

"Well? Did you?" McHenry asked again.

"Yes," she answered, wringing her blood-crusted hands.

"Okay." McHenry scratched more notes onto his notepad. "Why did that matter to Lyla?"

"I knew him . . . intimately . . . while he was married . . . to her mother. I really shouldn't say anything further unless you subpoena her records, but you do know who her father was, don't you?" Without waiting for an answer Jillian answered her own inquiry. "Calvin Kyle. Detective Calvin Kyle? He died in a house fire ten years ago."

Brighthouse's eyes instantly widened from their scrutinizing squint. McHenry had transferred to Philadelphia from out of state, so he wasn't familiar with the history of the department, wasn't familiar with the fire that had claimed the life of Detective Kyle. Brighthouse, however, happened to be overly acquainted with this particular incident, as it also claimed the life of his own father. It was probably due to his brain trauma that he hadn't remembered the name of the detective who'd tried to save his father, hadn't remembered seeing a dark-haired beauty at the funeral. Even at that moment, the scenes in his mind were blurry.

Jillian must have sensed McHenry's confusion, because she continued. "The fire occurred right after his wife was found dead of . . . self-inflicted knife wounds," she said before falling silent.

Brighthouse thought he might have seen a connection. Now he was sure of it. If he'd learned anything from LeeAnn, it was that Lyla had a twisted sense of justice, and an irrational need for control. He already knew Lyla couldn't stand how closely Brighthouse had been circling. Perhaps she'd blamed Dr. Atford for her mother's death and decided to exact revenge on them both simultaneously. If so, he needed to arrest Lyla Kyle.

53
Victory and Freedom.

CHAIN-LINK FENCES surrounded Lyla on all sides. Weeds reached new heights all around her. An abandoned swing-set to her right, an off kilter seesaw to her left, and directly in front of her an old metal trash can, years of rust flaking away to reveal more rust. At night, the jilted children's park was a haven for junkies and the homeless, often one and the same. During the day, it was deserted.

Lyla emptied the contents of the large paper bag over the mouth of the metal barrel, segments of rope and duct tape spilling out with Jillian's bathrobe. Hidden among the weeds and blocked from the street by her rented SUV, Lyla then removed her own clothes and tossed them into the trashcan, with several lit matches. Naked but for her bra and panties and faint smears of blood on her olive skin, she stoked the flames with a stick she found nearby.

With the evidence to her crimes licked by flames behind her, Lyla sashayed through the rough grass, wearing nothing but her undergarments. The stiff foliage itched her calves and ankles as she approached the back of the rented vehicle. She shrugged on fresh clothes, removed the molded pieces of masking tape she'd used to alter the license plates, and threw them into the fire as well, before hopping into the driver's seat. The marshmallow-sweet smell of burning paper wafted in through the vents of the dashboard. Reminiscent of ancient battlefields, Lyla waited a few more minutes, filling her lungs with the subtle smoke that signaled victory and freedom.

As she drove off, she peered into the rear-view mirror, watching the ashes and glowing cinders that broke free to ride the breeze above the metal drum. They fluttered behind her like dirty snow.

Lyla returned the rental in Delaware only to arrive at her house hours later and find she wasn't alone: her property was teeming with police personnel. *Brighthouse got his precious warrant.* At least her pod had made it over safely, although the sliding door was up and officers were pouring in and out of it like a busy two-way street. It was her understanding—after a chat with her high-priced attorney—that if she moved her items to the pod, they would have to amend their warrant to cover the pod. Apparently, that hadn't slowed them down. Lyla pulled up in front of the pod and waited for Brighthouse's smug face. It never came.

Instead, Blakely ambled up casually, wearing a solemn expression. Lyla could only assume they had found Brighthouse's wife's body. Lyla had hoped to have time to make her grand exit, but she would have to wait until the heat cooled. Cool like the breeze grazing her face as she rolled down her passenger-side window to speak with Blakely.

"You have to wait outside, Ms. Kyle. We have a warrant to search your home," he said dryly. From what she knew of him, this was very out of character.

"I figured as much. May I see it?"

Blakely whistled to someone who jogged over and handed him a thrice-folded set of papers. Lyla looked them over, smiled, and handed them back.

"You don't mind if I wait out the occupation of my home in here, do you?" she asked, gesturing to the interior of her Xterra.

"Suit yourself, Ms. Kyle. We should be done here very soon."

He turned to walk away, and Lyla called to him. "Hey Blakely, what's the matter? Your partner too cool to come out here and gloat?"

Blakely turned toward her with a look of fire—flaring nostrils and clenched teeth—contrasting with the moisture of the sadness in his eyes. "He's busy."

He turned his back on her again, and Lyla's suspicions were all but confirmed: Emma's body had been found.

54
Prey Just Beyond Reach.

BRIGHTHOUSE SCREECHED HIS Maxima to a stop behind Lyla's SUV. He breathed in and out a few times, reclaiming control of his nerves, though he was shaking so bad he could still feel his holster vibrating against his body, hear his gun rattling within it. He exited the car as calmly as he could muster, concentrated on smoothly closing the door behind him. He strode to Lyla's door, trying his best to project confidence and authority. He stood outside her driver-side door while she rolled down the window.

"Please exit the vehicle, Ms. Kyle."

"Officer Brighthouse. I was just asking about you. Tell me, what is it with you and your partner and all this 'Ms. Kyle' stuff? And what's with all the sour expressions?"

"Get the fuck out of the car, Lyla." Brighthouse unsnapped the strap on his gun holster, which was steady now, his body no longer trembling. "That informal enough for you?" he asked, his right hand hovering over the weapon.

"Fine, fine," she said with her hands in the air in mock concession. She reached to grab for her purse.

"Hands where I can see them!" Brighthouse shouted, unleashing his sidearm from the safety of its holster.

"Okay, take it easy, Dirty Harry. I'll leave my purse. But that means you'll have to shell out for dinner." Brighthouse ignored her joke. "Where are we going anyway?" she asked.

"You're under arrest."

Lyla laughed, and Brighthouse did all he could not to shoot her.

"Okay, care to let me in on the charge?"

Brighthouse spun her around, threw her face-first against the side of her SUV, and cuffed her tightly. Her wrists secure, he leaned in closely to her left ear and whispered, "You're under arrest for the murder of Emma Brighthouse. For the *murder* of my *wife*, you fucking bitch. Now," he leaned back, "you have the right to remain silent . . ."

Brighthouse peeled Lyla from the exterior of her Xterra and practically tossed her in the backseat of his car like a musty duffel bag, all the while reciting her Miranda rights. He locked the doors and drove off, ignoring Blakely, whom he spotted running about and waving his arms frantically, as if trying to keep a plane from landing on the double yellows of the road. Brighthouse's only regret was that he hadn't captured Lyla unnoticed.

At the station, Brighthouse led his prisoner to an unoccupied interrogation room, coincidentally next door to where Jillian Atford was being questioned. So many sets of eyes followed Lyla's movements, not because they knew who she was, or why she was in cuffs, but because she was stunning. Even bound by shackles, she captured the attention of onlookers like fireflies in a jar.

Inside the small room, Brighthouse uncuffed Lyla's dainty hands. Like most other perpetrators he'd seen, she rubbed her wrists soothingly for several minutes. Brighthouse stared at her while she acted oblivious to his presence. Finally she asked, "Now what?" sounding bored. Brighthouse's blood roiled, turning over and over with rage at her indifference.

"We wait. We wait until I can figure out how you're involved in my wife's murder." He spat each word through clenched teeth, virtually snarling like a chained Doberman whose prey idled just beyond its reach.

"You mean your 'estranged wife?'" she asked. She'd emphasized the word 'estranged,' added a high-pitched inflection to the word 'wife,' and finished with an annoying chuckle.

"How'd you—"

"Philadelphia. It's really quite a small town, dear."

"Here's what I have so far. You hated that I was onto you. Somehow, you figured out that I was still pining over my wife after our separation."

"Pining? How sweet."

"Shut up. So you murdered Emma to hurt me, but you framed Dr. Atford for it." He stood from his chair and circled Lyla. "I suppose setting up Dr. Atford wouldn't be that difficult for someone like you, who hides behind powerful drugs—and peanut oil—to do their dirty work."

"Is Dr. Atford here? Damn, I owe her a return phone call . . ."

Brighthouse kept circling, kept questioning, his movements tighter, nearer to the table now. He was about to pounce. "Dr. Atford was your father's mistress, wasn't she? The love affair that drove your mother to suicide, perhaps? Then your father died in a fire days later. That fire also killed my dad."

That last revelation got her attention. Lyla abandoned the act of needlessly admiring her manicure to meet Brighthouse's gaze.

The officer planted both palms on the table and leaned in close to his suspect. "That's right, Lyla. Same fire."

55
A Tree With Many Branches.

BRIGHTHOUSE PREPARED TO delve into everything he had learned about Lyla's parents' respective deaths. Everything LeeAnn had confided to him. Everything he suspected her of. Before he could speak, however, the door swung open and hit the adjoining wall with force; it was a miracle the doorknob didn't impale the sheet rock. Captain Torres stood in the doorway scowling, with Blakely towering behind him, apology clouding his eyes.

Brighthouse excused himself and Lyla grinned, as though she could sense he was in trouble. In front of his superior, he tried to hold his own, keep his head up, and meet the little man's assertive gaze. He figured he was probably failing at all three endeavors. He felt more like a drenched cat hiding in a trash-filled alley on a rainy night, having fled from a pack of wild dogs.

"What's she doing here, Brighthouse?" his captain asked with a stern, solid voice. Someone who didn't know him would probably infer he was angry because of his tone. Those who worked with him on a daily basis knew he spoke in severe tones all the time. Trying to make up for his height, Brighthouse always presumed. Right now, at this moment, however, he knew his captain was quite upset with him.

"I arrested her, Captain. I know she had something to do with this. Just hear me out—"

"There's nothing for me to hear. Blakely told me everything. Yet I heard nothing about actual evidence. Without evidence we can't hold her, Brighthouse. You know that. Plus, I hate to say it, but Dr. Atford looks good for it. Real good."

"I have seventy-two hours to hold her, Captain. Come on."

"No. *You* don't have seventy-two hours to hold her. The

department has seventy-two hours to hold her. And, as captain of this department—now listen to this part closely—we're not holding her. We have nothing. At least until we get the results of the search. Until then, let her go. Now."

No doubt Lyla had heard their slightly hushed yelling just outside the door. Presumably, so had Jillian Atford in the next room. Blakely stepped in front of Brighthouse, most likely to spare his partner any further embarrassment. He poked his head in the door. "Ms. Kyle, you're free to go," he said grimly.

"But don't go too far," Brighthouse called easily from over his captain's shoulder. He was rewarded with his boss's stinging glare; it felt like a jab to the face.

Captain Torres spoke briefly with Blakely about Jillian's interrogation so far. Then he turned to Brighthouse and pointed with a stubby finger. "You. Come with me to my office. No speaking on the way. I mean it. Not a word. Just one foot in the front of the other."

The captain's office felt cramped, but Brighthouse obeyed and sat silently and without protestation. The chairs were worn—so was the carpet and the desk—but all of it was somewhat camouflaged by a fine coating of dust.

"Jason, I want you to know you have my deepest, sincerest apologies for the loss of your wife. I don't propose to know what you're going through." Torres's voice was as soft as he would probably ever allow it to be. Still, Brighthouse felt he wouldn't appreciate what was coming next. "But I think you should take some time off."

Brighthouse was right; he didn't appreciate that at all. He jumped from his seat. Dust flitted around the room from the disturbance in the air. "Captain—"

"Listen, son," the captain gestured for the officer to retake his seat, which Brighthouse ignored, "you're too close to this whole situation. It's a tree with many branches and you've managed to build yourself a tree-house. Your wife. Your shrink. And now Blakely tells me your father is tied to this, too. Not to mention you just got over your first fatal shooting a couple of weeks ago. Your marriage, I'm sorry to say, was not on the up and up. It's too much. And I'm no stranger to your past, either."

"And what exactly is that supposed to mean, Cap?"

"I'm aware of the whisperings about your accident, is all—"

"It was an accident. Check my record. Ask Chief Tunney."

"All I'm saying is go home. Grieve for your wife. Maybe stay with your mom for a few days. Come back in two weeks."

"So I'm suspended?"

"Think of it as bereavement leave, Jason." He paused, sighed, and tapped on the desk. "But I do have to take your gun and badge. I'm sorry."

Brighthouse placed his things on the desk, and he couldn't help but notice his captain refused to look him in the eye.

56
Scraped Metal.

THAT MORNING'S ARRAIGNMENT sped by in a flash, the only fragment in a string of days that had. Having been arrested on a Friday afternoon, she'd had to endure the weekend alone in her cell until Monday. For Jillian Atford, the hours between had passed tediously, every torturous minute felt like trying to crawl through mud. No—like trying to breathe in it. Jillian was slowly suffocating.

She had wordlessly refused counsel, so rather than enter a plea on her behalf, the judge had assigned her a public defender to temporarily protect her rights, just for the purposes of the arraignment. The attorney assigned to her case had shown up for the hearing completely disheveled and unprepared. All he'd had to do was state "Not Guilty" for his defendant, but he hadn't even been prepared for that. Jillian fired him before the judge's gavel came down, signaling the end of the proceedings.

Exhausted, guilt ridden over Susannah Kyle, and unable to mention Lyla, Jillian had allowed herself to be assigned a public defender. Wholly regretting that decision, and needing to replace the incompetent fool she'd fired, she hired someone recommended to her by her tax attorney. On the phone, the woman's voice sounded reassuring already, steady and firm—the exact opposite of Jillian's, who fought to keep her hands still, never mind her quivering words.

Jillian only had two tasks for the woman at the moment: to make a phone call to a long ago friend, and to go to Jillian's house and retrieve a single photograph. She had placed everything related to Calvin Kyle in the trunk, but obviously whoever set her up somehow had access to it. She could no longer rely on its contents. But one picture, the last item to be placed into the trunk, she'd kept a duplicate of in her bedroom, wedged between the pages of her Bible.

She knew the choice of placement was ironic as the child was born out of wedlock, born of adultery, and born months after the death of his father. Yet he was her son. The son she'd lost. The son that kept her close to the only love of her life. That was enough of a biblical miracle for her, and she wanted to see him one last time.

When Jillian met the smartly dressed lawyer in the visitation area, she handed her client the baby picture without a word. Jillian grasped it tightly, the picture calming her. She found herself able to grip it with steady fingers. It was a link to Calvin. A link no one else would make, even though the infant had Calvin's dark, inky eyes and the beginnings of a strong brow. So handsome. She never even got a chance to name him.

The lawyer had been speaking to her the entire time. Jillian had tuned out the harsh, yet concerned, tone, until one phrase registered. "Jillian, you should change your plea to 'guilty' and save your life." She then went into detail regarding the DNA results from her clothing. Susannah Kyle's *and* Emma Brighthouse's. Just as Jillian had suspected, the District Attorney wanted to add the second charge and send her to death row. The lawyer kept imploring her to plead guilty. She said Jillian's son could visit. She begged Jillian not to leave her son motherless. She didn't know Jillian's son never knew his mother. Still, her attorney begged. Right up until Jillian fired her, too.

The woman sighed through tight lips, rose from the table, and said one last thing. "Jillian, I found that picture in your basement, in the trunk. The trunk was locked, and the key was where you said it would be. Nothing was amiss, as far as I could tell. It's my duty to tell you, that doesn't bode well for you or your claim that an unknown person had access to its contents and framed you for Emma Brighthouse's murder. I'm imploring you, please consider changing your plea. Good luck."

The woman nodded at Jillian with pity unhidden behind her polite smile. Two guards followed Jillian away from the conference room back to her cell, her hands obediently behind her back, but uncuffed. One guard offered a mirthless smile as he slammed the rusted gate shut in Jillian's face. She smiled back, her expression equally devoid of emotion.

Hoisting herself onto the inch-thick cot, Jillian propped the picture of her son up against the pillow—she was one of the few inmates who had one—and sat cross-legged, facing it. She studied the picture. In her mind, she aged the infant into a toddler, into a boy, then finally into a man. Jillian knew she would never see anything past her imagination; she'd given him up, thought it'd be too painful to raise him. Thought the authorities would eventually pin Susannah Kyle's death on her, and he'd be ripped from her arms to be raised in a string of destitute foster homes like she had. So Jillian had given him up. She'd saved him. And now she needed to save herself.

She hopped back down from the bed—if it could be called that—and shuffled over to the sink. Her reflection was barely recognizable in the scraped metal mirror, years of inmate abuse apparent on its surface. Jillian picked up the prison-issue toothbrush and held it between her thumb and forefinger, wiggling it. It was as long as her pinky and made of a flexible rubber. She assumed the odd little toothbrushes were issued to inmates because they couldn't be sharpened to a lethal point.

Disappointed, Jillian pressed a button on the sink and water spat out of the faucet. She brushed her teeth, but she wasn't sure why. She ignored the awkward size and feel of the toothbrush in her hand and focused on the rhythmic motion instead as she waltzed around the cell looking for another way out.

She spotted one.

57
A Taunting Mockery.

EVERY HOUR THE walls felt a little closer, the air a little staler. Brighthouse had been confined to his motel room for the past couple of days. It was tolerable compared to what Brighthouse would have felt had he decided to move back into his home. He went once. He was in and out in minutes, but when he left he was gasping, suffocated by the scent of dried blood, and lashed by the streaks on the walls. With the sight of each dark brown handprint, he felt like he was being slapped hard across the face, just to be confronted with more blood and another stinging slap. Brighthouse didn't think he could ever go back.

He sighed, sitting on the edge of the motel bed. His fingers were cold as they glided across the metal barrel of his father's old revolver, a Colt Cobra .38. He had tried this once before, after his father's death. Same gun. That time he had survived; he had the scar skimming around his scalp to prove it. This time he placed the barrel of the gun in his mouth and cocked the hammer, despite the awkward angle involved in pointing a gun at oneself. His finger hovered over the trigger. His hands trembled, and every few seconds the pad of his index finger just barely tickled the trigger.

Ten years ago he had welcomed his father's calming voice in his head, the memories of his father's instruction coolly teaching him how to shoot a weapon. This time, his father's voice was a taunting mockery, a nuisance Brighthouse wanted desperately to swat away.

He began to pull back—no, squeeze, just as his father had taught him—both eyes closed, but fluttering with tension. He prepared himself for the last thing he would ever hear: the explosion of gunpowder propelling the bullet through the barrel and shooting it into his mouth and out the back of his head, leaving a ghastly exit wound.

Instead, the next sound Brighthouse heard was pounding on the flimsy motel door, followed by Blakely's barely muffled voice on the other side.

He opened his eyes. He hadn't heard an exploding *bang*, hadn't smelled a tinge of smoky sulfur in the air, and hadn't seen a muzzle flash—at least, not yet. Brighthouse removed the snubby barrel from his mouth; saliva spilled from his lower lip where it had pooled during his moments of hesitation. He wiped it off with his hand and smeared it on the bedspread, then shoved the revolver under the pillow before rising to answer the door. Blakely was still grumbling, goading his friend to hurry up.

Brighthouse blinked his eyes dry of the gauze of tears brought on by coming so close to death, again. He opened the door. When his friend saw him, his brow wrinkled with worry. Blakely bit the inside of his cheek before rubbing his forehead smooth. He could almost certainly tell Brighthouse was in a low place, but he didn't speak; instead, he clapped a hand on his friend's shoulder.

"I have good news," Blakely said.

"Better be great news."

"It is. DiCicco received the results back from the state lab and they were able to confirm Alex Livanos was poisoned with that crazy paralyzing drug she was talking about. In response, DiCicco rushed all the evidence seized from Lyla's. Remember the tiles pulled up in the kitchen where you said she was scrubbing like a mad woman? Found another area like that in the studio upstairs, under the wooden floorboards. Lab said definitely trace amounts of blood present in both samples. Both compromised by bleach, so no DNA, but—"

"Then I don't see how this news is really all that good . . ."

"Wait, there's more."

Brighthouse rubbed his tired eyes with his thumb and forefinger. "You sound like an infomercial."

"Shut up. So you said she was scrubbing because she spilled paint. Red paint. The creepy paintings in her trunk were mostly red. Lab tested those—positive for blood, also. We're waiting to see if DNA can be extracted. In the meantime, Montoya is visiting the wives of Alex Livanos and Derrick Warner for samples so we have something to compare the results to. If all goes well, they may even start looking into her for the death of Dr. Ted Stone and Kevin White—the security guard—and our department will alert the DAs of the counties where the other cases you found through VICAP took place."

"Wow, that actually is pretty good news."

"Here's the best part: Captain Torres said you could come back . . . if you're . . . up to it. And if all this pans out, we'll be recommended to make detective. You did it. You and your wild hunches and ridiculous obsessions finally did it." He cleared his throat, "I mean, uh, you're very astute." He mocked him with a tight salute.

Brighthouse was silent, though slightly smiling. His dad would be proud. And Emma. Emma would be so happy. They could finally afford the baby she wanted.

Brighthouse noticed that his partner had fallen quiet also.

"I don't mean to ruin the moment," Blakely said finally, "but LeeAnn also let it slip that your wife was pregnant. She figured you had already told me. Man, I'm so sorry."

"Thank you, Byron. Did she say anything that connects Lyla to . . . what happened to Emma? Or are they still liking Jillian Atford for it?"

"She did tell me something, yes. I'm not sure how you're gonna respond, so I told you the best news first. You looked . . . rough when you answered the door." Brighthouse noticed his partner looking past him, into the depths of the room. He glanced in the mirror above the bureau, across from the bed, and realized the butt of his father's gun was peeking out from under the pillow. Brighthouse rolled his arms around one another, signaling Blakely to continue, and hoping to steal him away from the sight of the gun.

"They tested the blood on Atford's clothes and the murder weapon. The lab dug deeper when the DNA came back a familial match to Lyla. More specifically, the DNA matched Lyla's mother."

"I thought Lyla's mother committed suicide . . . Then again,

LeeAnn said she never did buy that story."

"Well, apparently Atford's shirt was worn when Susannah Kyle died, and when Emma . . ."

"You said the knife, something about the knife?"

"According to LeeAnn, it matches the set in Lyla's parents' kitchen. She said something about remembering the red handles from the crime scene photos. There was one knife missing at the time, but they'd thought that was inconsequential."

"Okay."

"Yep."

"So it looks like Atford killed Lyla's mother *and* my wife."

"Looks that way, bro."

"I need to talk to her."

"I knew you would say that," he said, slapping him on the back. "First, let's go get your badge and your *other* gun back."

58
Sever Ties.

THEY LEFT HIS father's old revolver behind. During the drive, Blakely informed his partner that Jillian Atford had been arraigned earlier that morning; but that was before the DNA evidence from the shirt had come back. The second murder charge was in the process of being added. Until then she was being remanded.

At the station, the atmosphere was different. Brighthouse hadn't expected to arrive to a chorus of cheers—and he didn't— but the absence of snickers and whispers was resounding. Heads nodded in respect at his approach, and were held high in his wake. And what Brighthouse had feared most of all upon entering the station for the first time since Emma's death, was nowhere in sight—pity.

Captain Torres greeted them with fanfare, his short, spindly arms extended to welcome Brighthouse back, his face genuinely beaming with pride. Wearing such an expression made the man almost unrecognizable to Brighthouse, aside from his beady eyes. With an arm stretched up and around each of their shoulders, he led them to his office.

"Hey, Cap, can't chat. We just stopped by to quickly pick up his shield and sidearm," Blakely quipped, accentuating the word 'quickly.'

Their captain's face fell into a frown of disappointment. "Really, gentlemen? I'd rather hoped you would have more time to discuss your futures." Before either of them could speak, he motioned for them to have a seat, and continued, "Officer Brighthouse, I'm pleased that you look so well. Your head seems clear, and we're all close to putting a serial murderer away for good. These are good times. We'll have to hold a press conference as soon as everything is settled. You're gonna get a haircut and shave by then, yes?"

Both officers nodded, standing to leave as Brighthouse's badge and sidearm were placed on the dusty desk. It was funny how, if the brass thought you were on the wrong track, they wanted to sever ties with you, suspend you, lock you away. If you were on the right track, though, they were quick to pat you on the back, take partial credit for having seen something in you, and parade you in front of the city as an example of what a fine institution they were running. Hypocrites.

Brighthouse couldn't help but wonder if that's what his father had meant, all those years ago, when he'd said he wanted something better for his son.

After being reunited with his gun, Brighthouse was promptly asked to turn it in with security at the front desk of the Philadelphia Detention Center. Blakely did the same, and they both signed in. They were escorted down a hallway of painted cinder block walls and dingy gray floor tiles. The two guards only spoke every fifty feet—when they arrived at another sliding metal door—where they shouted to gain entry. The sound of each door grumbling aside with a noisy buzz and clink soon became familiar.

The group progressed deeper into the jail to find Jillian's cell surrounded in chaos. Blakely stood back, his face creased in confusion, but Brighthouse pushed through the throngs of guards and emergency personnel. Emergency *medical* personnel. Bandages were scattered on the floor, stained dark red. Jillian was on the dirty floor of her cell. EMTs had cleared from her; whatever life-saving maneuvers they'd attempted had proved fruitless.

Brighthouse knew one thing: he was sick of seeing innocent women sprawled on the floor in blood.

He surveyed the cell, studying it from top to bottom. Jillian had bled out from a jagged wound on her wrist, so he searched for the sharp tool she'd used on herself. Nothing seemed culpable—until he saw the cot. A jagged piece of bed frame was twisted out of place, sharp, and covered in blood. Above the fatal piece of metal, Jillian had neatly folded the gray woolen blanket, and it appeared as if she had scrawled a message on it. In blood. Brighthouse asked one of the

EMTs for a pair of latex gloves, stepped over her body, and retrieved the blanket from its spot on top of the pillow. There was a photograph of an infant placed neatly atop the folded tapestry.

"Do we know if Dr. Atford had any children?" he called.

Everyone shrugged, and Brighthouse shook his head. *Great help, guys.*

He stepped outside the cell to the hallway and unfolded the blanket, which was barely large enough to cover the length of a child. Blakely helped him hold it open. The large, block lettering read:

I'm sorry for Susannah.
I'm sorry about Emma.
I'm with Calvin now.

The wording tugged at Brighthouse. *For* Susannah, but *about* Emma. Why didn't she use the same wording for both? Brighthouse couldn't dwell on it right now. He had a temptress to arrest.

"The DA's on his way. He's furious that this was allowed to happen," Blakely said, shoving his cell phone back in its belt clip. "But at least it saves you the trauma of a trial, eh buddy?"

Brighthouse nodded. His partner was right. He'd dreaded sitting through a trial, let alone the possibility of being called to testify. "And I guess I can't pin this one on Lyla," he mumbled to no one in particular.

"Doesn't look like you pin Emma on her, either, partner," Blakely said.

Brighthouse said nothing. The phrasing of Jillian Atford's final message still nagged him. He wasn't so sure about that.

59
Her Final Moments.

LYLA CAREFULLY WRAPPED the blown-glass oil lamps from her nightstands. She remembered when she'd found one of them at a craft fair in New Jersey. It looked almost exactly like her mother's. Ten years ago, after she'd stabbed a needle into her father's drunken body, she'd grabbed her mother's favorite possessions—then set the house on fire. In her haste to stage the scene before fleeing, one of the matching pair of lamps had spilled out of her bag, the oil immediately igniting. At the time, she'd thought of it as an unexpected way of including her mother in her plot for revenge. After the house was rebuilt however, she'd longed for the matching set. Lyla had been ecstatic to find the vendor at the craft fair, completing both her set and her recreation of the bedroom where her mother had spent her final moments.

Most of Lyla's things were already packed, and the police had destroyed everything else during the execution of the search warrant. She was loading her SUV with whatever she could and hitting the road. As for the stuff she couldn't fit, it was better off that she left it behind. If her goal was to domesticate, what better way to do that than to leave behind ties to her past and its indiscretions? Her mother. Her father. Her husband. CJ. And the rest of her many victims.

With that, Lyla gave the oil lamps a second thought. Though they were tied to her beloved mother, they were also tied to the night she killed her father, and an innocent cop trying to save his colleague's life, Brighthouse's father.

Lyla decided to leave the lamps behind.

***

Lyla packed the last of the boxes in the back of the Xterra—mostly art supplies and portfolios—and climbed in the driver seat. She figured she would head North to Canada, and figure out her plan from there. Once she did, she would ship her belongings out ahead of her and start her new life. She didn't know where she was headed, but the destination didn't matter because she only reached the edge of her neighborhood before she heard sirens and saw lights in her rear-view mirror.

Steering the car to the curb, Lyla awaited her least favorite cop and his acerbic partner. Behind her, the two of them split. Blakely flanked the passenger side and Brighthouse approached her side. When she rolled down the window Brighthouse just stood there, grinning, quite a mood change from the last time she had encountered him. She turned to Blakely who wore a less severe smile, but one of contented amusement nonetheless.

"I don't suppose you're just happy because the sun is shining and it's a beautiful day," Lyla said with a sarcastic smirk.

"Well it *is* a beautiful day, but only because I get to arrest you. Again. But this time you're not going anywhere." Brighthouse touched his chin, as if in contemplation. "Maybe that's *why* the sun is shining."

"It is a beautiful day," Blakely called from the other side of the SUV.

"Step out of the car, Ms. Kyle," Brighthouse said, opening the driver-side door for her. "You're under arrest for murder in the first degree."

"Number of counts to be determined," Blakely added.

"Did you get permission from your daddy, I mean, your captain, this time?"

"I got more than his permission. After the DNA came back on the paintings from your trunk, I got his blessing."

Lyla would never utter her true thoughts aloud—could hardly admit them to herself—but a breath of relief passed imperceptibly from her lips.

60
Blood in the Paper.

AT THE FAR corner of the bar, Brighthouse sat in the shadows while Blakely passed out slices of cake. A bartender—not Mickey—handed him a mug of Miller Lite. Cake and beer. An interesting combination. It was something of a tradition whenever a grueling case was closed, though Mickey probably would have snuck him a scotch. *Speaking of whom, where the hell is Mickey?*

This was the first such celebration in Brighthouse's honor. His father had enjoyed several. Brighthouse remembered because his father always brought home a generous slice of cake for his only son. Usually a corner piece with extra frosting.

Unfortunately, Brighthouse didn't feel like celebrating. Especially without Emma and with something still distressing him about Jillian's suicide 'note.' Every time one of his colleagues stood up and spoke, and everyone cheered and raised their mugs, clinking them in the center of the crowd, he simply nodded his head in their direction. He wanted scotch so badly, but tradition dictated he drink beer like everyone else.

The chatter of the jam-packed bar rose to a chant. At first listen it sounded like his name, but then he realized they were shouting, "Light-house, Light-house, Light-house." For once the nickname wasn't being used to mock him, but to praise him. For the first time he'd arrested Lyla Kyle a week ago, he cracked a smile.

Blakely moseyed over, sloshing his beer everywhere, and pulled Brighthouse to his feet by his elbow.

"The boys, and *Montoya*, want you to say a few words." Then he leaned in closer, and whispered so only Brighthouse could hear, "I know you're going through it, man, and the pain is still raw. Just say a quick piece and we'll get you out of here."

Brighthouse sighed and waved to the mass of cops. As he made his way to the head of the bar, he stopped and removed his father's photo from the wall of the fallen, cradling it to his chest. He stepped up onto the footrest that rounded the perimeter of the bar so he could be seen and heard by his admirers.

"My whole life I've wanted to be like my father," he began, holding up the photo. "To have hunches. To solve cases. I've certainly had my share of hunches," the crowd roared with laughter, "but not all of them led to anything. In fact, very few of them did. I was beginning to think I hadn't inherited whatever innate sixth sense came so easily to my father. It turns out, I did. I just needed to sharpen my skills."

Brighthouse paused, staring down, splitting his focus between his father in his dress blues and his half-empty beer. Out of the corner of his eye, he could see everyone waiting: Blakely, McHenry, Montoya, Swartz. Captain Torres. Even Chief Tunney, the man who had made Brighthouse's career possible, was standing in the shadows, grinning proudly. They were all waiting, all pleased. His lower lip quivered and he bit down on it in protest. Brighthouse couldn't deal with this right now. It felt wrong to celebrate.

"As many of you know, I lost my wife, Emma, during this ordeal. If you'll excuse me, I have to make the final arrangements. The services will be held two days from now. I hope to see plenty of familiar faces. Lord knows, I could use all the support I can get. Goodnight."

Brighthouse stepped down, knocked back the rest of his beer, and walked toward the door, snatching his jacket from the back of a stool without even bothering to stop. The crowd held their mugs up to him in honor of his accomplishment, and in appreciation of his loss. Blakely jogged up behind him.

"Where we going, bro?"

"Listen, I understand what you're trying to do, but I'd rather be alone." He handed him the framed photograph. "Take care of this for me. I don't know where Mickey is, but he'd have a fit if he knew I'd taken it down."

"Okay, no problem. Listen, I get it, you wanna be by yourself, but I have to ask how you're getting home."

"Driving. I only had two beers. I'm fine. And it's not like Mickey was here to slip me a J&B on the rocks. Do you know where he is? It's not like him to miss one of these nights."

"I haven't heard anything, but serving you a scotch would've been against tradition," Blakely said, casting a solemn glance around the bar before briefly lowering his gaze to the floor. "I'll check on you later," he said at last, peering up at Brighthouse.

Brighthouse opened the front door, and the clattering of disturbed bells erupted. Behind him, though, the bar had fallen quiet. Even in the face of his somber words, the hush over the crowd, following such reverie, was eerie. Hand still on the door handle, Brighthouse didn't turn around, not yet. Instead he listened as someone raised the volume on the TV in the corner.

The media had taken to referring to Lyla as the Murderous Mistress, on account of her fatal entrapment of married men. At first it seemed like the newscaster was continuing the ongoing reporting of Lyla's arrest, but there was urgency in her voice. Her report was breaking news. Her report was 'just in.'

"Another victim has been discovered. We're told the circumstances are consistent with the Murderous Mistress killings," she said, sounding out of breath. She must have rushed to the scene to broadcast live on site, in front of the prison where Lyla was being held. "A source close to the case, who spoke on the condition of anonymity, did mention a new element, something not seen with the previous cases." The reporter peered down at her notes before continuing. "Apparently, a newspaper was laid near the victim. Our source says there was blood in the paper—I'm sorry—a substance *consistent* with blood. The substance appeared to be smeared over an article written about the Murderous Mistress killings. Obviously, Lyla Kyle is in custody and this raises quite a few questions. Could this latest murder be proof of Lyla Kyle's innocence? Or did she have a partner? Or perhaps there's a copycat out there. At any rate, authorities are not commenting at this time. This is Ayana Steele of

Action News and we'll have more on this story at eleven."

The cacophony of sounds that had filled the bar only moments ago—chattering, laughter, cheering, toasting—never returned.

The silence was deafening.

**Note from the Author*: Now that you have finished reading *Blood in the Paint*, won't you please consider leaving a review on the website from which you purchased your copy? Reviews are the best way for readers to discover up and coming authors, such as myself, and, personally, I would really appreciate it. Thank you.

Jordanna East

About the Author

Jordanna East readily confesses she started writing a novel one day when she was broke and unemployed. Her cable had been turned off. SHE WAS BORED. Longing to use her minors in Psychology and Criminology, she ventured outside the box; she plopped down on her bed, started writing, and she hasn't stopped—even though she now has cable. Jordanna currently lives with her husband and their two cats, both named after food.

Released in June 2013, *Blood in the Past* is the prelude novella to the *Blood for Blood Series*, and takes place ten years prior to the events of *Blood in the Paint*. Jordanna highly recommends you read it if you haven't already, though she may be biased. The next full-length novel in the series, *Blood in the Paper*, is in the works. Also be on the lookout for two multi-author anthologies featuring Jordanna's short fiction and *The Word and The Way*, a serialized novel involving an off-the-grid religious cult plagued by power hungry members, sexual abuse, and murder—and one young couple desperate to escape.

Contact the Author

Jordanna East loves to hear from her fans. You can find her everywhere:

http://jordannaeast.com

http://www.facebook.com/JordannaEast

http://www.twitter.com/JordannaEast

https://www.plus.google.com/JordannaEast

http://www.goodreads.com/JordannaEast

Or email her directly:

jordannaeast@gmail.com

Acknowledgements

Just like last time, I didn't do this on my own. I would like to thank my editor, Lauren "McStellar" McKellar, who did a fantastic job even though her laptop was lost midway through her process. I really enjoyed working with her and it was fun teaching her about apartment building mailboxes in the US. Kit Foster, of Kit Foster Design, for creating my cover, my author logo, my press logo, and any other kooky thing I ask for. Thank you to Karen Perkins of LionheART Galleries for formatting my documents because I'm not technologically inclined enough to do it myself. Even if I were, she'd still do a better job than me. I would also like to thank my beta reader team, Amanda Surowitz, Rhonda Ramsey, Tonya Kerrigan, and Karen Einsel for taking the time to read, critique, and question my story. I would especially like to thank Rhonda for being there for me every day, right there in my idiosyncrasy drawer. Thank you to Chief Bill Whinna and Detective Jake Massing of the Westville Police Department for meeting with a relatively unknown author, answering my questions, and assuring me my story was sound. A huge thank you to the members of the Crime Scene Writers Group on Yahoo—specifically Kelly Whitley, Melissa Maygrove, Lee Lofland, Wes Harris, and Wally Lind—who provided me with their experience and expertise in medico-legal procedures through an invaluable online forum. It goes without saying that any mistakes found are mine alone and are a result of my own misinterpretation of everyone else's facts. Thank you to the members of the South Jersey Writers Group and the New Jersey Authors Network for all of your inspiration and opportunities. Last, but not least, thank you to all the readers, reviewers, bloggers, and social networking fans and followers I've befriended over the last couple of years.

Thank you to my friends and family who have supported me. You know who you are and exactly what you've done for me.

Finally, I'd be nowhere without my husband, Justin. He cheered me on whenever I lost confidence, he never let me give up, and he bought me a new laptop when the last one became the bane of my existence. I can't think of a single other time in my life where I would have been happy and content enough to let my creativity take over. I owe it all to him.

www.ingramcontent.com/pod-product-compliance
Lightning Source LLC
Chambersburg PA
CBHW050014180626
46810CB00002B/415
9780989581035